THE WOMAN WHO
MADE MEN CRY

The Woman Who Made Men Cry

THAMES RIVER PRESS
An imprint of Wimbledon Publishing Company Limited (WPC)
Another imprint of WPC is Anthem Press (www.anthempress.com)

First published in the United Kingdom in 2012 by

THAMES RIVER PRESS
75-76 Blackfriars Road
London SE1 8HA

www.thamesriverpress.com

The moral rights of the author have been asserted in accordance
with the Copyright, Designs and Patents Act 1988.

All the characters and events described in this novel are imaginary
and any similarity with real people or events is purely coincidental.

A CIP record for this book is available from the British Library.

ISBN 978-0-85728-245-3

Cover design by Laura Carless

This title is also available as an eBook.

THE WOMAN WHO MADE MEN CRY

William Coles

THAMES RIVER PRESS

Further Praise for William Coles

The Well-Tempered Clavier

"What a read! Every schoolboy's dream comes true in this deftly-written treatment of illicit romance. A triumph."
—Alexander McCall Smith

"This is a charming and uplifting read."
—Piers Morgan

"An outstanding debut novel. A wonderful story of first love. Few male authors can write about romance in a way which appeals to women."
—Louise Robinson, Sunday Express

"Charming, moving, uplifting. Why can't all love stories be like this?"
—Tunku Varadarajan, The Wall Street Journal

"A beautiful book, managing to use a simple narrative voice without consequently bland style – honesty, beauty, and passion pervade the novel but so do humour, youthfulness and energy."
—Stuck in a Book

"My own piano teacher was called Mr Bagston and frankly I don't think any power on earth could have persuaded us to create a scene of the kind Coles so movingly describes!"
—Boris Johnson, Mayor of London

"Passionate and excruciatingly compelling."
—Curledup.com

Dave Cameron's Schooldays

"A superbly crafted memoir."
—*Daily Express*

"Try Dave Cameron's Schooldays for jolly fictional japes. It helps to explain the real Dave's determination to whip us into shape."
—*Edwina Currie, The Times*

"A piece of glorious effrontery… takes an honourable place amid the ranks of lampoons."
—*The Herald*

"A fast moving and playful spoof. The details are so slick and telling that they could almost have you fooled."
—*Henry Sutton, Mirror*

"A cracking read… Perfectly paced and brilliantly written, Coles draws you in, leaving a childish smile on your face."
—*News of the World*

Mr Two-Bomb

"Compellingly vivid, the most sustained description of apocalypse since Robert Harris's Pompeii."
—*Financial Times*

For my two New York amigos, Geoff Stead and Tunku Varadarajan

ACKNOWLEDGEMENTS

Like Kim, I was also the New York Correspondent of the *Sun* between 1997 and 1998 – though my love life was never nearly as exciting as his. This story, however, is nearly all true. Most of it happened, including almost all of the details of Kim's insane love affair. Even the extraordinary ending is true. It just never happened to me.

I would like to thank my fellow foreign correspondents, who all became part of the warp and weft of my New York adventure. They include my News Corp. colleagues Tunku Varadarajan, Geoff Stead, Cameron Stewart, Oliver August and David Yelland. Then there were my direct rivals – Allan Hall, Andy Lines and Nick Hopkins – who treated me far better than I deserved; thanks, chaps! And also in Manhattan in 1997, there were four terrific women in my life, Shannon Sweeney, Amy Finnerty, Karen Plitt and Lizzie Warburton. I thank you!

My thanks, as always, to my agent Darin Jewell; and to Jeremy Hitchen, story-teller and bon viveur; and last, but of course not least, my especial thanks to Margot, my wife. Merci mille fois!

CHAPTER 1

She did not set out to make men cry. She was too kind for that.

I know of a few women who would love to be able to make men weep. There is something extraordinarily powerful about the sight of a strong man in tears.

But not Elise. For although I have seen her reduce a man to tears in minutes, she always seemed vaguely embarrassed. She is the young girl who's made the birthday boy cry.

And how did she do it? Or, to be more precise, how *does* she do it? It seems to be a power that has only grown with age.

Well, predominantly, she just listens. She listens, she absorbs, she takes it all in. And then she asks questions. Always, always, back come the questions, and often they are very simple questions. There is nothing much to it at all. She asks a question, gets a reply, and then comes straight back with another question.

She asks the questions because she's interested. And within just a few minutes, that man is back there in the very moment when he lost his first love, or was thwarted by his brother, or beaten by his father. And then, well, the tears come, and because men cry so infrequently, when the tears come, they're difficult to stop. It's like turning on an old red-rusted tap: it takes as much effort to stop the water gushing out as it does to start the flow in the first place.

That, as far as I can tell, is usually what Elise does when she makes men cry.

But there are other ways.

And the first time she did it to me... well, that was another way altogether. It happened over ten years ago, and I daresay that the effects of those tears continue to reverberate even now. Somehow it feels as if those tears caused a tectonic shifting of the plates, so that always lurking there in the depths of my dark heart is this determination to pay her back in her own coin.

Though now that I think of it, rather than giving you these opaque glimpses of what happened all those years ago in New York City, why don't I take you there right now?

How very appropriate. We shall start not with the beginning of the relationship, but with the beginning of my tears.

But before we start, I would like to put these tears into context. I was not by any means a pushover. In fact, quite the opposite: I was a hard-bitten reporter in New York, and it was as if I had been through a baptism of tabloid fire which had left me so tempered as to be untouchable. I was the perfect reporter, wholly objective, and never once letting my feelings get in the way.

And then along came Elise... and my life has never been the same since.

It was in Manhattan, 1998, early April, and it was a Thursday. Oh yes, I may not be able to remember the exact date, but I can most certainly remember the day. It was a Thursday, and even now, as Thursday afternoon starts to turn into Thursday evening, I still get this Pavlovian response. A queasiness begins to develop in the pit of my stomach; that feeling you get at the end of the most blissful summer holiday as you realise that the party is well and truly over. Well, it's a bit like that, only with the knowledge that this same feeling is going to occur again, and again, and again, every single Thursday night, and that there's not a thing you can do about it. How pitiful that sounds. For of course there was something that I could have done about it. And my only excuse is that I loved her. I loved her from the very first.

Now at the time, I wasn't just a hard-bitten reporter, but a hard-bitten foreign news correspondent for the paper with the biggest bite in the business: the *Sun* newspaper. I daresay you've already got your own opinion about that paper and there's nothing much that I can say that will change it. We'll come back to it later.

I had been in New York for over a year and was living in a flat on one of the brownstones on the Upper West Side. It was a stone's throw from where John Lennon was shot dead at the Dakota.

I'd been out to Central Park with another foreign correspondent, Steve, a stocky barrel of an Australian. I was still recovering from a serious operation – of which much, *much* more later – and Steve had pushed me around the park in a wheelchair. We'd had a few beers, and for an hour had been skirting around the one tortuous subject that was uppermost in my mind: Elise.

Steve was trying to persuade me to go out clubbing. I wasn't interested.

"Seeing what she'll be doing tonight, I don't think Elise is in much of a position to complain."

"I love her," I said simply.

"Bet she says she loves you too." He scratched at his wild spike of hair.

"It's what she wants."

But that was just the point.

When we made our deal together, Elise had been quite clear. She'd not just wanted it. She'd insisted on it. She had been adamant. I don't know if I can express myself any more clearly: Elise had gotten exactly – just *exactly* – what she had wanted.

Though I still couldn't help but wonder: was it really what she wanted? I am sufficiently intuitive to be able to divine that a girlfriend's words may not be entirely in line with her feelings.

Steve wheeled me back to my apartment and helped me hobble up the stairs. Elise, as I'd expected, had left. There was the scent of fresh perfume in the air, one that I didn't recognise. It might have been Chanel. I slumped into the sofa. Steve got a couple of beers from the fridge. He tousled my hair as he switched on the TV. It was Seinfeld. I didn't watch it.

Steve had just been complimenting a poster on the wall. It was that classic 1930s picture of the workmen high up on the Empire State Building, perched out on a girder as they have their lunch. One small slip from oblivion.

He broke off. We'd both just heard the sound of singing from the bathroom. It was Elise. She was singing Frank Sinatra's 'New York, New York': "I want to wake up in a city that never sleeps—"

"She's still here?" he said, incredulous.

I nodded.

"You're mad!" hissed Steve.

For a while I didn't say anything. The TV images washed over me.

"You're out of your mind!" He drank his beer.

"It's what she wants."

"Is it?" he said. "Is it?" He looked at me over the top of his beer bottle. "It was what she wanted in February. Has it been set in stone?"

"No, really," I said. "It *is* what she wants. It's the agreement we made."

Now to clarify. I was neither forced nor hustled into making this particular agreement. Perhaps that's why, even now, I've never really got over it. Eyes wide-open, I happily acceded to Elise's wishes.

But with Elise now actually in my flat... that put a different complexion on things.

Perhaps, by staying in my flat, she was pushing for me to take control: go striding into the bathroom like some knight errant and take her in my arms and bawl: "We're having none of that, my girl!" Because yes, I am aware, that although women are always ultimately the mistresses, it is also true that they occasionally like their men to be the master.

From the bathroom, I can hear the sound of the toilet being flushed; a last moment to check her hair and make-up in the mirror; the door is opened: and out comes Elise.

Perhaps it was the knowledge that for that night, Elise was untouchable, because I had never seen her look more beautiful. The clothes themselves were nothing much, just jeans and boots, a camel hair coat and some frilly top which revealed a glimpse of flushed skin. Around her neck was not her usual silver crucifix but an expensive gold necklace of entwined vine leaves. I did not recognise it. Her auburn hair and make-up: all done just so.

She was not vampish or overly glamorous, and yet the very fact that she was so unattainable made her look like the most exotic creature I had ever seen.

"Hi Kim," she said. Forced brightness. "Hi Steve."

"Oh, hi." I half got out of the sofa, suddenly awkward, unsure of what I should do next. Should I kiss her? Launch myself into her arms? Throw myself at her feet and beg?

I glanced momentarily at Steve. Though he said nothing, I could tell he was urging me to action.

Elise paused at the door. Perhaps she, too, was uncertain, was unsure about whether to take the next step. A strange thought occurred to me: had she, perhaps, performed this peculiar charade with some other besotted boyfriend.

Now that, I do not know. But I do remember her waiting there by the open door, almost challenging me to pluck her up. On the one hand, wanting to go: on the other – and I'm sure of it now — quite yearning for me to insist that she stayed.

And I, meanwhile, am still sitting uncomfortably on the edge of the sofa, still there with that pathetic empty beer bottle in my hand, not quite believing that it has really come to this. Though still a part of me is the objective, dispassionate reporter, not so much in the moment, as aware that this *was* the moment.

"Well..." said Elise. There was a sort of smile on her lips. I could see it start to crumble at the edges. Perhaps, and I've never thought of it like this before, she knew she was going to be hurting herself just as much as she was going to be hurting me. "I'll be off then."

She still lingered in the doorway, and oh, to have been able to have analysed all of the thoughts that must have been running through her mind at that moment. Bravado and excitement for sure, perhaps even lust. But I also had the sense of a little girl who is in the very act of defying her parents; she's about to pull the switch, she wants to pull the switch: and yet a part of her longs for her parents to assert themselves and take control.

And so there she stands, swinging this way and that in the turbulence of all our unspoken emotions: hurt, fear, lust and this quite terrifying dread that she might actually have to see it through.

And out the door she goes.

"Get after her!" said Steve. Instantly. "Stop her on the stairs!"

But, I don't know, it feels that the dice have already been cast. Though looking back, while she was on the stairs, the dice were still in spin, still undecided as to which way to fall.

"I can't." I slipped back onto the sofa. "It's her call."

"Go out and get her!"

"Too late." I was zoning out, slamming down the shutters as I stared sightlessly at the TV. "She's gone."

Steve stalked over to the little kitchenette. "You're an idiot," he said. "You're both idiots." He snapped the top off another bottle of

Budwar. "You two… you could have had something quite good. And now you'll never know."

Well… perhaps he's right, and perhaps he's wrong.

As it happens though, I've only spent the past thirteen years analysing that night – and indeed all of the other Thursday nights after it – and this, just for the record, is my position: when your girlfriend or your wife or your loved one is swearing blind that there's nothing she wants so much in this world as to go off and bed another man… well she might well mean it. And she might not. But the one thing I'm sure of is that you have to fight it, fight it with every last breath in your body.

This is not just for the woman. It is also largely for your own sanity.

Only a patsy steps aside to let his loved one go off into the arms of another.

And so, I guess, I was that patsy. But love does strange things to you, does it not? And when you're in the heat, it is difficult to see things with quite that crystal clear clarity of a decade's hindsight.

CHAPTER 2

I've tried to analyse it since. Why did I do nothing? Why did I let Elise leave for her assignation when every last fibre of my being was telling me to drag her into the bedroom and do... do those very same things which the Frenchman was about to do to her. So many reasons... I suppose I thought that it was what she wanted. Along with that, she was her own woman and the cage door always had to be left open. And although it caused me no little hurt, I was also doing my best to live in the moment. When Elise and I were together, it was always wonderful: and when we were apart, well, how could Elise's actions affect my pleasure of the moment?

I came up with all manner of philosophical tricks in order to kid myself, but ultimately I suppose that I felt I was not good enough for her.

There was one other reason, perhaps, why I allowed it.

About three years earlier, my disastrous first marriage had come to an end. And although now is not the time to go into it, let us just say that this car-crash of a marriage had left me a little vulnerable. I was a plunger. When I had even the first whiff of true love, I would dive straight in without ever once thinking that it might first be wise to test the waters.

It never ceases to amaze me how love continues to turn my life upside down. The first time it happened, when I was a seventeen-year-old schoolboy and fell heels-over-head for my music teacher, well... I don't know. Passion combined with the most extraordinary jealousy, such that it sometimes felt as if my heart would crack in two.

But the next time that I fell for a woman, I had been half-expecting that the love would be not quite so... what is the word for it? Enthralling? Exhilarating? Intoxicating? All those, of course, but ultimately for me, it has also always been devastating. That seems to have been the nature of my love affairs. Never just the toe in the water, I always tend towards the full-body immersion: and every time, it seems as if I've been as much in love as I was with my first grand love, India. But the corollary is that when it all comes to an end, as all love affairs must, that the hurt is just as deep as it was that first time around.

Yes, the hurt is always the same. But what had happened over the years was that I had become much more adept at dealing with it. My emotions were kept lashed tight together behind this imperturbable façade. So another girl had dumped me and another relationship had bitten the dust and with practice I had become quite adept at dealing with it. I would go off to the pub, drown my sorrows and wallow in a week of torment, until a week, a month, a year later, and with still nothing learned, I'd dive in all over again.

And yet the thing about Elise was that I was in uncharted territory. She'd had her Thursday trysts before. But up until that Thursday in April, she'd never prepared herself for the Frenchman from within my own flat. And certainly for me, that was part of the kick of it: the knowledge that that very night, this beautiful woman was going off to sleep with another man. It was a new experience, a new emotion: just how was I going to feel when it actually happened?

At first, still there on the sofa watching wall-to-wall Seinfeld, I could only marvel at the sheer and utter ridiculousness of the position. It was Thursday night and my – yes, *my!* — girlfriend was out seeing another man. She'd been gone about half an hour now. Save for his name, I knew none of the details. He was called Georges. Feel that word, let the R roll off your tongue. Such an earthy name, the name of a man who likes to get his hands dirty, who embraces life; and a Frenchman too.

So... Thirty minutes for her to get there. But where was there? Did he have an apartment? A house? Was he rich? Did he have a string of lovers? Or were they meeting up in their favourite Soho bistro, sharing a bottle of chilled Sancerre and a dozen oysters before tumbling into his nearby bed? It was the not knowing which was almost worse than anything else. For in my fevered imagination, Georges was this multi-millionaire Gallic hunk: open with his emotions, living in the moment, rather than just purporting to be; a very accomplished lover. In short, Georges was, as I pictured him, almost everything that I was not.

As I sat there on the sofa, the thoughts crashed through my head like the coaches on one of those mile-long freight trains that stretch across America. One thought after the next, after the next, and for a moment you can spot it, analyse it, but only for a moment as in the next second another gory image is running through your mind. Perhaps worst of all were the pictures I was somehow miraculously able to conjure up. I have always had a particularly vivid imagination, and that Thursday it seemed that I only had to have the very whisper of a thought and the next moment there was the image, live, in colour and in 3D, being acted out on this enormous movie screen at the back of my brain.

I'd wonder, say, if Georges ever fed her oysters, with his strong, gnarled fingers clutching onto the shell as she supped the salt and lemon through wet-glossed lips: and then and there I can see the actual movie of them doing exactly that, with Elise caressing Georges' stubbled cheek as the tip of her tongue peeps from the side of her mouth. And what, I wonder, is going on beneath the table? And there, immediately, I can see it: their legs interlocked at the knees, hands clasped together and pressed tightly against his thigh. And for the rest of it... for what happened later on in the night, when they went back to Georges' flat... you can only imagine how I tormented myself with visions of all of those things that they were doing to each other in the bedroom.

Steve had brought me back another beer. To his mind, the whole thing must have been inexplicable. But at least he had the good grace to keep his own counsel.

"Do you want takeaway or shall we go out?" he asked. "I could even cook... if you're in the mood for a burnt egg."

I pondered. Already my bright-eyed bushy-tailed façade was dropping back into place. "What about curry?" I said. "Tandoori lamb-chops, four each, and a magnum of Musar."

I had just got up and was stomping off to get my coat from my bedroom. He touched my arm. "I'm sorry," he said.

Always, always, it's the niceness that gets me in the end.

When it comes to insults, I am Mr Teflon, armour-plated and invulnerable. But it's when people are kind to me that I crumble.

Even before I'd shut my bedroom door, the tears were spiking at my eyes. I threw myself onto my bed – the very bed where I had been making love with Elise not twenty-four hours earlier – burying my face into the pillows. I could smell her scent. Still on the pillow-case, there was a strand of long auburn hair. My fingers touched something crisp next to the sheet. She'd left a note.

She was, I think, trying to be kind, and just as always happens when women try to be kind to me, it only made things worse.

"I'm sorry," she'd written. "I need to sort these things through." She signed off with her name and with a solitary kiss. I still have the note. Of course I do: I have kept every single love-note that has ever been given to me by a woman. And as I look at it now, I still have no idea.

I know precisely *why* I started to date Elise. But I still really have no idea why I *continued* to date her. So that is the point of this little book. It is an exploration of my love for Elise. It is also, in part, an attempt to set the events of the past few months into context. But I am afraid that in large part, I am writing this book in order to help me keep a tenuous grip on my own sanity.

Why did I put up with it?

Why do I continue to put up with it?

I have no answers. All that I have are my own questions.

CHAPTER 3

I still find it incredible at how a love affair can unravel so quickly.

Most times, it seems that I have barely set sail before the storm clouds start to loom upon the horizon.

Perhaps I should make one thing clear. Since the thought is doubtless already in your head, I might as well bring it right out into the open. I make no bones about it: when it comes to matters of the heart, I am one of the most feckless, reckless fools that ever walked the earth. They say that a man with wisdom is able to learn from the harsh experiences of others. I, on the other hand, have been incapable of learning a jot from even the harshest lessons that my own life has thrown at me.

So, despite all my busted love affairs, I still had high hopes when I started out with Elise. How much of a plunger am I? Let me count the ways: within a week of our first kiss, I was already conjuring up dreams of marriage, children and cottages with clematis climbing up the walls. That is a tendency I have had with most of my previous girlfriends. I fall in love very, very fast. I'll be damned if I ever see a therapist, but I'm sure that it would be their primary contention that I'd been so starved of love after my mother's death that now I'm like a shipwrecked sailor who will cling onto any rock which will have me.

Perhaps it is so. But I'm not interested in root causes. I'm interested in the story. And what a story we had waiting in the wings for us that January.

In terms of sheer acreage of news-space, I think that it might even have beaten 9/11. At the beginning of 1998, the story had only just broken the surface. Looking back, I was a fisherman who'd had a very slight tug on the end of the line.

I remember thinking that the story might have legs. But I could never have dreamed it would turn into such a monster. For a paper like the *Sun*, it had everything: scandal, intrigue and sex in high places. For nine golden months, the world was transfixed by the story of President Clinton's love affair with his Monica.

In the end though, it's always the detail that counts. All these years later, what is that we remember of Clinton's affair with his intern? We remember the sex acts. We remember Monica's cheerleader smile. And we remember a little blue dress that nearly brought down a president.

When it comes to playing my trade, I pride myself on being the most fastidious observer. I miss none of the details.

How ironic it all now seems. For when it comes to matters of my own heart, I can somehow contrive to miss the elephant that is standing right in front of me.

I make no bones about it. But there it is. Because right from the very first with Elise, there were certain matters which should have rung alarm bells.

Of course it was all just part of the perpetual ongoing war between journalists and the public relations people who spin for the stars. It is a strange relationship that we journalists have with the PRs: we both need each other, we both feed off each other, and yet we are forever at loggerheads. I'll try to sum it up in a sentence: we journalists like our stories to have spice, while the PRs prefer them unseasoned.

One thing I can tell you is that just as with love, all's fair between the stars and the press. So I don't know why I complain. Perhaps I fell in love with Elise so completely for the very fact that she was the first PR in years to have got one over on me.

But I'm done with all of this musing about ridiculous hypotheticals. You've had a small taste of her.

Now let me formally introduce you to Elise, the love of my life.

We had already spoken about three times on the phone and she had sounded brisk and professional. In those days before Google, there was no means to check out what she looked like, but in my mind's eye I pictured one of those Manhattan show-ponies, striding to work down Fifth Avenue in high heels and a designer suit.

Elise had a star who wanted to promote his latest film, and who was therefore prepared to give up one hour of his time for an exclusive interview with the *Sun* newspaper. I forget why I was doing the interview. Normally those sort of stories were covered by the showbiz team, but we tabloid hacks are nothing if not versatile.

Now, do please excuse me if I don't actually name this star. The reason is that, even a decade down the line, this star is still a star. I have also had to alter some of the details of what happened, but the essence is absolutely as it occurred.

For the purposes of this story, however, this star is going to need a name. I shall call him Nick Spitz.

Elise had arranged for us to meet in the bar of one of New York's grand old-style hotels, the St Regis. It is the place, they say, where the Bloody Mary was invented. The plan was that we would get acquainted over a drink in the Old King Cole Bar and then we would move on up to one of the St Regis's suites for the actual interview. The meeting had been set for lunchtime, but at the last minute, Elise had postponed it until eight p.m. And, not that it made any real difference, eight o'clock in the evening in New York just happens to be one o'clock in the morning in London.

This rescheduling was not ideal for me, as I had to postpone a dinner date, but I will come to that later. When it comes to dealing with the stars, it would be rash indeed to ever imagine that you are an equal. Stars may go through this whole charming routine of being just another regular guy, but you only have to read the riders, or sub-clauses, in their contracts to realise that these people are anything but regular guys. They are not like the rest of us mortals. Everyone must know their place.

I turned up to the meeting with time to spare. I had also done my homework, spending the afternoon poring over a few score of Nick's cuttings. As for my clothes, I was wearing a few mementoes. Whenever my mad-masters despatched me across the Americas, I would buy a piece of clothing with which to remember the story by. So that night, I was sporting a burgundy velvet Versace jacket in memory of Gianni Versace's murder in Miami; on my feet were ostrich-skin cowboy boots bought on an astronaut-hunt in Houston, Texas; and around my waist was a Dallas Cowboys belt... although, now that I think about it, that belt was perhaps a little showy. Elise always hated it, and I have never worn it since. But no tie though, thank God. Ties are absolutely mandatory in the *Sun*'s head office in London, as are suits, but in New York the foreign correspondents may wear what they please.

And I was drinking – of course – a Bloody Mary, or Red Snapper as they like to call them in the Old King Cole Bar. It didn't taste even half as good as the Bloody Marys that my father used to knock up before Sunday lunch.

I propped myself up at the bar, admiring the mural of the merry old king. When you meet a big star, it is better if you are already standing, so that you don't have to flail around levering yourself out of a low-slung chair. Likewise, I did not touch the stick of celery. The last thing I needed was to be greeting Nick Spitz with a clump of celery in my mouth.

And in he came, on the very dot of eight o'clock, that alone revealing that Elise had some considerable clout. Dragging a star along for an interview is like taking an unruly child to school: in the end they'll all go, but only after a lot of complaining.

You may not have seen an A-list star when they are supposedly 'off duty'. When they are on show on the red carpet, then they're obviously the star. They look the part and they do what they're supposed to do. But even when they're not on public show – like having a drink at the St Regis – they still twinkle. It's still all an act, but just a lower key form of act.

What the A-list stars have in common is this astonishing charisma. I don't think they've always had it. Charisma seems to come with the job. The moment Nick entered the room he seemed to suck the very oxygen out of the air. All about the dimly lit bar, conversations started to flag, and elbows were nudged. As if by osmosis there was not a person in the room who was not immediately aware that we were in the presence of a star.

Nick scanned the bar, spotted me and glided straight over.

"Kim?" he asked, hand outstretched, and with the biggest smile on his face as if he were greeting his oldest schoolmate. "How ya doing? Good to see ya!" It was all an act, of course, but the real stars never for a moment stop acting.

I may have been a hard-bitten hack but I was nonetheless charmed. It is difficult not to be when you are under the full focus beam of an

A-list star. I liked his low-key way of dressing: just jeans, black boots, a plain pink shirt and a grey V-neck.

We shook hands, a nice firm, dry handshake of which even my father would have approved, and although my eyes were fully locked on his, I was also aware of a presence hovering at his side: and this, of course, was Elise.

I hope you will excuse me when I say that I was not overwhelmed by Elise's looks on our first meeting. She was a beautiful ice-queen. I took in auburn hair and a grey dress and coat, though there was this indefinable thing that somehow also registered. It was nothing more than a tweak at my Stone Age antennae... but there was this hint, this presentiment, of the most sensuous sexuality. She was a sexual being.

We shook hands – "Hi Elise", "Hi Kim" – and then both reverted our attention to the star. I ordered another two Bloody Marys and as the room watched, we slipped over to a snug table in the corner. I marvelled at how Nick handled the room. Every step of the way, he was twinkling, his eyes roving around the bar as he smiled at the ladies. He even shook hands with a couple of fans.

Even after we had taken our seats, I was still blown away at how unbelievably *cool* Nick was. With his specially tousled hair and his cheery smile, it was as if he just couldn't believe how good it was to be there with Elise and me. He sat with one leg slung over the side of the leather armchair, hands behind his head, and that's when I noticed a four inch boot knife strapped to his ankle. It was odd, the sort of thing that a private detective might wear. I wondered if it was a memento from one of his old films.

"Cheers!" I was melting under Nick's charm offensive.

"Happy days!" he said. We chinked and sipped, and for a minute or two we chatted like the great friends we were about to become.

Elise delved into a little black leather briefcase and brought out a couple of sheets of paper.

"You couldn't just sign these?" she said to me. "One for you. One for us."

"Sure," I said. "No problem."

The papers were passed over with a Mont Blanc pen. I was just about to sign when this little voice whispered that it might first be wise to read the contract.

"Better give it the once over," I said.

"You go right ahead," said Elise. Her voice was a mid-Atlantic hybrid: New York with an earthy tang of English. "It's the new holding contract the we've introduced. No big deal."

I started reading. It was all fairly standard: an exclusive interview to be granted to the *Sun* newspaper, said interview to be run within the next week, and no less than a two-page spread.

And then I got to the last sentence.

"I can't sign this!"

"There's a problem?" said Elise.

"You know very well I can't sign this."

"Oh dear." She gave a little sigh, flicked her hair and sipped her Bloody Mary.

I looked at the last paragraph again, where, at the end of the contract, were two of the most offensive words in a reporter's lexicon. Though I'd hazard that if you're not a journalist, you probably won't even have heard of them. Certainly not "No Comment": we don't mind hearing a "No Comment" at all. There are a dozen ways we can get round a "No Comment".

No. The last two words of the contract and the two words that were starting to give me palpitations were these: 'copy approval'. They may sound innocuous enough, but they possess the most unbelievable power.

"Copy approval?" I said. "I can't sign away copy approval. I'm just a reporter."

"Why don't you call up your editor?"

I had been completely outflanked.

I laughed without any humour. "At one thirty in the morning?"

"If you can't sign it, Kim, that's not a problem."

Stupidly, I brightened, as Elise continued: "There will be more than enough British papers which would just love to have an exclusive interview with Nick, copy approval included."

"What about…" I was searching for a way out. "Can I do the interview tomorrow? I'll have had time to run it past the boss."

"Perfect," she said. Her smile seemed to get even bigger. "Except Nick is flying to Aspen first thing."

"A phoner?"

"It's now or never, Kim," she said. "It's just the standard thing we include in all our contracts these days. We never enforce it. We just want to cover all the bases. I'm sure you can appreciate that."

You can have no concept of how vexing it all was.

For what Elise had sprung on me was the ultimate PR weapon. It was the PRs' Patriot missile, guaranteed to take down all known hostile fire from a tabloid enemy.

I'd heard of it, of course. Very occasionally, if the star was big enough and the story warranted it, an editor would hand over this extraordinary magic bullet that is known as 'editorial control'. It meant that before a story could go to print, it first had to go through the PRs, who could then excise as much as they saw fit. I've even seen them pull an entire feature.

Editors hate it, but these days there isn't much way round it. Either hand over the copy approval, or hand over the exclusive interview to a rival paper.

But there in the St Regis, copy approval was still relatively new. And it was certainly not the sort of thing that could be handed over willy-nilly by a mere reporter.

"Isn't there a sign above the doorway into the *Sun* newsroom?" Elise said. "What does it say?"

I rolled my eyes. Above the double doors into the *Sun*'s newsroom there is indeed a sign and when I first read it, I could not help but hold my head up high. For any other business on earth, it would have sounded ludicrous, but at the *Sun*, it seemed like the most magnificent call to arms: 'Walk tall, you're entering *Sun* country!'

"I'm going to get into a lot of trouble for this," I said.

"What you're going to get is the interview," she said. "Don't worry. You can write what you like."

So I drained my Bloody Mary and signed: signed with a flourish.

And that is modern journalism for you. As you read your papers or listen to the radio, you have no concept of how many deals have had to be done before a particular interview gets the go-ahead. Whether it's showbiz, politics, or some random punter who happens to be wallowing in her fifteen minutes of fame, there are always deals that have to be done.

It's not perfect. I certainly don't enjoy it. But if you want something badly enough, then usually you have to compromise.

Just like in a relationship.

CHAPTER 4

The star, Nick, was transformed. Whatever happened now, whatever he said, whatever he did, none of it was printable unless she first gave it the green light.

When we were in the lift, he started playing the goat. This is also all standard for a superstar. It's as if they're trying to show you that, along with being a star, they can also fool around. And yet it never quite fits: and it is then that you realise that even the horseplay is just an act. It is just another persona that the star has decided to adopt: the party guy who is out to have fun.

Nick started flicking at Elise's hair with his finger-tips. "I've never seen such perfect hair," he said. "Is it a wig? What happens if you get a hair out of place?"

"You don't want to know."

Nick tugged her hair. "Wiggy!"

"Look, don't touch," she said.

Nick continued to flick her hair. She stared at me. Glacial. Daring me to say a word.

The moment the lift doors opened at the top floor, she was out and marching off to the penthouse suite. She flashed her passkey over the lock and held the door open to usher us in.

"You've got twenty minutes, Kim." She locked the door with the passkey. "Better make sure we're not disturbed."

Another four minutes to ensure that we all have our drinks from the mini-bar – water now for Elise, Bloody Marys for Nick and me – and finally, finally, we are sitting at the round table in the dining room with Nick in the middle, now not so much a star as a suspect with his lawyer.

I took in a little of the suite as Nick fussed with his drink. Save for the gigantic modern four-poster bed, we could have been in practically any five-star hotel in the world: the usual huge television, creamy walls, balcony and soft, low lighting. Not that I was much interested in the décor. I only had another fifteen minutes in the room.

I switched on my tape recorder and placed it on the middle of the table.

"Fire away, Kim!" said Nick. "Give me your best shot!"

"I'll see what I can do."

Elise smiled as only a PR can when she's got what she wants more than anything else in the world: total control.

I dived in to see if there was anything new that I could learn from Nick and his latest sci-fi movie.

Route one for a tabloid journalist is to press the interviewee on his co-stars. You can sometimes get a slight sense of friction, and, very occasionally, a star will tear into an ex-colleague or an ex-lover to reveal the tiniest glimpse of what life is truly like inside the Hollywood goldfish bowl. It is those little scraps that fall from the star's table that we mongrel hacks feast upon.

"Your co-star, then, Nick?" I asked. "How did you get on with her?"

"I just loved her," he said off pat. "Just the funniest woman. Every day, she just creased me up!"

And on... and on.

I drew a blank with the supporting cast. They had become such close friends that most of them had been skiing with Nick over Christmas.

I drew a blank with any injuries or indeed hardships that Nick might have suffered during the filming.

I drew a blank with his ex-wife: "We're just the best friends!"

And I also drew a blank with his all-but-estranged mother: "She's my mother, I love her! What else can I say? She's a wonderful woman. I respect her."

I was dying inside. I was having an exclusive interview with one of the world's top stars, and with only two minutes to go, I had absolutely nothing to show for it. And there I'd been quibbling over copy approval in the bar, when he hadn't said a single word that was worth printing.

And Elise? She was still sitting there picture perfect as she basked in her star's glory.

In desperation, I tried talking about dogs. Nick had a famously volatile Alsatian. "Has Blondi had any more scrapes?" I asked.

"Blondi!" he said. "No, since I had him done, he's much calmer."

My ears pricked up a little. It wasn't going to set the world alight, but at that stage, it was about the best I had.

"Are you going to follow suit?" I asked.

Nick rocked with laughter, ignoring my question to tell an anecdote about Blondi. It was quite funny, I suppose, the first time I'd heard it: except that I had read that exact same story, word for word, in the cuttings that afternoon.

Elise looked at her watch. "Time's up!" she said. "I do hope you got what you wanted Kim."

"Thanks for seeing me." I had a fixed smile on my face as I tried to mask my boiling rage. I'd got nothing. Not a single thing. How could I make a story out of that pap?

I retrieved my tape-recorder – though did not turn it off – and tried one last cast as I shook hands. That is another thing that we journalists love to try: as the interview comes to a close, just as the star's guard is coming down, we fire off a last question.

I can still picture the room: Nick and Elise standing at the table, seemingly delighted that the interview had passed without mishap.

"So Nick" I said, hand upon the door-handle. "Who's the most annoying star you've ever worked with?"

"Most annoying star?" he repeated, turning for a moment to gape at Elise.

She played with the crucifix about her neck. "Get away with you!"

"All right!" I said. The mood was infectious. "How about the least annoying star you've ever worked with?"

"Get out of here!" Elise laughed. "You've had your interview: now scram!"

Nick was off to the lavatory. He waved. "Good seeing you, Kim!"

And that, I suppose, was when my exclusive interview suddenly started to get interesting.

CHAPTER 5

Elise had left the passkey slotted into the door-lock. Opening the door should simply have been a matter of pulling the card out.

Except that nothing happened. The lock light continued to glow red.

I shrugged and gave it another try.

"Something wrong?" said Elise.

"The lock's jammed," I said. "Is it the card?"

"I hate these new locks." Elise gave the card a try. "What's wrong with an old-fashioned key?"

She swiped and swiped again, but the door remained locked.

Elise went over to the phone to call reception. I noticed the way she elegantly peeled off her diamond earring as she brought the handset to her ear.

It seemed that a power-cut had caused a glitch in the computer – or perhaps it was the other way round – and every door on the top floor was locked.

"I hope you haven't got anything planned," she said. "We're stuck."

"Oh."

I was, of course, delighted. What journalist in the world wouldn't love to be stuck in a hotel suite with an A-list superstar?

"I wonder how Nick will take it," Elise said.

He bounded out of the lavatory, his face flushed. There was perhaps a little dusting of cocaine on his nostril.

"Still here?" Nick asked me.

"Afraid so," I said. "We're locked in."

"Locked in? We can't be locked in!"

"It's the whole of the top floor," said Elise.

He snatched the passkey from her hand and started jabbing it in and out of the lock. "But I've got to get out of here!" He hammered at the door with his fists. "I've got to get out."

I was fascinated. Over the years, I had heard occasional gossip about Nick's temper. But to witness it up close was extraordinary. It was like a switch had been flicked.

He snatched up the phone and was screaming four-letter foulness at the receptionist. Elise calmly stooped to the wall and unplugged the phone from its socket. Nick continued to jabber at the handset before realising it had gone dead.

"Just take a seat, Nick," said Elise. "Have another drink. They'll get us out as soon as they can."

Nick stood panting, eyes rolling in his head. With the dead phone still in his hand, he considered what to do next.

He took five smart steps and launched a thundering drop kick at the door. Nothing happened. He attempted another drop-kick, and then another. The door didn't move.

Elise went over with a bottle of water from the fridge. "Have a drink," she said. "There's nothing we can do."

"Don't touch me!" He brushed her hand away. "I just need to think."

I watched, ever cool, ever clinical, as he marched over to the balcony window and opened it. A rush of cold air swept into the room. He stared about him from left to right; tested the balcony rail; looked over the edge. I wondered what might have happened next. But Elise was done with the charade.

Very business-like, she went out onto the balcony, caught Nick under the arm and dragged him inside.

"Sit down," she commanded. "Do not get up."

Nick looked about him suspiciously. He was about to get up and then thought better of it. "Can I use the phone?" he asked.

He had a curt muttered conversation. Elise drank water straight from the bottle. For the first time, I noticed her lips. There was a trace of, I don't know, gloss or lipstick and I idly wondered what it would be like to kiss her. That is what I do when I am daydreaming in the company of a beautiful woman. I wonder what it would be like to lean over and, ever so gently, steal a kiss from those moist lips.

We might have talked, but Nick flicked on the TV and started scrolling through the channels. By chance we came across one of his earlier films. He knew it instantly.

"This was my first hit!" he said. "This was where I met Barbara!"

He was entranced as he stared at the TV screen. It was the film which had turned Nick into a star and his ex-wife Barbara into an even bigger star. He was the cop, she was the lieutenant. The on-set chemistry between the pair had been quite electric. By the time the movie had wrapped, the pair had each split from their long-term partners and were all but engaged.

The wedding was lavish. The couple had three children. And then, rather sadly, Nick fell for another of his leading ladies. Barbara might have taken him back, but Nick was already dead set on Megan, his newer, younger love. The divorce had gone through a couple of years earlier. It had been as acrimonious as they come.

And yet as Nick watched the TV, it was becoming increasingly clear that he was still besotted with his ex. He was mesmerised, the fights and the shouting now all but forgotten as he was once again reminded of Barbara's beauty. I'll never forget the sight of him sitting there, constantly sipping from a tumbler of whisky, elbows on his knees.

I'd never before watched a film in the company of the actual star of the show. My eyes flicked back and forth, one moment looking at Nick on the TV and the next looking at the man himself. Occasionally Elise would conspiratorially catch my gaze; it was surreal.

Nick clapped his hands in ecstasy. "Our first kiss!" he said. "Our first kiss, there on film! We were so tense we must have had thirty takes. And at the end of it all, you know what they did? They went with the very first one!"

It was a perfect first kiss. A peck, followed by another, firmer peck, and then a third kiss, more lingering still, before a final sigh as Barbara was enfolded in Nick's arms.

Elise continued to top up Nick's glass. Between the three of us, we were working our way through the entire mini-bar.

The film came to a close. I was all but holding my breath.

"So good," Nick said. "Still the best film I've ever made."

Elise sat on the side of his armchair and stroked his shoulder. "It's my favourite."

"God we were good together."

I can't remember exactly how it happened, but the mood in the room suddenly turned maudlin. Perhaps it was the drink, or perhaps it was the movie, but the combination of the two was having a disastrous effect on Nick.

"What was I thinking of?" he said. "What was I doing? Split with Barbara, to start seeing this... this bitch! I must have been mad! I don't see my kids! I don't see my kids anymore! I don't see Barbara and I don't see the kids!"

He burst into tears. Elise passed him a box of tissues. I didn't know where to look. I hate to see a woman cry, and it is even more excruciating to see a man in tears.

As the tears started to dry up, Nick began to talk. "It was the biggest mistake of my life," he said. "She'd have had me back. Barbara would have had me back! Let me tell you something. Never, ever get divorced. No matter how much shit you have to put up with, anything is better than divorce." He drank more whisky. "What a screw-up. What a total, total screw-up."

I said nothing. I didn't know what to say, and anything that I did say was going to be just too awful for words, so I kept my mouth shut. Elise continued to stroke his shoulder as he became more and more despondent.

At length, Nick stood up and weaved to the bathroom. We heard the sound of water. He was running a bath.

Elise and I stared at each other. I blew out my cheeks and exhaled. It was not going to be me who broke the silence.

"Well..." she said.

"Well..."

And again: silence. I think we were both utterly speechless.

"I think I could do with some fresh air," she said.

We stood out on the balcony, icy rain spitting into our faces. Elise let out a monstrous sigh, burying her face in her hands, before sweeping her hair back through her fingers. "I've never heard him quite as bad as that before."

"What happens next?"

"Who knows?"

"You're doing a great job of holding it all together."

She gave me a wan smile. "It's in my nature. Besides: it's what I'm paid for."

We stared out into the rain. I wish that I had the gift of honeyed words, but I do not. It was easier, safer, to say nothing.

When we returned to the suite, Nick was still in the bathroom, though the taps had been turned off. We watched some TV for a few minutes, though by now Elise was drumming her fingers with impatience.

"How long's he been in there?" she asked.

"Ten minutes?" I said.

She sat in silence for another two minutes before abruptly getting to her feet and knocking on the bathroom door. "Nick?" she said. "Nick? Are you okay?"

No reply.

I joined Elise.

She knocked again, much louder. "Nick?"

We pressed our ears to the door. There was not a sound to be heard.

Elise bit on her lower lip. "I don't like this."

"Could he have fallen asleep?"

"We better check."

The door handle rattled as she shook it. "Nick!" she called out.

Nothing. Not a sound.

"Okay," she said, matter-of-factly looking me straight in the eye. "Break down the door."

"I think you're right."

I tossed my jacket onto a chair and leaned against the door, probing for the position of the lock. It seemed to be flimsier than the main door into the room. Elise stood to the side.

"Here goes." I charged at the door. It trembled as I hit it with my shoulder. The sound of splintering wood.

"Nick?" called Elise.

"If that didn't wake him up, then… then we've got a problem."

I had a renewed sense of urgency, charging the door one more time, driving my shoulder in low with my full bodyweight behind it. The lock snapped, the door boomed open, and I sprawled head first onto the bathroom floor.

It was carnage.

Nick had slashed a wrist and was lying unconscious in the bath, the water wine-dark with his blood. White pills were scattered all over the floor. His skin was pale and waxy as white froth bubbled at his lips.

Elise leapt past me, hauling at Nick's body.

"What have you done?" She cradled his head in her arms. It was one of the most pitiful scenes that I have ever witnessed.

"Do something," she said. "Get something for his wrist."

I darted back to the lounge area, eyes scanning the room before I spotted the phone. I unplugged the cord at both ends.

Nick's head lolled forward as we heaved him out of the water. As I dragged him over to the wall, Elise lifted his feet. Blood still oozed from his wrist, the very reddest vermilion as it dripped onto the white tiles.

I grabbed a hand-towel, pressing it against the wound before cinching it tight with the phone cord. Elise, squatting beside me, watched my every move. Nick's boot-knife was still lying by the bath. I picked it up and cut the cord.

Elise left the bathroom, and barked staccato sentences as she called an ambulance from her mobile.

I looked at my makeshift bandage. It seemed to be a decent enough job. Blood wasn't seeping through the towel. I tried to recall my first aid lessons from half a lifetime ago. Was there more I could do? Perhaps try and make him throw up the pills. I didn't know.

I wrapped him in a towel and, not knowing what else to do, just sat next to him, the two of us shoulder to shoulder. How strange it all now seemed: one moment interviewing an A-list Hollywood star, and the next fighting to save his very life.

Elise, still on the phone, popped her head around the door. "They'll be here shortly," she said.

There was the sound of a thundering crash as a sledgehammer was driven into the door of the suite. Then there was another crash, followed by splintering wood. I'm hustled away into the lounge area, as white suited medics pile into the bathroom. After the calm, everything is a sudden whirl of activity. Nick is being wheeled from the suite in a gurney, and a hotel executive is apologising.

I was done.

I gave Elise a hug and slid off into the night. I walked back home through Central Park, revelling in the rain.

I had been in bed for an hour when Elise called.

"How is he?" I asked. It was nice, lying there snug in the dark talking to Elise.

"He'll pull through," she said. "I'm sorry, did I wake you?"

"No, can't sleep."

No, I could not sleep. It wasn't just the sight of Nick Spitz's limp body lying there in the bath. Or that trail of blood on the tiles as we'd dragged him across the floor.

The one thought that kept coming back to me was this: why had this Hollywood superstar tried to kill himself? He'd seemingly had it all: wealth, fame, adulation. And yet even all that had not been enough. What more did he want? What more did he expect? I just couldn't work it out. Did his life have to be perfect in every way? Maybe it was just the booze and the 'black dog'.

Eventually though, not then, but a little while later, I did come up with an answer. The money and the fame are all fine enough. But if there's no love in your life, then it all quickly turns to bitter wormwood.

And Nick's problem was that he'd actually found the love of his life, only to end up spurning her. That is, I'm afraid, what men do. We find these great loves, and then, because it's in our perverse nature to always want more, we shun them for something else. Not necessarily something better, but something different.

I understand it. I know about the sheer insanity of lust and desire; and along with that, the quite extraordinary things that a man will do for love. That is something that I do know about. And this, I suppose, is the story of how I dealt with it.

CHAPTER 6

My office in those days was a delightfully collegiate environment on 'The Avenue of The Stars', or Sixth Avenue as New Yorkers still like to call it.

It was from here, not a block away from Times Square, that Rupert Murdoch ran his fiefdom. In our skyscraper were the various newsrooms of Murdoch's magazines and papers. Occasionally, I'd waft into the *New York Post*'s newsroom to see a couple of friends and would rock with inner glee as I watched the staff descending into a deadline frenzy.

Amidst all of this media bustle, there was one small oasis of calm on the fourth floor which was inhabited by Murdoch's handful of New York Correspondents. We had two men from the *Times* in London, as well as Steve and five other Australians who were writing for Murdoch's Australian papers. There were also three Americans to keep the office running smoothly, as well as a Canadian office boy. Freelancers would occasionally pop in to use our computers.

As for myself, I was responsible for all of the *Sun*'s news coverage in North America, South America, Canada and the Caribbean. Even now, it still remains my dream job. I had bosses who precisely shared my tastes for the exotic, the bizarre, the sleazy and the scandalous, and they had a seemingly limitless budget to send me wherever they pleased. From one day to the next – one *hour* to the next – I had no idea where fate might next be taking me. One moment I might be playing chess with the man from the *Times*, and the next I'd be desperately hailing a cab to pick up my bag and passport.

This, then, was the extraordinary world that I inhabited in New York City. It may give you some small glimpse into the whys and wherefores of my crazy relationship with Elise. Crazy; there's no other word for it. But when you spend your life living on adrenalin and when you can only see as far ahead as the next story, then somehow even the craziest relationships seem to make sense.

I may only have had three hours sleep, but I was still out of bed at six a.m. By six thirty, I had showered, shaved and still wearing my Versace jacket for luck, was catching a cab to the Mid-Town. I am not a morning person. If there was a downside to being the *Sun's* New York Correspondent, it was having to get up so early; the Australians, filing to the other side of the earth, could roll into the office whenever they pleased.

I always loved that drive in to work, whisked in silence through skyscraper canyons as a hint of mist lingered over Central Park. I bought two bagels and two coffees at the street vendor and three minutes later I was sharing them with Justin, the man from the *Times*.

I had my morning conference with the *Sun's* two main rivals, the correspondents from the *Mail* and the *Mirror*. Our editors would have preferred it if we'd been at each other's throats, but we found life in New York much more conducive when we co-operated. Exclusives could be forgotten within the day. But a missed story in the *Mirror* would have had my mad-masters grinding their teeth for weeks.

Most days, I would share everything with my rivals. But I was not about to tell them about Nick Spitz. No: that glorious story, I was hugging to myself.

And that's when it hit me. Most American hospitals have a hotline straight into their local newsrooms. Why wasn't it all over the radio stations?

I switched on the two TVs and the radio. There was nothing at all on Nick Spitz.

The enormity of it all was still sinking in: but a few hours earlier, I had helped save the life of one of Hollywood's biggest stars. I had it all to myself.

My fanciful dreams. Forgive me if I indulge myself for a moment. You will soon understand why.

It was about then that I realised that if the story was going to be running across the front page of the next day's *Sun*, then I would need to move fast. The tabloids may be famous for their brevity, but when it came to the big stories, they wanted every last detail. Nick's drama of the previous night might easily run to five pages... perhaps over 4,000 words.

My hand stretches for the phone. I'm about to make the call that will change my life.

And just as I'm about to pick up, the phone rings.

"Hi Kim," she said. "It's Elise."

"Elise?" I stumbled over her name. "Hi, how are you?"

"A little strung out," she said. "But how are you?"

"I'm good." My eyes flickered over at the TV; another smash in the Lincoln tunnel. "How's Nick?"

"He's asleep. He'll be fine," she said. Her voice sounded oddly flat. "I was wondering if you'd started the story yet. When do you think I'll be able to have a look?"

"A couple of hours," I said.

"Yes." Again, it sounded all wrong. There was a long, deadly pause. "Actually, Kim, I wanted to speak to you about that. I've been talking this through with my colleagues. And we have decided... we have decided that what happened last night may be problematic. I'm very sorry."

"Problematic?" I said. "What do you mean?"

"I don't think we can run it. I'm sorry."

"I'm sorry?"

Elise cleared her throat. "We don't want you to run the story. I am very sorry."

"What? What! How can you spike the story? He nearly killed himself! We saved his life! That's what happened! You can't deny it!"

She sighed. "Kim, I'm sorry about this. But we do have copy approval, and we can't approve anything like that. It would be a disaster for Nick. You know that."

White knuckles gripping the phone. She was spiking the biggest exclusive of my life. If I lived to a hundred, I'd never be able to top it.

"But ... but!" I was so outraged I didn't even know where to begin. "So what if he'd died?" I said. "You'd have tried to cover that up too?"

"He didn't die though, did he?" She was speaking so calmly: quite different from myself. "But this story could break him. It really could."

I was silent as I probed the matter further.

"I've already told London," I said. "I've got to file by nine."

And now there was a pause from Elise as she digested this fresh piece of information. "No you haven't," she said.

"On the contrary." I lied smoothly. "I called up the news desk as soon as I got in. I told them everything."

"You didn't, Kim," she said. "I know you didn't."

"Honestly: I've got ninety minutes to file."

"You're lying, Kim," she said. "Three reasons. First, you wouldn't have lost it like that if the story was already a go. Second, I've yet to hear a man use the word 'Honestly' when he hasn't been lying. And third, well, let's just put it down to a woman's intuition. But even if you have told the office – which I don't believe – you've still got to run the copy by me. And it's probably best you know now: I won't be approving it."

I could squirm and I could writhe, but how she had me skewered.

"Okay then." I took a deep breath, making a conscious effort to calm down. "I won't bother sending you the copy. I'll send it straight to London. What you going to do about that?"

"You won't do that," she said, her voice as smooth as honey. "You'd be finished. We'd not only sue your newspaper, but we'd sue you personally. Nick's got deep pockets." She switched tack. "I'm really sorry."

"My heart bleeds."

"Kim, I don't think you understand. I'm quite happy to talk it through with you. But this is not a subject for negotiation."

"Don't you get it Elise?" I said. "This story is bound to come out anyway! The New York hospitals leak like a sieve…"

"He was taken to a private clinic."

"But it doesn't make any odds whether we run it or not: the story's going to come out!"

"But not from you," she replied.

"I've got the tape!" I said triumphantly. "I've got the whole thing on tape! How are you going to deny it!"

Another silken pause. "Have you now?" That's all she said.

I slammed the phone down and walked out, pounding out my rage on the iced pavements as I headed off to Times Square and down Broadway.

It may sound laughable coming from a *Sun* reporter, but I was genuinely shocked. I knew the celebrity PRs could twist and fabricate as well as any Downing Street spin-doctor. But Elise wasn't even trying to spin the story; she was denying its very existence.

At first, I was set on just filing. Put in a brief call to the news desk. Tell them I had a belter. File the basics in thirty minutes, then leave it to the lawyers to sort out what we could and could not publish. That is my natural reaction when it comes to brinkmanship. Rather than be blackmailed, I'll bring the whole house tumbling down on my head. Have this PR luvvie calling me up at seven thirty a.m. and telling me – telling me! – what I could and could not write? Just what sort of patsy did she take me for? So they'd be suing the paper? Suing me personally? Well wouldn't that just be a case worth watching?

I had a disquieting thought. What was the last thing Elise had said? I'd told her that the whole thing was on tape and… How had she replied? "Have you now?"

In sudden alarm I patted my jacket pockets. The recorder wasn't there. I did that frantic searching thing you do when you realise you've lost something important. Could it have fallen out in the bathroom? In the suite? Could… Could Elise have slipped it out of my pocket?

Now, thirteen years on, I am able to smile about it. What a match we were for each other. At every turn, Elise had out-thought me. I'm not sure it's a compliment but, as they say, we truly deserved each other.

I'd walked about four blocks. My steps faltered. The disappearance of my recorder was putting a completely different complexion on things. Because if Elise had the tape… then what exactly did I have to stand up my story? It would be my word against the two of them… and both of them would be more than capable of lying through their perfectly capped teeth. Don't think it doesn't happen. In all the current turmoil of phone-hacking and computer-hacking, most people imagine that it is the tabloid reporters who are the unprincipled hounds. But compared to the PRs, we were as blameless as the Vestal Virgins. Our stories do at least tend to have a basis in fact, whereas the PRs' sole aim is to protect their client... I'll leave it at that. Even as I write, I can feel my blood pressure soaring.

As I started to walk back, I continued to inspect the dilemma from all angles. I'm still not sure that I did the right thing. But at the time, it seemed I had no option but to bow to the inevitable. Who knows how my life might have turned out if I'd just walked tall, filed my story and to hell with the consequences. They might have run it; they might not. Nick might have sued; he might not. Though there is one thing of which I am reasonably sure: would Elise and I have started dating? Most definitely not.

CHAPTER 7

I could hear the phone ringing even before I'd got back to the office.
Time to face the music.

I picked up.

"Kim! Where the hell have you been? It's gone one thirty!"

It was one of my many masters, Kent. There were four news editors on the *Sun*, of whom Kent was *the* news editor. In the peculiar ranking system of a national newspaper, that probably put him at about Lieutenant Colonel. But above him there were various Brigadiers, Generals and, of course, the Field Marshal himself, the editor. Like the officers of old, all an editor has to say is, "Make it so", and it will be made so.

As for my position in the *Sun*'s ranks, I was a subaltern, usually only answerable to Kent, the news editor. Usually.

Usually.

"Hi Kent," I said. "Just got back."

"We've got no splash," he said, straight to the point. "Did you get anything good out of Nick Spitz last night?"

"Well…" I had not expected to have to commit myself so quickly.

To tell or not to tell? Why didn't I just come clean? Tell him everything: tell him I'd signed away copy approval; tell him I'd lost my tape recorder. It would have caused the most almighty row, but at least it would have then been up to London to sort it all out. Bigger brains on bigger salaries would be left to deal with the problem.

But I didn't.

I suppose that like most men, I have a natural aversion to admitting when I've messed up. Though if I'd had even a couple more minutes. To think it matter over, I would have realised that I was already up to my neck in it.

"There were a few lines," I temporized. "Probably not enough for a splash."

Kent was straight back at me. "What's the best line?"

"It was… He said that he'd given his dog Blondi the snip and… he might be going the same way too."

"File as soon as possible."

I remember pawing at my lower lip, already wondering if I'd done the right thing. Was it too late?

"Kent," I said. "One other thing. I had to sign a contract. They've got copy approval. Otherwise there wasn't going to be an interview."

"You cleared that?"

My most hideous fears were being confirmed in full. "Well, no, I didn't. It was gone one o'clock before they'd even produced the contract. I… didn't want to disturb the boss. There was nothing contentious… it's fine."

Kent let out a whistle. "You didn't even call the night desk?"

"There wasn't time."

"Christ!"

So, precisely one hour to file my world exclusive interview with Nick Spitz, bearing in mind that I had no record of the conversation and only the very shakiest recollection of what had been said. How my time in New York all comes back to me: the phone perpetually ringing as I rush to meet my daily deadline; a series of desperate sprints to catch the next plane; and that constant refrain from the news editors, "File as soon as possible".

I hadn't even turned on the computer before the phone was ringing again. I picked up, bracing myself.

"Hello?"

"You did what?"

"Oh, hi. Trisha."

This time it was the Head of News.

"You gave them copy approval? Are you out of your mind?"

Steve came into my office. He sat on the desk and started chewing his nails.

"I'm sorry," I said, striving for a note of sincerity. "I'm very sorry."

"Well let's see the copy," said Trisha. "This is hopeless! Absolutely hopeless!"

"Yes Trisha," I said. "Thank you Trisha. I'll file right away."

I replaced the handset. Steve spat out a nail onto the floor.

"Do you have to?" I asked.

"That sounded like a boss to me," he said. "Who was it it?"

"The head of news," I replied curtly.

His fingers tapped out a tattoo on the desk. "The head of news? And might that be Trisha?"

"Yes." I took a sip of revolting cold coffee before spitting it back into the cup.

He turned to admire the map of America on the wall. "That wouldn't be the same Trisha who you slept with after a Christmas party?"

"I told you *that*?"

Steve smirked. "I bet she's one of your biggest fans."

"I wouldn't bank on it," I said.

Indeed so. It is more than possible to be a fan of an ex. But to be the cheerleader of someone with whom you had a one-night stand... well... it is not impossible. But it is less likely.

CHAPTER 8

Let me describe a newspaper deadline. In the right circumstances, they are very exciting. In a small way, I guess it's like running in the Olympics. So long as you've done the training, been on the right diet, had enough sleep, then you at least know you're in contention. You've done everything you can do: and as for the rest, well, that's as arbitrary as falling in love.

With a tight deadline, you are aware that this vast machine is waiting for your golden copy to drop into the news editor's inbox. I am told that I get so tense my face goes white. My language becomes very crisp and curt. And for the space of one hour, my entire life seems to concentrate on this one laser-like point: the story.

I've seen reporters stall. It happens because the reporter hasn't developed the necessary skills. A tight deadline is like a crucible. Your every weakness will be discovered. If the story's big enough and the deadline's tight enough, then your brain can go into spasm. It's like a mental cramp. You can't write a word. It's a disaster. Kiss goodbye to the prospect of ever covering a big news story again for a tabloid.

So at that moment in my little windowless cubby-hole in New York City, I was trying to get my priorities right. I had to win round Elise.

I hoped she wasn't one to nurse a grievance.

"Hi Elise" I smiled into the phone. You can hear a person's smile.

"Hi Kim." Not exactly warm. Not hostile either. Waiting to see which way the wind blew.

"Well you've got your wish. As yet, London is still none the wiser about Nick's suicide attempt."

"Oh Kim!" she said. More than anything else, she sounded relieved. "Thank you." It is, perhaps, one of the few uplifting traits of the strange little world that I inhabit that you can be as rude as you like to someone and yet within ten minutes, it's all so much water under the bridge.

"Though as I'm sure you're aware, I no longer have my tape recorder," I said. "I've got to file the whole of last night's interview. They seem especially interested in the fact that Blondi is getting the snip, and that Nick Spitz will be following suit. There is also the matter of your copy approval."

"I better come over," she said.

"And I don't have long."

"Give me fifteen."

Even then, even though the mad-masters would soon be shrieking down the phone, there must have been a faint scent of love in the air. The story would have to wait. It was time for a tidy-up. Although the office was only the size of a small bus-shelter, it was awash with newspapers. There were hundreds of them stacked in piles by the far wall.

I'd bin the lot.

Steve wandered in with my coffee. "Now give us a hand clearing all this junk out," I said.

"Don't you have a deadline?"

"There's always a deadline," I replied with more swagger than I felt. "Fetch a trolley from the *Post*."

"So it's someone important coming round?"

"It's nothing to do with that."

"She must be beautiful too." Steve smiled, his single golden canine glinting. "I'll pretend to be the office boy."

"Go to!" I said. "What are you waiting for?"

Steve padded back with the trolley and we started loading it up with old newspapers.

Steve paused over an old copy of the *Sun*. "Your story!" he said. "The Boston nanny, Louise Woodward! Don't you keep your front pages?"

"Fish and chip paper," I said dismissively. Yes, it's a strange attitude that we have to news. When you're in the moment, it seems there is nothing so important as your story. You'd do anything for that exclusive. And then a week later, it's gone, just another ephemeral news story that has been sucked into the black mist of history.

As Steve continued to shovel out the newspapers, I started work on my desks. This was the hub of the *Sun's* US Empire, three desks, set out in a U-shape, with a black swivel chair in the middle. They were entirely covered with paper.

My first instinct was to bin everything. But then I caught sight of a bill and a cheque and realised that there might actually be something of import in amongst the junk. I swept it all into one of the filing cabinets.

"Now that's my kind of filing." Steve heaved the last of the newspapers onto the trolley. "Shall I get some flowers? A little posy of roses by your computer? It might help strike the right note."

"Don't you have some work to do?"

"Who is she?" he asked. "If she's coming in this early, she's either a hack or a PR."

I wiped away at the computer screen, amazed at how much dust had accumulated there in the last eight months.

"She's…" I trailed off.

Elise was standing in the doorway, wrapped up in a white ankle length coat. I don't know how she'd done it. She can barely have had three hours sleep, and she still looked sensational.

"She's a PR," she said. "Good morning."

"G'day!" said Steve.

"Aussie or Kiwi?" she asked.

"A Kiwi? Do I sound like a Kiwi?"

"You better say 'fish and chips' and then I'll be able to tell. How do the Kiwis say it…" She made a grotesque imitation of a Kiwi accent. "Fi-ushhh and Chi-upps."

"Fish and chips?"

"So you're an Aussie?"

Steve witheringly shook his head as he pushed off with the trolley.

"Morning Kim." As Elise walked into my office, she ran a finger along the edge of the desk and sniffed at the amount of dust. "Late night?"

"An outbreak of hives," I replied. She'd taken off her coat, hanging it on the door. Underneath, a blue silk shirt hung loose over her trousers. "It's what happens when I've been grievously let down."

"Does it happen a lot?" She kissed me on the cheek and as she did so, she laid one hand lightly against my chest.

"Only when I'm dealing with PRs."

"We'll just have to see if there's any way that I can make it up to you then." Deliciously, she cocked an eyebrow. I did a double-take. And looking back, I think *that* was the moment when it dawned on me that she was no mere Manhattan show-pony. She was beautiful. In a mere matter of seconds, I had completely reappraised my view. In fact, I was surprised that I had not noticed it before. Perhaps I had been so much in Nick's thrall the previous evening that I had not had the eyes to see her.

"What did you have in mind?" I took my seat, looking up at her.

Elise perched on one of the desks, stretched over, and very gently rubbed the lobe of my right ear between thumb and forefinger. "I wonder."

And *that*, I suppose, was the moment when I realised that she was unlike any other woman I had dated. I don't want to make her sound like a wanton. But there was this definite frisson of overt sexuality.

"That is unusual," I said. "Very unusual. Nobody's ever done that to me before." I stretched up and took her the lobe of *her* ear between thumb and forefinger, gently returning the compliment. She still wore her diamond studs. I was careful not to pinch the skin.

"You stroke my ear, I'll stroke yours," she said, again stooping down to take my ear. We were each stroking the other's ear, eyes quite locked onto each other.

"Quite erotic?" I said.

I was aware that her pink lips were only two feet away. My ear had become one vast erogenous zone.

"Only quite?" she said. "I thought you had a story to write."

"Do you do this to most guys you meet?"

"No," she said. Her eyes never once left mine.

"Standards must be slipping."

"And not usually before breakfast."

"You probably haven't written a splash before breakfast either," I said. I glanced briefly at the door. Steve had done a glorious double-take as he'd walked past. "Ready to start?"

"Any time." We broke away from our ear stroking. Elise eased herself back to sit on the desk, her legs swinging.

I was still tingling as I tried to analyse what had just happened. I think it was the sheer unexpectedness of it that had floored me. The one moment, I'd been in deadline mode, gearing up to write a story; and the next this woman had started stroking my ear. I wondered if it was a come-on. Of course she was flirting with me. That's what female PRs do with male journalists. They use their feminine wiles to get what they want. She'd probably stroked the ear of every other male hack that she'd met...

It was difficult to know what she meant.

You see, there was one other matter to throw into the mix. In the same way that every dog immediately knows its place within the pack, so I was aware that Elise was a little out of my league. It's difficult to put my finger on the specifics. But somehow, within just a few seconds of meeting someone, you generally know where you both stand. And Elise... she seemed like a woman who knew what she wanted from a man. I sensed a wealth of experience. She was used to dealing with much older men; older, richer, more powerful.

Did she sleep with her stars?

Well as to that, I just don't know. I've never asked her. I've never *dared* ask her, for fear of what I might learn.

But the one thing I know I was right about was her predilection for older, more powerful men. I was a very atypical boyfriend. Sometimes, even thirteen years on, I still have no idea what she saw in me.

And yet there at eight a.m. in my New York office, Elise was openly, brazenly, flirting with me. What was that secret pulse which connected us?

I started typing. It was not the most sparkling intro I'd ever written. But then I wasn't paid for my intros; I was paid to bring in the stories.

Elise read out loud over my shoulder, "'Hollywood sensation Nick Spitz was last night preparing to have the snip, after following the lead of his pet Alsatian Blondi.'" She swept her hair over her shoulder. "Almost as impressive as your touch-typing."

"Took me ages to get a job," I said, still typing away. "I went to secretarial college. If my Fleet Street career goes belly up, I could always be a temp. Right, are you going to make up some quotes for me now?"

She did just that. It was better by far than anything to have come from Nick during his desultory interview. She even threw in a line about Nick paying a trip to the sperm bank, just in case he had second thoughts.

"Are you happy to approve that copy?" I asked.

She scanned it one more time, playing with the silver crucifix about her neck.

"Your copy is hereby approved," she said.

"You know they'll re-write it all in London?" I asked.

"Surely," she said. "A small price to pay for... last night's accident."

"It's all going to come out," I said. "It won't be me leaking it and it probably won't be you either. No, the person who will leak this story is Nick himself."

That was another worrisome nag. Just another of the niggles that had cropped up ever since Elise had come into my life. It's hard enough keeping a secret if only two people are involved. But to have at least five or six people in the know? And a sensational secret?

I filed and called up the news desk. Did they say "Thank you"? Let me put it like this: do you say thank you to the faithful family car for never breaking down and for starting up without fail every morning? No, you do not. All you do is kick the car when, once every five years, you're left stranded at home because the battery's flat.

Elise yawned and stretched, her hands interlocked as she pushed up to the ceiling. She looked up, her hair turning into this shimmering auburn waterfall. She didn't seem to be aware of her breasts straining against the blue silk. I admired them. That is what guys do. It would be stupid to pretend that we do not.

"A great morning," she said.

"Quite a lot's happened since I met you twelve hours ago."

"And thanks: you know, for last night. This morning. Do you have time for breakfast? Do you even do breakfast?"

"I think I do breakfast."

And, just as happens in all of the corniest films, the phone rang. Not that it was that surprising, seeing that, day and night, my phone never stopped ringing. But I do sometimes wonder if things would have turned out in quite the same way if I had not been saved by the bell.

Saved by the bell? No, I wasn't saved.

I was merely postponing the inevitable.

"One moment…" I said and picked up.

"Hi!" I said. "I am *so* sorry about last night! Even if I told you what happened, you'd never believe it, and if you did believe it I'd have to kill you! But…"

I felt a very gentle rub on my ear lobe. I glanced to the door and caught a glimpse of a wave as Elise disappeared.

Being a woman, she had divined immediately that this was not entirely a social call. And being Elise, she was not a woman who ever played second fiddle.

It was my Jess, my girlfriend. Or just to clarify – since in New York it is essential to be aware of all these tiny nuances – Jess wasn't quite *my* girlfriend. She was *a* girlfriend.

CHAPTER 9

When I'd arrived In New York a year earlier, I had found the rules of dating both strange and exhilarating.

In Britain, the rules of dating – at least as far as I knew them – were that you took a girl out for dinner. You might kiss or you might not, but by the time you were sleeping with each other, you were 'dating'. By making love, you had committed to the project, and too bad if you changed your mind, because the voyage was already underway. Over time, your lover's little tics and habits might become progressively more vexing, but still you stuck with it: because that's what you did when you were dating, and it seemed more palatable than the alternative, which was 'breaking up'. And so it continued until all these peeves reached such a critical mass that you were done with the whole thing. With a sigh of relief, you'd swing the axe and officially become 'single' again: only to be snapped up a couple of weeks later by one of the beautiful girls who had been waiting so patiently in your heart's pending tray. That was me. That was a lot of British guys that I knew. We were serial monogamists, ping-ponging straight from one committed relationship to the next; we endeavoured not to be unfaithful.

You could look at the dainties on display. If you liked what you saw, you might be allowed a sniff, even a touch. But if you wanted to have a taste, then you had no option but to buy the whole box.

And New York City? Well they've always been ahead of the curve by about fifteen years, and as far as I can see, they were spot on target with this particular trend.

In New York City, you could take a bite from the pastries without having to buy. If you liked, you could come back to the patisserie a week, or a month later, and have another bite... or perhaps even try something fresh. There was a downside. All too often, when you came back for that second bite, you could discern that another man had had his lips to the pastry; not that you could ever be certain. It would have been unseemly to ask, and just as unseemly to tell.

Not that I was by any means a player. But friends like Steve might have two or three different dates in the week, and maybe he'd sleep with them, maybe he wouldn't. His dates neither seemed to mind nor care. So Steve had never committed himself to any one woman, but why should that stop them from having sex with him? I don't doubt the women were enjoying the Manhattan feast just as much as Steve.

Fidelity was of course still an option. Once you had found a keeper, you would take them out for an expensive dinner and politely ask if you were 'dating exclusively'. If the reply was in the affirmative, that meant that, with immediate effect, all other pastries were off limits.

And if you had *not* had this conversation, then it was tacitly acknowledged by both parties that you were most definitely not dating exclusively. This exclusivity conversation – and I say this from personal experience – was as big a transition as to that next step up, the engagement.

One last point, as I feel I need to be accurate on this matter. I was not a bed-hopper, though in theory I would have loved to have been. I would have loved to have been taking a bite from every one of New York's sweetmeats. But it's never been my style and the reason is because, as you know, I'm a plunger. I fall in love. And once I've fallen in love with a woman I want her all for myself.

And with Jess, I'd never fallen in love. Most likely that was why we'd never pledged our fidelity. I fancied her. She was a beautiful woman. We had sexual chemistry by the lorry-load, but that other kind of chemistry was more elusive. I just couldn't see myself falling for her. Part of the problem, I realise now, was that she was too damn nice. I am drawn to women with an edge; women with baggage.

But our no-strings relationship seemed perfect for my needs at the time. The practicalities were that from one day to the next, I never knew whether I was going to be in America, let alone New York. The reality, though, was that I was keeping my options open, and that Jess was keeping me warm at night until the day that I met 'The One'.

So, bad karma all round. Not that my behaviour was *too* awful. But it wasn't great either. It was something that I am not overly proud of. And what occurred afterwards... well now that I look back, it all seems like the most perfect payback.

I arranged to see Jess that night, and after the mad rush of filing my story, there was a pleasant lull to the day. I went out and bought a bagel, before spending a few minutes indulging in that state-of-the-art activity that was then quaintly known as 'surfing the net'. In those days in 1998, we journalists had no conception of what an incredible tool this little toy would become.

There was only one site that we bothered to look at, the Drudge Report. I'm not sure how old Matt Drudge is doing these days, but in the first years of the internet, he was a pioneer. Drudge had a mole in Washington who was passing on weapons-grade material about Bill Clinton's trysts with Monica Lewinsky. And the sheer beauty of it all was that the American press didn't deign to touch a word of it, deriding Drudge's leaks as mere tittle-tattle. The Brits scooped them every single time, and more astonishing still: it turned out that every last word of the Drudge Report was true.

What a mad year it was. Not that I believe in omens or augurs, but the whole craziness of the President's affair turned out to be the most perfect symbol for my own love life. From January to August, you kept thinking that the Clinton story could not get any more bizarre. Then up would pop some extraordinary new detail which would cap everything that had come before. Cigar sex! Pizza sex! Phone sex! The man must have had a death wish. How I know the feeling.

Steve mooched in. He had a bongo board under his arm. It was like a skate-board, but instead of wheels it had a free-rolling wooden cylinder underneath. Snatching up my half eaten bagel, he balanced on the bongo board, his legs moving from side to side while his torso remained quite still. Deceptively simple. I'd tried it a month earlier and had nearly knocked myself out after over-balancing and taking my foot off the board.

"I don't like raisins," he said.

"What would you prefer then?" I asked. "Maybe just a plain bagel, with, say, some salmon and cream cheese?"

"That'd be great." He continued to roll from side to side.

"Pepper and lemon as well, please."

"It's lucky I'm so congenial."

I continued to scroll down the screen. He licked his fingers one by one before slicking back his hair.

"What's on Drudge? Any more smut on Clinton?"

"He's talking about a blue dress that was worn by Monica. It may contain evidence of Clinton's DNA."

"Evidence of his DNA? What the hell's that mean?"

Well indeed so – but who, then, could have predicted the precise form that this DNA evidence would take? Who could have guessed that that dress would very nearly bring down the President?

Steve's reverie about Clinton's DNA had sent him off on another flight of fancy. "Speaking of DNA. Nice woman," he said. "Where have I seen her before?"

"I have no idea."

Back and forth he continued to roll on the bongo board, hands behind his back. "And she liked me too."

I snorted. "How many women have you got on the go at the moment?"

"Three. Nearly four," he said, jumping off the bongo board to admire my map of America. It was bristling with pins, each one marking another goose-chase across the US-of-A. "There's always room for more. What's her name?"

"I don't think I should tell you."

"You're being a bit of a dog in the manger! What about Jess?" He took out a pin from Nebraska and pushed it into the as yet untouched Alaska.

"Do you have to do that?"

"I'll buy you a pint." He took out one of several pins in Los Angeles and planted it in Ohio.

"It's even nicer to know that I have it in my power to deny you this pleasure."

"Have it your own way," he said. "You'll only get burned."

"Why do you say that?"

"It's in your nature. Call it intuition. You have the smell of a guy who's always going to get burned."

I clicked off the Drudge Report and shut the computer down. "You are so full of hot air!"

"Trust me on this Kim: listen to Gypsy Steve," he said. "Stick with your Jess. Give me the hottie's number. In the long-run, I'll be saving you a lot of pain."

"And what do you know?"

"I know a little about women, and I know a lot about you," he said. "What are you, thirty-two? Thirty-three? You've got that quietly desperate air of a man who's getting ready to take the plunge. Only thing is, you're going to be plunging for the wrong woman."

It's so difficult to tell, isn't it? We date ten, twenty people; maybe more. Eventually, if we're lucky, we commit. But is there some time switch that kicks in and urges us to settle down, or is it that we've met the right woman? And after that... well it's only the biggest, most important decision in your life, and you've got to pray to God in his heaven that you've backed a winner.

But you never forget the others, you know. Especially after you're married. For it's only when you're fully committed and in so deep that there's no way out, that you can indulge in that meaningless luxury of wondering how things might have turned out if you'd shackled your vessel to another craft. You start to wonder. Would the voyage be any more pleasant? And the views, they would certainly be different. But would they be any better? Would there be more adventure? Would your twin vessels have already crashed upon the rocks, or might, perhaps, you still be agreeably sailing on into the twilight?

And when you get that chance to go back and to have a taste of that old life, do you take it? Are you tied by convention and morals and marital scruples, or are you the master of your own destiny? Do you still have the verve, the nerve, to seize life by the throat? Well... do you?

It was gone seven p.m. when I started walking out across Central Park. This is my favourite park on earth. It is difficult to believe that it is bigger than Monaco. Just a few hundred yards in, you can almost make believe that you're in the countryside, and then you look up to see that you are surrounded by this forest of sheer-sided canyons and winking skyscrapers.

Jess's flat was about a mile from mine in the much more genteel Upper East Side. She called it a flat, though it was actually a bedsit, her sofa turning into a fold out bed. She had a cat too, I remember that; a cat which had spent its entire life cooped up in this one-room prison. The cat was mad and very possessive of his mistress.

By the time Jess buzzed me up, I was pink with the cold.

Jess kissed me on the cheek. Not the lips: that would not have been appropriate. In fact, to parody dear President Clinton, it would have been wrong. Only couples who were dating exclusively greeted each other with a kiss on the lips.

"You're freezing!" she said. "Let me get you something to drink. A whisky? Or something hot? A toddy?"

"You're so sweet." I took off my coat and gloves. The cat was warily stalking about the edge of the room, knowing, as he did, that he might soon be consigned to the bathroom.

"I'll get you a toddy," said Jess. She tucked a lock of her blonde bob behind her ear. She had spent some time, I could see, on her make-up. And I liked what I was seeing. A very short black skirt, tight, and cut way above the knees; black tights; black boots; and a grey cashmere turtle-neck. Like that boy in the patisserie, I stretched out to take the most succulent pastry on display.

Although according to all the rules of New York dating, I was quite within my rights to take a bite, there were, inevitably, certain subsidiary rules. So, to continue the patisserie analogy, what these subsidiary rules entailed was that, though I could still most definitely have a bite from the pastry without paying for it, I first of all had to tell the shop-owner what a wonderful pastry she had; how fine it looked; how I longed to taste its sweetness. Basically: if I wanted to have sex with Jess the very moment that I walked through her door, then that required the inclusion of that deathly term 'exclusivity' into our relationship.

Not that I was going to fail for want of trying.

I joined Jess as she busied herself with the kettle and the lemon squeezer, clasping her waist with both hands as I nuzzled her neck. It didn't feel wrong. It felt like the most unbelievable piece of bravado, as if I'd chanced my arm with one of the secretaries, sneaking up and giving her a cuddle as she'd worked the photocopier. I was not at all sure how Jess would respond. We'd not had the requisite dinner. I was not committed.

Such a powerful tool is sex, is it not? And at least from my limited perspective, women can turn it on at will... and turn it off, though this devastating weapon must be used judiciously. Keep a man hanging on too long, and he'll just go sow his oats in some greener field. But if you can tease a man to the very brink, and then give him his due reward; if you can act the houri, but not too much; if you can be both saint and sinner, and yet never let a man guess your dreams; then you'll be a woman, my girl, and men will pour their riches at your feet.

Jess let out a little moan of pleasure as she leaned against me, but only for a moment. Even as my hands were slipping down her waist and to her hips, she was easing away from me.

"Still cold?" she laughed.

I kissed her neck. "So cold."

"How thoughtless of me," she said. "Here's your toddy."

She sashayed over to the sofa. I can still picture that heel–toe, heel-toe catwalk sway; it must be nice to know that your every move is being watched so closely, that your very walk makes you so desirable. But, to my knowledge at least, I have never experienced this. I am just another lumpen male who has very little idea of what it is that makes me desirable to a woman. I fire off random shots into the darkness and very occasionally, I suppose, I end up with a hit. Yet it has always seemed to be in the lap of the gods as to what I've ever brought down... or how I did it.

We sat beside each other on the sofa. My toddy was too sweet; with age I have found that I prefer things bitter. "Lovely," I said. "Cheers."

Jess sipped from a glass of American fizz, and even that simple act seemed to have an erotic charge. She raised her eyebrows and smiled elliptically: look, but don't touch; at least, not yet.

"You were being very mysterious about last night," she said. "What happened?"

"I spent the evening with Nick Spitz," I said. "It was appropriately bizarre."

"Nick Spitz? Nick Spitz!" she said. "You spent the evening with Nick Spitz?" She unfurled those long sheer legs, crossing them towards me, so that her knee just touched my thigh. "Is he as gorgeous in the flesh? What happened?" She spoke with a perfect BBC accent, so English as to be indefinable. She'd come out to New York a year before me in 1996. She did something with computers. I was never able to fathom quite what.

"What happened..." I tailed off.

So now we each of us had something that the other wanted, Jess with her sex, and me with that altogether less tangible bargaining chip, information. She took my hand, held it to her cheek

"To think!" Jess said dreamily. "I am now touching the very hand that Nick Spitz shook last night."

"I haven't washed it since."

"Well what happened? Tell me." She looked up at me with these huge baby-doll eyes. "Tell me what happened."

"It's a long story," I said. "A very long story. And as yet it still remains very much classified information. I thought you were hungry."

Her thigh was now pressed against mine, as she played with my fingers. You think the London dating scene is complicated, with all the "Will he, won't he" machinations of girls waiting by the phone for the call that never comes? In the New York dating pool, it was like being buffeted by an unending series of currents, eddies and rip-tides. You were constantly swirled from one direction to the next. And even when you thought you were home and dry, a tsunami could still knock you clean off your feet before sucking you back into the deep.

"What did you do with Nick?"

I am nothing if not contrary. Not five minutes earlier, I'd wanted nothing so much as to be making the most ardent love with Jess.

But now... as she kissed my fingertips and writhed against me... I was wondering how best to fob her off.

I'd briefly considered telling her the truth, but what an almighty hostage to fortune that would have been

"It all got a little bit physical," I said, leaning over to kiss Jess's forehead. "I'll tell you all about it over dinner."

She gave me one of those looks: searching, weighing me up, weighing up whether I was to be trusted. "Really?" she said. "You'll tell me over dinner? You, Kim, will tell me what happened with Nick over dinner?"

"The story, the whole story and nothing but the story."

I helped Jess smooth down her skirt as she stood up. My hand lingered.

"He is handsome though, isn't he?" she said as I helped her slip on her astrakhan coat.

"Very," I said. "Though actually rather short."

"Can you give me a clue?"

"All right then," I said. "It involved a lot of drinking and some rope."

"Really? Rope and lots of drinking? With Nick Spitz? I don't believe it!" I still remember her excitement at the thought that she was going to be the recipient of a genuine exclusive. The cat entwined himself around her legs as we walked out of the flat.

"It's as true as I stand here."

All the way to the Thai restaurant, Jess had her arm tucked tight into mine. She was still trying to wheedle the story out of me.

I hadn't even taken my coat off before my mobile rang; as ever, it was my mad-masters from London, come to spoil my little party.

"Good news, old boy!" It was Campbell, the night news editor; perhaps a major in the *Sun*'s hierarchy. "You're off to Minnesota! The last flight leaves in two hours. Call when you get to La Guardia!"

Jess and I had been through a number of variations of this phone call, so she should have been used to it. But her disappointment was evident; all those high expectations which were about to be dashed.

"You'll tell me what happened with Nick Spitz?" she said. For the first time that night she kissed me on the lips. "You promise?"

"I promise," I said, clutching at her hand as I hailed a cab. Just another of the many promises that I have made and then broken. Break enough of them and you soon get used to it. But by the time I next saw Jess... well, there was no need to spin her any more lies.

CHAPTER 10

During my two years in New York, I had to sprint for so many flights that I have been left with a pathological hatred of cutting things fine.

Today, even though I might just be catching a short domestic flight up to Scotland, I like to be in the airport at least two hours before take-off. I chat to the check-in staff. I amble through security. I savour the simple pleasure of buying myself a coffee.

I still have a few memories that make me inwardly shudder. And that flight to Minnesota provokes not so much a shudder as a spasm. Running, running, running, in this flat-out sprint until I actually believed I was going to faint.

It's different if you've managed to check your luggage on board. Check your luggage on board, and they can bellow all they like over the Tannoys, but they will not be leaving without you. As we seasoned travellers know, they can't fly if they've still got your bag in the hold; it takes an absolute age to unload a specific bag.

But if you *don't* have any hold-luggage, well that's a different matter entirely. You can be checked in and through security, but if there's even the prospect of your plane missing its slot, they'll dump you off the flight without a second thought.

On that drear January night, I'd met up with Ali the photographer with thirty minutes to spare. Neither of us had managed to get anything into the hold.

"You'll have to hurry now!" the check-in girl called after us.

She was right.

Ali was a doughty freelance photographer in New York, though effectively on the *Sun* staff. She was in her forties, married and reliable; I did not fancy her. We'd worked together so often, and in so many exotic places from the Keys to all over the Caribbean, that I would have been driven to distraction if Ali had been a beauty. My libido is a bottomless pit. Everywhere I go, anywhere in the world, I see beautiful women and I wonder... what with a little chat and a fair wind... then perhaps... Just hark at me! Don't I sound like some paunchy dribbler in the throes of a mid-life crisis? Well perhaps not the paunch. But as to the mid-life crisis... as you shall soon see, I think we'd have to put a definite tick in that particular box.

Both Ali and I had small overnight bags, but she also had a much heavier bag with her cameras, her lenses and her computer. It had no shoulder strap. I carried it.

We were jogging up the escalators. Security in those days pre-9/11 was much more rudimentary. We breezed through and searched the signs for the departure gate. It was one of the last flights of the evening. And then we came to the horrible realisation that it was *the* very furthest gate in the entire terminal.

Most times, when you set off jogging for a plane, you're reasonably confident that you're going to make it. You have a feeling that you've got time in hand. But this flight to Minnesota... I was not at all sure. The flight board sign was bleakly blinking red. We had barely started towards the gate when our names were blaring out over the Tannoys.

I'm now not just jogging: I'm running. Running hard, with my bag over my shoulder and Ali's camera bag clutched to my chest. Some years earlier, when I'd been at school, I had picked up a severe knee injury. A little memento from another love-affair and another life. But the worst of it was being physically unable to get enough air into my lungs. In those days, I didn't exercise much. I was thirty-two years old, and still thought I was on the very cusp of youth, with no need for stretching or running or gyms or any of those other things that we do to help stem the tides of time.

We were about halfway to the gate when I realised I couldn't take another step. Ali's bag crashed to the ground. All I could do was stand there panting with my hands on my knees. I was that wheezing red-faced traveller who suddenly realises his youth has passed him by.

"Jesus!" I wheezed. Spittle dribbled down my chin. I didn't have the energy to wipe it away.

Ali looked on sympathetically. She said not a word.

We started off towards the departure gate, not so much a lope as a brisk walk. We carried her camera bag between us.

We made it and were chivvied through the gate. As soon as we were on the plane, the door was slammed shut behind us. The other passengers smugly scrutinised us as we walked to our seats. The luggage lockers were all full and I scrabbled for somewhere to stow the bags. The sweat dripped down my face and my shirt was completely saturated: though by the time we landed in Minnesota I knew it would be crinkly dry. I was asleep even before we'd left the ground. And as I dropped off, I made a pledge: get fit.

We'd had to catch the last flight to Minnesota because otherwise we'd have been too late for the next day's story. It was one of those weird ones that only ever happens in America; though once it *has* happened in America, then the rest of the world just dives on in.

So at ten a.m. that Wednesday, Ali and I were queuing up outside what was then the world's biggest shopping mall. It was big enough to fit a good-sized park in the middle, complete with a rollercoaster ride. It was ghastly, and as such, the perfect setting for Minnesota's wedding of the year. Charlie was to marry his Lucy and hundreds of people had turned out to watch the freak show which had been organised courtesy of the local radio station.

I saw Charlie first. He was a strapping redneck with a buzz-cut. They'd dressed him in black tails and a white bow tie, as if he were about to take part in a ballroom dancing competition. Charlie stood with his best man on a podium outside the mall entrance, and behind them was a makeshift altar that was covered with the radio station's logo. The organisers had ticked every cliché in the book. Lucy was wearing a white puff-ball dress, with a veil and a garland of flowers in her hair. Her six bridesmaids were in pink and walked up the Mall steps to the strains of Mendelssohn's 'Wedding March'. One of the mothers was patting the tears from her cheek. It was very solemn. The crowd, the guests; everyone was so serious. Was I the only person who wanted to howl with laughter at the sheer tackiness of it all?

Charlie and Lucy made their vows. They were proclaimed man and wife. The Minister gave Charlie permission to kiss his bride.

And this is the moment that we've all been waiting for. Some bumpkin yells out, "Go get her!". The Stars and Stripes crackles overhead in the wind. Like morning mist, a hush descends upon us.

I'm craning my neck to see what happens next. Lucy hesitates a moment before fumbling with the hem of her veil. She leans forward slightly, and then with both hands lifts the veil over her head. For the first time, we see her face.

And for the first time – ever – Charlie sees the face of his bride.

That's right: before the wedding ceremony, Charlie and Lucy had neither met nor spoken to each other. His first glimpse of her was when she lifted her veil. She was one of those cute American cheerleader types. She had a lovely smile. She obviously seemed pleased with the husband that had been handpicked for her by the radio station.

Charlie was also pleased. He let out a whoop and pumped his fist in the air before sweeping Lucy into his arms. The next moment they were vigorously snogging. Ali, squatting at the foot of the podium, was capturing it all on film.

Later came the interview. I did not have to do much probing. They were happy to talk. Lucy was still smiling as she held her husband's hand. "I woke up two weeks ago and heard about this wedding offer on the radio," she said. "They were going to pay for the wedding and the honeymoon, *and* they were even going to find me a husband! I just thought, 'Why not?' I mean this whole marriage thing: it's all one big crap-shoot, anyway."

And *that* was the moment when I also fell a little in love with Lucy.

It's all one, big crap-shoot. Indeed it is, Lucy, indeed it is.

Ali and I were talking about it over dinner that night. I'd filed a 2,000-word spread for the Saturday paper and we were settling down for a boozy night in Minnesota.

We were in one of America's ubiquitous business hotels with a low-lit dining room and a lot of meat on the menu. Ali topped up our glasses. It was our second bottle of Merlot. She always matched me glass for glass.

"What do you know?" said Ali.

"What do *I* know?" I said. "Well I *was* married. Does that count?"

"Not for much," she said. "So you had a tough time of it first time round. And from that one disaster you've extrapolated Kim's universal theory of marriage."

"Good title."

I helped myself to some of Ali's crackling. I think she used to order the roast pork just for me. She ate the meat, but would never touch the crackling, leaving it on the side for me to snatch up at the end of the meal.

I chewed on a shard, letting the fat linger on my tongue.

"Just take a look at India," I said. "Got around a billion people. Not too much divorce –"

"That's because most of them *can't* divorce."

"Irrelevant. The point is, most marriages in India are arranged by the parents. When the bride sees her groom, she'll know him about as well as Lucy knew her Charlie."

"It's a bloody crazy way to marry someone and you know it," said Ali. "Are you just playing devil's advocate again, or do you really believe this shit you're spouting?"

"I believe a bit of it," I said. "Okay, let's forget today's marriage, which was just a publicity junket for the radio station. What I'm saying is: I reckon your parents, or your best friends, would probably be better at picking your life partner than you would. Well not necessarily you, obviously, as you're happily married to Patrick, and you're both delighted to be living in your own squalor. But most people – especially most men – would be a hell of a sight better off if their wives were picked by their mates."

"Genius," she said. "So how do you work that out, Mr Crackle-Head?"

"Mates and family, they're going to be objective," I said. "Wholly objective. And let's face it: they can hardly be any worse at spouse picking. What are the figures now? Two out of five marriages ending in divorce?"

"You know, I always took you for more of a romantic," she said.

"It's precisely because I *am* a romantic that I know what I'm talking about!" I said. "I fall head-over-heels for every single girl that I've ever dated. Even when I kiss a woman, I fall a little in love. I am so quickly besotted with a woman that I can't tell who are the keepers."

"You are sad." Ali finished off her glass, eyes never leaving mine. She held up the empty bottle. "We getting another?"

I nodded. "It's true that your friends may not know every last thing about this prospective life-partner. But on the flip side, they won't be blinded by beauty. They will not be swayed by the tyranny of sex."

"Swayed by the tyranny of sex?" Ali rolled the words around her mouth. "Where the hell did that come from?"

"You want me to spell it out?"

"Yeah, go for it," said Ali. "Tell me about these tyrants."

"It's pretty simple, Ali," I said. "Guys are prepared to put up with quite a lot if they're having good sex. It addles their brains! It's a drug... and they'll do what they can to keep getting it."

"And in your book, that means marrying the wrong woman."

"Oftentimes." I leaned back as the waiter poured more wine. "Thank you."

"Well I'm glad I'm not your girlfriend."

"Why not?"

"You'd be an absolute nightmare to go out with."

I don't know. Perhaps she was right; perhaps she was wrong. Even for us emotional icebergs, it's very difficult to tell whether we can cut it as a boyfriend.

CHAPTER 11

My mind yo-yoed on the way back to New York the next day, the one moment embracing an idea, and the next discarding it.

I was going to get fit, or at least fit enough to be able to run the length of an airport terminal without collapsing. But how was I going to get fit with my injured knee? Did I go out and buy a new one?

As for my love life, I was going to quit hedging. I was going to commit. How could I ever expect to bring out the best in a woman if I'd not first committed myself – exclusively – to her?

But was Jess the one?

And if not her, then who else?

Surely though it would be kinder, fairer, to break off with Jess?

But why to blazes did I have to commit to anyone?

Why, just three years after the end of my first marriage, was I so eager to dive in again?

I could just write something glib: I love being in love.

It's time to go a little deeper. This, by the way, is not to excuse what has happened. But it may help you better understand it.

My mother died when I was six years old. My father, a stiff army officer, came to my boarding school to tell me the news. It was the first time that I'd seen him cry. She had died of cancer. For many years, I'd thought it was one of those arbitrary tragedies that can occur to any of us. I had a picture of my mother which I treasured. We were by the sea, and though I was five years old, she had me scooped up into her arms as if I were a newborn. She looked happy and was laughing at the camera. I adoringly gazed up at her. Sometimes I even used to make myself believe that I could remember that grey day on an Isle of Wight beach. As I grew older, I did not think of her so much, but when her name cropped up, I would give her the mental genuflection that is due to an angel. How could she have been anything else but an angel? She was perfect in every way.

About three years ago now, I was having lunch with my father's mother, Clemmie, and her sister, my great-aunt Agatha. They had spent their lives immersed in the army, either following their father or their husbands around the world, though my grandmother was by far the more affable. Having children had forced her to unbend; she'd developed a sense of humour and, perhaps rather to her surprise, found that she enjoyed it. Her elder sister Agatha would have found life less grating if she'd been born a Victorian. She believed that children should be seen and not heard, and was still having some difficulty in coming to terms with the possibility that I might have grown up.

I was treating them to Sunday lunch in the Wolseley: so much more civilised than the adjacent Ritz with all its stuffy rules about jackets and ties. High ceilings, comfortable cosy tables and the buzz of people enjoying themselves.

As we waited for our three roast beefs, I'd happened to ask Clemmie about my mother. Her name was Sylvie.

My grandmother's mouth puckered up and she dabbed at her dry lips with a napkin. "I did not know her as well as I would have liked," she said. "I wish that I had got to know her better. She was a very passionate woman, always so enthusiastic. I liked that about her."

"So do you have any memories of her? What do you remember of her?"

"Yes." Again, the little performance with the napkin. I can sense Agatha fidgeting next to me. "I remember when you were born, Sylvie had this look on her face as if she were holding a priceless treasure, which of course you were, at least in those days. Your parents still hadn't decided on a name for you, and I asked Sylvie if she had anything in mind. She said she rather liked the name Kim, and I suppose I must have been much starchier in those days, because I pulled a face and said that it sounded rather effeminate. But she quoted me Kipling and I'm glad she did because I think it's a lovely name. It suits you."

"And what about when she died?" I said. "What was that like?"

For the first time that lunch, Clemmie glanced at Agatha who was methodically buttering a tiny scrap of bread.

"It was very hard," she said. "It was particularly hard for your father. He always seems so strong, but underneath..." she paused.

"I'm not sure that the army was the best career for him." She mused for a while. "Or for Sylvie."

"How long was she treated?" I said. Perhaps I had never really talked about my mother's cancer before. I don't recollect it. But it seemed then as if I didn't know even the most basic details of what had happened to her.

"Ohh," said Clemmie. "Not long. It was very quick."

Agatha popped the bread into her mouth and chewed very briskly. She seemed to be shaking as she swallowed, as if she couldn't hold something in any longer. She broke off another piece of bread and was still staring at her hands as she spoke. "Well I think it was a very selfish thing to do," she said. "I don't care what anyone else says."

It was so fantastically jarring. All about us are these convivial diners enjoying their lunch, my grandmother is pleasantly reminiscing, and from out of nowhere comes this… this extraordinary statement.

"I'm sorry?" I asked.

My grandmother winces. Something occurs beneath the table. Agatha busies herself with her bread. Clemmie picks up her napkin. Not another word is said.

Though I was not going to let the matter drop. Later, after we'd dropped Agatha off, I drove my grandmother back to Kensington. She had a flat in an Edwardian apartment block I followed her up in the lift.

Nothing is spoken as the lift grinds upwards, but the tension is crackling off the walls.

I follow my grandmother out of the lift, and as she opens the front door, she has this air of resignation. She leads the way through to her pristine drawing room. Light floods in from the floor-to-ceiling windows; the steady tick of the grandfather clock. She sets her stick by the fireplace and lowers herself into one of a pair of wingback armchairs. How I remember those chairs. They seem to be part of the very fabric of my memory. If I picture my grandmother, she is sitting in that chair.

I take the matching wingback on the other side of the fireplace. Very gently, she is rubbing the back of one of her hands with her fingertips. We have not spoken now for a full five minutes.

"Perhaps," I said. "There's something you'd like to tell me."

She's now turning her wedding ring in her fingers. She has worn it for over sixty years. It is gold and wearing thin at the edges.

"I'm sorry." She looked at me for the first time since we'd left the Wolseley. "I'm very sorry."

At first falteringly, she told me the story; the true story. As I write it now, it just seems like another of those random tragedies that occurs to people; very different from cancer, yet still just as arbitrary. But of course it was anything but. It was Sylvie's choice. And I understand why my father and my grandmother lied: because how, exactly, do you tell a six-year-old boy that his mother hanged herself in the woods? And once you've started the lie, it's difficult to stop, and although one day you would like to be able to sit the boy down and tell him the truth, that day never comes. I don't blame them. It would have taken my father more courage to tell me about my mother's suicide than he ever showed on the battlefield.

At first it was like this very distasteful piece of news which, given time, I would be able to digest. And digest it I did, though for months I was in shock. In a single afternoon, my mother had been swept from her pedestal. Far from being snatched away from me, she, herself, had consciously abandoned her six-year-old son.

I forgive her now; how could I not? Who knows the demons that were tormenting her? And in time, it just became another piece of unpleasantness about my life. I no longer flinched at the memory. Yet there were consequences. If you have children, there are always consequences to each and every action that you take, and even after you're long dead, those consequences continue to reverberate.

Ali gave me a peck on the cheek as she dropped me off outside my flat. It was lunchtime on Friday, and I felt oddly deflated; it was often like that at the weekends in New York: you've spent all week haring hither and thither and then suddenly you're back home and with absolutely nothing on the agenda. That's what happens if you're a newsman. You rarely bother to organise anything in advance. It's Kim's First Law of Journalism: the more money you spend on a ticket, the less chance there is of you ever using it. Book two fifteen dollar tickets to the cinema for the weekend and it's odds on that come Friday you'll be sitting there in the back row with your beer and your hotdog. But spend, say, $500 on four tickets for the opening of "The Lion King", the musical, and it's pretty much a cast-iron certainty that you will not be there to escort your father and stepmother to the show. During the previous year, I'd blown off so many friends that there were now at least a dozen of my flat keys floating around the office; at least my guests had somewhere to stay, even though they weren't able to see me in person.

My flat was not squalid, but it was grubby. Heaven knows why I never had a cleaner, but I didn't, and the result was that the grime continued to accumulate, but so slowly that I was not aware of it, like a dad not realising his daughter has shot up six inches in the last year.

I took a load of clothes down to the washing machines in the basement, ever hopeful that I might have a chance to chat to the beautiful Norwegian who lived on the second floor. I had only met her once by the driers, but I was ever the optimist.

So: Two in the afternoon on a Friday and the most frenetic city on earth is there for the taking. Call up Steve, Justin, or another of my play-mates, and drink red wine until midnight? Visit the Museum of Modern Art? Call up Jess and see if we could pick up where we'd left off…

My mobile went. In those days, mobile phones were still sufficiently rare that a phone call meant action. Friends were not in the habit of just calling for a chat.

It was Elise, about to ask me to immerse myself in the hostile element.

"Great story," she said. "I'm so pleased."

For a moment, I could not fathom *what* she was talking about. Only for a moment. All that drama with Nick Spitz seemed like a lifetime ago; like hacks the world over, I'd forgotten all about it. Not that I'd forgotten about Nick in the bathroom. But as for that load of bilge that I'd filed with Elise, I'd moved on.

"Cool," I said. "What did it make in the end?"

"Don't you even read your own paper?" she said.

"Nope," I said. I wondered if I should have a beer. "Can't be bothered. By the time I get the papers, they're always about five days old. I have reached the journalists' Nirvana. I chase the stories.

I write them to the best of my abilities. Then as soon as I've filed, I let go. I neither know nor care whether it ends up on the spike or the front page."

Elise snorted her derision. "Hmm," she said. "New York Correspondent of the *Sun* newspaper says he doesn't care about splashes?"

"Well, Elise darling, as I recollect I had a pretty good splash on my hands three days ago, and somehow I was persuaded not to write anything about it."

"Point taken, although you didn't have any option," she said. "So are you interested in hearing what it made?"

"Five pars on Page Three?"

"Centre spread," she said. "And a picture byline. You looked rather... dashing. Not that I would have recognised you. But dashing, nevertheless."

"That picture was taken a long time ago," I said. "Before I'd started dealing with PRs like you. Stick it on your bedpost as a memento."

"I could do," she said. "Though I'd prefer to persuade the memento himself to come out for a drink. To celebrate."

"Sure," I said, cool as you please.

And that, for your information, was the all-too-brief moment when our relationship fundamentally changed from the professional to the personal. I'm not bragging. I'm just telling you like it is. And in New York in 1998, a drink was never just 'a drink'. If I had to paraphrase its meaning, I would say that it went something like this: "I quite like what I saw of you this week, and I don't find you entirely distasteful, so why don't we give it a go, and just so long as you don't suddenly morph into a monster then I may be persuaded to add your name to the list of people that I am currently dating." There was, naturally, no mention on the subtext of 'exclusivity'. That was all a long, long way down the road.

"Got anything on tonight?" she said.

"From this moment, Elise, I am entirely at your disposal. I've just got in from Minnesota. It's my golden night; I don't have to go into work tomorrow morning."

"You work Sundays, huh?"

"Doesn't everyone?"

"Okay, well why don't you swing by Dexters. Do you know it? In the mid-town. A little old-fashioned, bordering on the quaint, but I like it."

"Sounds just like me," I said. We arranged to meet up at four thirty that afternoon, and even as I scrubbed myself first-date clean, I tried to recall what Elise looked like. Very straight, glossy, auburn hair: I remembered that; and the crucifix; and that indefinable air of sexuality. How long could I wait before I kissed her? I am terrible like that. I should wait much, much longer before I kiss a woman. But I cannot resist myself. I am the schoolboy, illicit in the pantry, who dips his finger into the icing on the cake.

If I can, I like to walk to a date. It helps settle me, gets the endorphins pumping and, or so I'm told, gives my skin a glow of healthiness. I wandered through Central Park, the tips of the high-rises winking at me through the trees in the twilight. It is a remarkable sight. On all sides you are surrounded by this absolute forest of sheer-sided sky-scrapers. And when you walk down these die-straight avenues, it feels like you're in the most precipitous canyon, scoured from the rock by long dead rivers. There is no city to touch it. And the energy too: it is palpable. You can feel it pumping off the buildings, energising your every cell. Many friends who visited me in New York used to think that I was on drugs. But it wasn't cocaine and it wasn't drink, it was the very city itself.

I don't know if it was the rushed flight to Minnesota, but my knee was cramping badly. By the time I'd reached The Plaza Hotel on Central Park south side it was so painful that I could only walk with my leg out straight. I hailed a cab for the last few blocks.

I was carrying on like an arthritic pensioner, my dead leg flailing out to the side. If I'd had a walking stick, I would have used it.

I'd never been in Dexter's before, but it was the sort of place my father would have loved, with dark wood panelling and various snugs about the walls. Elise was on a bar stool chatting to the Latino barman. By her side was a bottle of Krug in an ice bucket. I may not know much about expensive designer clothes, but I do know a little about expensive alcohol. Krug is right up there. I have been on a number of first dates in my life, but that is the one and only time that anyone has ever bought me Krug. She had high hopes; I do not know if I have ever been able to match her expectations.

I cupped my hand round her waist, and even before she had turned around, I kissed her on the cheek. She was prettier than I remembered.

"Join us," she said.

"I'd love to," I said. She poured like a professional, tilting the glass and letting the Krug glide down the side before giving the bottle a slight twist. I always love to watch an expert about their business.

"You've worked in a restaurant."

She returned the bottle to its bucket. "I'd be the Chief Sommelier at The Plaza if I'd stuck with it."

"The Plaza's loss is PR's gain." I was trying to get my coat off, but it was awkward with my screaming knee, and even more so when I tried to ease myself onto one of the bar stools.

I let out a sigh of relief and we both looked at each other and smiled... and I still don't know if it was the relief in my leg, or that enigmatic smile, but I did exactly what I'd been telling myself not to do. I leaned over and kissed her on the lips.

It is a weakness I have.

When I meet a beautiful woman and there is any sort of chemistry, then I just want to kiss her. In the past, this has led to problems. Some women, whether or not they've liked me, have found it very disarming to be kissed by a man they've only just met. Others, of course, like it, for to kiss someone is to cut to the chase. It puts your cards on the table. Your meaning is both clear and undeniable. So many times, when I was young, I would go on date after date with women, and would not kiss them until I was absolutely, positively certain that my feelings of ardour were eagerly reciprocated. What a waste! What a waste, what a waste! I hate to think of the scores of kisses – and, indeed, all those other things that might have ensued – which must have passed me by. Whether you like someone or whether you don't, a kiss is always a compliment. Without a word, it says, "You're beautiful".

So, within two minutes of hobbling into Dexter's bar, I had done exactly what I had promised myself I would try to avoid. For although I love that first kiss with a beautiful woman, I also enjoy the chase. I like the cool looks over the drink, the hands that linger and the knees that touch beneath the drapes.

But, when it comes to matters of the heart, I have little self-control. When I am with a beautiful woman, my first thought is, "I wonder what it would be like to kiss you"; and, more often than not, the thought is father to the deed.

I only kissed her for a second. I drew back, and then I did the unexpected: before she'd had a moment to draw breath, I kissed her on the lips a second time.

And... rest.

I slid back into my chair, with this impish smile playing on my face, and Elise, I have to say, had this little smile too as she nodded at me. She nodded and she nodded, and if I had to hazard what she was thinking then, I would guess that it was something on the lines of: "I've got your number, Mr Man From The Tabloids."

"And you haven't even touched your Champagne yet?" she said, cool as you please as, like a connoisseur, she held her glass by the base and sipped.

I took up my glass and we chinked. "What will I be like when we've finished the first bottle?" I said.

"The *first* bottle?"

I smiled and drank the champagne. Krug is, I'm afraid, entirely wasted on me. I like the message that a bottle of Krug sends out; it betokens that you are held in high esteem. It promises much. But as a drink: no!

But if a lady has gone to the trouble of buying Krug, I will drink it with a will; I will eulogise about its fine ethereal bubbles and its taste; and I will go to the expense of buying another bottle. But it is a very costly way of telling a person that you think they're worth the most expensive bottle of wine in the house. And I'd already told Elise that with my first kiss.

After you have unexpectedly kissed a woman, there is often a pause. A few moments are needed to rearrange your cards, and decide if a new line of play is in order. All the swirling undercurrents of desire and fear are still in play; but with just a single kiss, they suddenly merge into the background.

Elise drank more champagne. I liked it that, even as she tilted her glass, her eyes never left mine. I remained silent. The ball was very much in her court.

"I don't think I'd expected to be kissed *quite* so early in the evening," she said. Her fingers strayed to her crucifix; I have seen it so many times since.

"Did you like it?" I asked. And again, like the kiss, a direct question was cutting clean to the chase. I wasn't so much asking if she liked the kiss; I was asking whether my ardour was reciprocated.

"It showed promise," she said, and ever so slowly, she leant over, rested her hand upon my knee, and in turn kissed me. "I like the champagne on your lips."

I enjoyed the kiss. But I winced as she touched my knee.

"What's wrong?" she said.

"Just my knee," I said. "An old war wound. I've had it for years. It's a little tender at the moment."

"What sort of war might that be?" she said. "Why don't you get it sorted?"

I just gazed at her, fascinated. I couldn't believe that there seemed to be this entirely mutual attraction between us. All thoughts of Jess were erased from my head; Jess was lovely, a very special woman. But she was not to be compared to Elise.

"I don't know why I've never had it done. It happened half a lifetime ago; not so much a war as a skirmish. I can't run or walk very far. I suppose I've got used to it..." I trailed off. I was mesmerised by her lips. My eyes kept drifting down to her mouth. "I have this most extraordinary desire to kiss you again, Elise, and it is a feeling that will not be assuaged?"

"Assuaged?" she said. "That's a big word for a Red Top reporter."

I kissed her again, holding it a moment longer.

"The more I kiss you, the more I long to kiss you," I said.

"And a poet too?"

"Come live with me and be my love, and we will some new pleasures prove, of golden sands and crystal brooks..."

"With silken lines, and silver hooks," she finished the line. "Now John Donne? Aren't your talents wasted on the *Sun*?"

We kissed and opened our eyes at the same moment. She winked at me.

"I have a friend," she said. "A doctor who does hips and knees. You might like him. I'll fix up a meeting. He'll give you a good deal."

She bent down to her bag, a Louis Vuiton, and pulled out a Moleskin notepad. Like me, Elise was a note-taker. If there was anything that needed to be actioned, down it would all go into her little black book.

"Let's have your address," she said. "I have a feeling I'm going to get to know it quite well."

We drank a second bottle of Krug, and then fit for almost anything, Elise took me for dinner.

CHAPTER 12

Tabloids like the *Sun* have a fairly arbitrary system of expenses. You can claim any number of dinners with your girlfriend as 'entertaining a contact'. You might even be able to claim going to a show on Broadway. The only proviso is that you have to keep on bringing in the stories. So long as you keep filing those exclusives, the managing editor is not going to kick up too much of a fuss for a couple of dinners a week on your expenses.

I tucked the receipt for the Krug into my wallet. Would I be able to claim? Possibly: if I could bring in a front page within the next week. It would have been more helpful if the receipt had not specified that I'd been drinking Krug. Still, cheap at the price? Who but a penny pincher would cavil about buying Krug if they'd just kissed one of the loves of their life?

We walked for about 200 yards, me hobbling along as Elise held my hand.

"You poor thing," said Elise. "Perhaps we should be going somewhere a little closer?"

"I'm in your hands."

"There is one place that's nearby…" she tailed off before giving me a wicked smile. "It'll give us lots to talk about."

"Why's that?"

"It's called La Nouvelle Justine," she said elliptically.

The worm of a memory vibrated. Had Steve told me about La Nouvelle Justine? Or was it the name itself: Justine? A picture of soporific school classrooms came to me, as if the very name Justine had once provoked a quiver.

The Maitresse d' was wearing a tight black leather skirt and singlet. She had metal spikes in her tongue and a silver chain that went from her nose to her top lip.

"Have you been here before?" she asked.

"I've heard of it," said Elise.

"Welcome." Her nose chain jangled as she spoke. She looked us up and down. "You'll fit in just fine. It's all there on the menu."

We were led downstairs to the basement restaurant. But the more my eyes adjusted to the light, the more I could see that it was quite unlike any other restaurant that I had ever been to. Like the Maitresse D', the waiters and waitresses were all dressed in skin-tight leather. At the far end of the room was a wall-to-wall mirror with a large eight foot crucifix in front of it. I thought that I heard a shrill scream. It seemed to be cut short.

I cupped Elise round her waist as I helped her to her seat, and then, watched by Elise, I took a moment to study the room more closely. And that's when it came back to me: I may not have heard of La Nouvelle Justine, but I certainly remembered Justine. She was one of the favourites of the Marquis de Sade.

Not far from our table was a man in a pinstripe suit. In the daytime, he was probably a banker or a lawyer, but just then, he happened to be on all fours on the floor while one of the waitresses swatted at him with a leather paddle. Another man had been trussed into a straitjacket and was being spoon-fed like a baby. And over by the crucifix, a waitress was busily manacling a man's wrists.

While all these extraordinary acts of petty perversion were going on, Elise never stopped looking at me.

"Anything take your fancy?" she said.

I had my poker face on. The more extreme the moment, the less reaction I show. I may not be very good when it comes to revealing my emotions. But I am the master of the waxen mask of indifference.

"Like a session on the Cross?" I said. "My treat."

Elise scanned the menu. "Wouldn't you like to try 'Bad doggy in the dog house'?"

"Wouldn't you like to try, 'Bad baby won't eat her supper'?"

Elise laughed and stood up. "Come on, let's get out of this place."

"Not even a drink?"

"I don't think so."

I followed her up the stairs. My eyes followed the hem-line of her skirt. I wanted to kiss the back of her knees.

"Not for you?" said the Maitresse D'.

"My friend is still in shock," said Elise.

I cocked my eye at Elise as we walked out. "So what was that about?" I asked.

"I thought it'd be fun."

"Did I pass the test?"

"I knew you wouldn't fail me."

We stopped midstride. For although I have no problem at all with women leading me a merry dance, they must also know that there is a price to be paid.

I drew Elise towards me, holding her tight in my arms.

"Has that restaurant been giving you ideas?" she said, her lips not inches from mine. She breathed the words into my mouth.

"I hope so."

It was the first time that we'd ever held each other like that, and it was much more than just desire. There was also this air of devilment.

Holding someone special for the first time: it is one of those charged moments that I never tire of. And even as I held this she-devil in my arms, I was already well on the way to falling in love. No other woman that I'd met would have dreamed of taking me into a sadomasochist club.

Looking back, I can see that Elise was the perfect match for me. Whatever I had, whatever I did, Elise had it also; though ten-fold. She was all the things that I was, only more so. I was that man who'd sowed the wind, so carefree when it came to a woman's love, and what a whirlwind I was about to reap.

When it came to repartee, Elise could match me blow for blow. I used to believe that I had chutzpah; Elise was the Queen of it. Where I had been merely thoughtless in matters of the heart, Elise was positively cavalier. And whereas I sometimes lied to spare a hurt, Elise was about to give me the most complete master class.

It's all to come; it's all to come. The more you fall in love, the more it hurts. And if you are ever lucky enough to find that perfect love, then it will take some little time to mend your broken heart.

From the first with Elise, everything seemed to fit just perfectly.

For just as things ought to be when you've met the one, everything clicked perfectly into place.

In her high heels, she was just a little shorter than me. I drew her close. She slid one hand round my back and with the other, she caressed my cheek; we kissed once, twice; little pecks that gradually became firmer, moister, and then in perfect synchronicity we feasted on each other's lips and mouths. What an odd little sight we must have made on that street corner, eyes shut, thinking of nothing else but the warm lips and the soft tongue that probes so delicately.

One day, when I am rich, I will have a plaque put up on that street corner, as well as a cross in the pavement, to mark the exact spot where I realised that miracles *could* happen: and that, although bruised from my first marriage, my heart was by no means broken.

We kissed for a long time before, sated, we stopped.

Elise stroked the back of my neck as she kissed me one more time. "You kiss so well."

"And what does it bode for the future?"

"Heartbreak and misery," she laughed. "At least for one of us."

"Why not both?"

"Perhaps," she said, and I can still remember how, almost absentmindedly, she kissed me as she spoke. "Though not at the same time."

CHAPTER 13

We did not sleep together that night. That would have been a waste. By the end of that evening, after we'd eventually found a restaurant that served just food and drink, I think that we both realised that we might, just might, be onto something special, so there was no need to force the pace. Not that I didn't want to make love. I would have loved to have done it that very night. But I was endeavouring to smell the flowers along the way.

Over the next few days, we talked a lot on the phone and we sent a lot of e-mails. But we weren't able to meet up for another week because Elise was out chaperoning her stars in Los Angeles.

She also arranged for me to meet up with her friend the knee specialist. His name was Anthony Steele and he had an office in one of the mid-town skyscrapers, not far from where I worked. A few days after my date with Elise, I took an early cut from work to see him.

I could tell he was rich even before I saw him. The reception was lavish, with a thick, thick carpet, expensive pictures on the wall, state-of-the-art coffee machine, and a picture-perfect view out over the East River. It reeked of money; not that I'm over-awed by money. But I am aware of the power that it brings. The receptionist was pretty. She made me a coffee as I waited. Behind the glass reception desk was emblazoned an array of certificates, presumably earned by the four or five specialists who worked in this medical hub.

The doctor did not keep me waiting by so much as a minute; at exactly three p.m. one of the doors opened, and he was striding towards me, hand outstretched.

"Kim?" he said. "Good to see you."

"Dr Steele." We shook hands.

"Call me Tony."

I don't know what I'd expected from Anthony Steele, but I had not expected this. I suppose I'd rather presumed that he'd look like an academic, with gold-rimmed glasses and a stripling's body. But this man... he was a beef-cake. He was taller than me by a good three inches and looked like he spent a lot of time in the gym. I guess he was about ten years older than me, with a full head of greying hair, which did not so much age him as make him look distinguished. His skin was all but lineless; he not only topped up his tan, but moisturised regularly. And is there anything else that I can recall about this all-American hunk? He had a wedding ring, a large plain band of gold; an expensive Rolex plus diamond cufflinks; and underneath his white doctor's coat, he wore a lilac shirt with a striped club tie. You could tell that even a minute of his time was not going to come cheap. Had it not been for Elise's introduction, I wouldn't have gone near the place.

With his hand on my shoulder, Tony guided me into his office. It was designed to create maximum shock and awe as his speechless patients stretched for their cheque-books; the contrast with my own windowless hole was stunning.

The room was even larger than the reception, with a wall of windows, a cream sofa and a couple of armchairs. Over to the side, almost as an afterthought, was a large oak desk and an examining table. On the desk was a number of framed pictures of a beautiful brunette woman and four angelic children.

I'm trying to analyse the feelings that were welling up in me. Tony exuded power, but I was aware of something else. At first I couldn't put my finger on it, but as we chatted about inconsequentials, I began to get a waft of President Clinton: this guy may have been married, but he had this air of latent sexuality. As he talked, I found my mind wandering. I wondered if he had made love with the receptionist on the sofa on which I was sitting, or perhaps even a patient.

I couldn't ascertain exactly what it was that defined this man as a sexual being. But I was aware of it. My antennae hummed and bristled as they picked up all the strange vibes. It was not just his age, his money and his looks; I was in the presence of a greater power. Women, I was sure, turned to mush in front of this masterful man. I, however, did not. Even though his words poured out in this smooth, effortless burble, I found that he unsettled me.

"So how do you know Elise?" he asked, one leg cocked over the other, his hands clasped at the knee.

"We worked together on a story," I said. "When she heard about my knee, she said she'd put me in touch."

"She's a great girl," he said. "Let's have a look then."

I felt oddly self-conscious as I took off my trousers. He passed me a white gown and we went through to an adjoining room for the X-rays. Two shots, bang-bang, and then I was back in Tony's office, following his instructions as I lay down on the examination table in just my pants. What was making me even more unsettled was that I didn't know why I was feeling so edgy. What was it about this competent doctor that was throwing me?

Tony was tutting as he returned to the office with the X-rays. "That must have been some accident."

"It was." I crossed my arms.

He placed the X-rays on the desk as he stood next to me. "You don't work out much."

"Don't really have the time."

"Sure you don't," he said. From his tone he might as well have added, "You total loser."

"I'm just going to feel your knee," Tony said. "Tell me if it hurts." He worked his fingers round the sides of my knee. Very soft fingers; how the ladies must have melted to his touch. I winced as he probed across the knee-cap itself. He left off to examine the X-rays one more time.

"They should have done something about this years ago," he said. "Can you walk a mile without it flaring up?"

"Not often," I said.

"Should have had it fixed." He tutted again. "How long ago was it?"

"Fifteen, sixteen years ago."

"Let me tell you the position then, Kim," he said, perching himself on the edge of his desk. "This knee is not going to get any better; it's going to get worse. The good news though is that it's now a relatively simple operation to put in a new knee."

"And how much is that going to cost me?"

"Thirty thousand dollars," he said.

"Thirty thousand!" My head jerked off the pillow.

"Sometimes it's covered by insurance."

"I doubt whether it's covered by mine."

"Sure." He shrugged, crossing his legs at the ankle. "If you want to get a new knee in New York, then you know where to come. But it's so bad, your National Health Service may swing to giving you another one; join the waiting list now, and they might fit you in within the next decade."

"I'll think about it," I said.

"You're so very welcome."

As I got dressed, he went over to the window. A sudden wild thought came into my head: did he do that with his lovers? After making love on the sofa, did he stand there at the window, staring out over the river as he waited for the ladies to dress and leave?

I slipped on my ostrich skin cowboy boots. They usually gave me a bit of a 'what the hell' swagger, but in the office of Dr Tony Steele they made me feel like a clown. "How much do I owe you?" I asked.

"On the house," he said, turning towards me.

"Really?" I said. "Thank you."

As I opened the door, he came over to shake my hand. For the first time I noticed how his fingers quite dwarfed my own. "A pleasure," he said. "Write me a story some time. Elise says you're very good at that."

"I might do."

He gave a wave as he closed the door, and, even now, I struggle to recollect an experience which I have found more unsettling. I did not like him and I hated not having to pay. It may just have been as simple as Elise repaying the favour that she owed me, but it felt as if I was now personally beholden to this spit-polished American. I did not like it at all.

Before I'd even entered the lift, there was one thing that I had resolved upon: no way, no how, would I be going back to Dr Steele. Regardless of his exorbitant 30,000 dollar fee, the man gave me the creeps; and the worst of it was that I had no idea why.

CHAPTER 14

And what, meanwhile, was I going to do about Jess? Ever since my Friday night with Elise, Jess had been weighing very heavily on my mind.

Under normal circumstances, my position would have been quite clear. I would have carried on dating Jess and on the days that I didn't see her, I would have been free to be with Elise: and, like every other gadabout in Manhattan in 1998, I'd have continued running those two horses together until Force Majeure or circumstance compelled me to do otherwise.

That's certainly what I would have done before I'd met Elise. My life was in such a state of flux that having two lovers in New York almost seemed like the most sensible solution. Why commit to one woman when you never knew where you were going to be from one day to the next? And, further to that, by specifically *not* committing myself to one woman, then I'd be less likely to fall in love... less likely to get hurt... and, indeed, less likely to cause it.

From almost every angle, it made much, much more sense to continue to date Jess whilst at the same time embarking on a second voyage of discovery with Elise. That was the American way. It may seem squalid now, but in 1998, it was how young single people in New York chose to lead their lives; and after all, we were only following the lead that had been set for us by the Fornicator-in-Chief, President Clinton. Now there was a man who made a grab for everything that passed him by. Why shouldn't I?

So to repeat: From *almost* every angle, there was no pressing need for me to commit myself to Elise. We'd had two evenings together, and though they'd been fantastic – *extraordinary*, even – did that mean that I had to pin all my hopes and dreams on this one woman?

Well… yes it did. I believe I may have mentioned it: I am the plunger. Looking back now, I can see that with Jess, I'd been marking time. I enjoyed her company, but there was not that spark, that edge, which was ever going to make me fall in love.

But with Elise, even though I had not even the remotest scintilla of evidence that she was ready to commit to me, I wanted the decks cleared. From the very first, I wanted to give our relationship every best chance. And that meant Jess had to go.

A man like Steve would not even have considered it a problem. He would have bedded Jess the one night and Elise the next, and though he may well have preferred one to the other, would have judged that it was better still to be having sex with the both of them.

Hindsight, they say, is supposed to be twenty-twenty. But it's not. It's nearly as murky as trying to glimpse into the future. For I wonder, you see, if I made a strategic error; I wonder if, by doing what I did to Jess, whether I altered the actual mechanics of my relationship with Elise. It certainly made me more vulnerable, more likely to fall in love. Perhaps that's a good thing, perhaps not. Because although hindsight is useful, it's not going to tell you how everything would have turned out. You throw a rock into a pond, and sometimes even 13 years later, you can still feel the ripples.

But anyway, in the week before my second date with Elise, I had to gird my loins to throw a very large rock into my Manhattan mill-pond. I did not like it one little bit. I have always been absolutely hopeless at dumping women. I hate it. I hate the tears and I hate the guilt. Once, in times past, I was so gutless that I even used to pray that it would be my ex-loves who did the dumping.

With Jess, however, I had no alternative but to do it face-to-face; and the sooner I did it, the sooner I could offer up my heart to Elise.

Jess had been calling up for some days, asking when she would see me next. I had ducked out of various evening commitments, but after four days of prevaricating, I had steeled myself to do the deed. I'd arranged to see her at a bar near her office as soon as she'd clocked off from work. I hoped that, by the unusual choice of time and meeting place, she might divine that the axe was about to fall.

"Can't wait to see you!" she'd said; I felt like the slaughter-man sent to kill the children's pet lamb.

We'd arranged to meet in an Irish bar with shamrocks on the door and fiddles and leprechauns on the walls. How the Americans adore their Celtic antecedents; they love it if they can claim some Scottish or Irish ancestry. Don't hear very much, though, of Americans vaunting their English pedigree do we now? That's how it is when you're English. No one likes us; we don't care.

I'd arrived fifteen minutes early and had rehearsed exactly what I wanted to say: buy her a stiff drink; do the deed quickly; express both gratitude and sorrow; get the hell out of there and in thirty minutes I could be out drinking with Steve as he again reminded me that I was a complete idiot.

That was the plan. That *was* the plan. I was so nervous that as soon as I'd set foot in the place, I'd downed a Gin and French. You see, it wasn't that I disliked Jess. I was fond of her. I fancied her. It was just that I happened, for one reason or another, to be just that little bit more fond of Elise, and in my old-fashioned English way I wanted to be free to love her and her alone.

I'd thought it was going to be bad.

It wasn't bad.

It was excruciating. I have a few horror-show memories of my time in New York and this one has got to be right up there.

I was watching the door as Jess came in… followed by four of her workmates.

"Kim!" she squealed, throwing her arms round me as she smothered my lips. "I have missed you so much!"

I was introduced to her workmates, three women and a guy. I ordered two bottles of white wine. As we sat at a table, Jess stroked my thigh.

She was leading the party, screaming with laughter as she regaled us with stories, and all I could think of was the deed that had to be done.

"You're quiet," she said. "Something up?"

"Been a tough day," I said. "Had a really early start."

"Let's go back to your place then," she said. "It feels like I haven't seen you in ages."

"Yes."

I couldn't think what to say. It felt like I'd been prepping up for this moment for the last four days. And now that it was upon me, I was determined to see it through. But I couldn't do it in the Irish bar; I couldn't do it outside. But her place? My place? Should we go to the neutral territory of another bar?

"You poor thing," said Jess, kissing me again. She downed her wine in one. "Let's get you home. I'll call for a takeaway."

There was some ribald innuendo as we waved them goodbye, Jess clutching onto my arm with both hands. It was pouring with rain, hammering it down on the pavement; we tried for a cab, but it's every man for himself when you're hailing a taxi in the rain in New York. Men and women think nothing of racing across five lanes of traffic to stop a taxi in its tracks.

We ended up on the subway, with Jess snuggling in close as I braced myself on a strap handle. I stroked her wet blonde hair. What the hell was I doing? I was going back home with this beautiful woman. We could have a wonderful night. We'd eat and make love and no-one would be any the wiser. What was the especial urgency to end it all now? And surely, to live in the moment, you had to snatch up every grain of happiness that came your way? Why not postpone it for a day or two? How could it possibly make things any harder?

We squeezed under a micro-brolly and walked the last few blocks home. Jess was so warm, so giggly, that under normal circumstances, all I would have been thinking of was getting her out of her clothes just as soon as we'd walked through the front door. Where could be the harm in it? Was I not versatile? Couldn't I change my plans on the hoof? And that other whispered thought, so soft that I could barely hear it: was Elise really so special that it had to be her and no-one else but her?

My Norwegian neighbour Ingvild was coming out of my brownstone as we walked up the steps.

"Oh Kim," she said in her lovely singsong accent. "Hi!" She seemed pleased to see me... Well of course she was. Now that I had both Elise and Jess in my life, Ingvild had inevitably decided that it was me she wanted above all others.

"Hi Ingvild, how we doing?"

She laughed and stroked her hair. "Not as well as you, I see."
Inside the porch, I flapped the rain off the umbrella.
"Who was that?" said Jess.
"One of the neighbours," I said. "Ingvild. She's from Norway."
"She's pretty."
"I don't really know her."

Jess pushed me up against the wall as she tried to nibble at my lips.
"I'm going to have to watch you."

I extricated myself. Could I really do it that night? She'd be
devastated, utterly devastated.

"Just got to check the post." I delved into my pigeonhole; the
same bills that I'd left there the day before.

We went upstairs and with every step this thumping nausea was
growing in my heart. I'd do it when we got in. No matter what
happened. We'd walk in and before she had a chance to do anything –
anything at all – I'd say the fateful words, "Jess, I've got something
to tell you", and that would tell her that finally the axe was about
to come. But I'd have to be fast. I dreaded being pinned up against
the wall as Jess worked her fingers through my wet buttons. In this
topsy-turvy world that I now inhabited, it seemed only natural that
Jess would be making the first move.

At the top of the stairs, I busied myself with my clutch of keys.
"Come on!" said Jess.

I opened the door. Even as we walked inside, Jess was peeling off
her coat. She let it fall to the floor. Her flared brown trousers were
so wet that they clung to her calves.

"Jess, I've got something to tell..."
My phone rang. Jess looked at me. Hesitant?
"Excuse me."

It was London. Of course it had to be London. Always eager
to intrude into my most private moments, it was one of my mad-
masters from the *Sun*.

"Hi Kim." This time it was Trisha, the head of news, my onetime
ally with whom I'd shared a one-night stand. What an error. When
it comes to my romantic life, it always it seems as if my errors have
massively outweighed my few successes. I may have won a few

battles along the way, but in the end it always feels like I end up losing the war.

Though it is possible, I suppose, that the blunders tend to make for the deepest scars.

"Hi Trisha," I said. "How are you?"

"What do you know about this movie star who tried to commit suicide in a hotel in New York?"

"What!" It was like we'd been chatting at a cocktail party and she'd suddenly punched me in the gut.

"You know about it?" she said. "Who is it? What happened? Why didn't you mention it?"

Well, she may have caught me unawares. But I was not that much of a greenhorn.

"What's happened?" I watched as Jess went into the bathroom.

"Do you know who it is?" said Trisha. "Which hotel was it?"

"Can we start at the beginning?" I asked. It may sound extraordinary, but what with all the events of the previous week, and Elise coming into my life and Jess about to leave it, I had completely forgotten about my insane evening with Nick Spitz.

"It's a paragraph in the *Mirror's* showbiz column, their Wicked Whispers," she said. "'Who is the Hollywood A-lister who attempted to commit suicide in his luxury hotel suite in Manhattan, only to be rescued by the hapless hack who was interviewing him?'" She paused. I listened intently. "What have you heard?"

She was giving me one last chance to come clean. It wouldn't be too late. It would still be a world exclusive. But on the other hand... it would torpedo any chance of a relationship with Elise.

I didn't take long to decide which way to jump.

"A Hollywood star?" I tried to sound as if I were scouring my brain. "It's not ringing any bells."

"Really?" she said. "You don't know?"

"If I knew anything – anything at all – then I'd have told you."

"See what the rest of the pack have to say."

"Of course, I'll get back to you first thing."

She switched her line of attack. "Weren't you interviewing Nick Spitz last week? In New York? Which hotel?"

"I interviewed him in the St Regis; but, as I say Trisha, nothing happened."

I could sense her sifting through what I'd said. Like all the best executives, she had that gift of knowing when people were lying to her. "You're not telling me something. What are you holding back from me, Kim?"

"Me?" I said. "Nothing."

"I don't know why, Kim, but as a general rule I don't believe a word you say. This conversation is no exception."

"I'll put some calls in."

I sat on the sofa, burying my head into my hands. How had it got out so quickly? I hadn't breathed a word. And I was fairly sure that Elise hadn't talked. Which meant... it must have been the paramedics. And if it was already being whispered in under a week, then it wouldn't be long before the rest of the story came out.

As I pondered my options, Jess came out of the bathroom. She glowed. She'd taken off her wet clothes and was wearing my old blue bathrobe. She'd towelled and her tousled hair lay wet about her shoulders. It is one of the eternal truths of my life that a woman's beauty grows exponentially when she is out of bounds to my touch. It's bad, of course, when I see an old girlfriend for the first time since we've split. But it's worse by far when we're in the process of splitting up. During those awful few minutes, they are magically transformed into my Helen of Troy.

"Sounds like trouble," she said.

"It's always trouble," I said. "New York is trouble."

"Poor you." She came over, hugged me, and kissed me on the cheek. "What were you saying, before that call? You had something to tell me?"

"Ohhh."

She looked expectantly up into my face. And looking back, why didn't I just kiss her? It was what I wanted. It was what she wanted too. But it was like I was being pressured by some hidebound sense of morality, as if it were somehow virtuous to deny myself this fleeting pleasure.

I hemmed. I hawed. I dithered at the brink, hating the thought of that electric cold water. I could almost hear my father crowing at me: "Get on with it: man or mouse!" I swung my arms back. And launched myself in.

"Yes," I stumbled. "It was just... I've got so much on at the moment... I'm so busy... I don't feel I'm being fair to you... So it might be easier if we saw a little less of each other... I'm sure you're seeing plenty of other guys..."

"I'm not seeing anybody," she laughed. She seemed so trusting as she looked up at me. How I longed to kiss her. How stupid it all now seems: what was I thinking of, breaking this woman's heart, and all in a pathetic attempt to do the gentlemanly thing? And what a thank you I would soon be receiving for my pains.

"I love it when I'm with—" Jess trailed off. For the first time I saw the hurt register in her eyes. "I'm so stupid. You're breaking up with me."

"Well..." It all sounded so lame. Where was the cold steel that I'd planned to deliver? I'd wanted one swift savage blow and to have done with it. And now it was being eked out to the last drop. "I'm so busy. I've got so much work on. I'm sorry. I just don't have time for you."

"You've found somebody else," she said to herself. What was so truly awful was that she was so nice about it. "I knew you would." She sniffed and wiped a tear from her eye. "I hope you're very happy together."

She slipped away into the bathroom to put on her wet clothes. I heard her blow her nose and then she came out, her eyes red from the tears.

I had already rehearsed what I wanted to say. "Goodbye and thank you so..."

I tried to clutch at her; was I making the biggest mistake of my life? Who knows... but that was definitely the moment when the wind changed and my course changed with it.

Jess ducked my kiss and left my flat. I stood at the top of the stairs watching her go down, her wet brown flares flapping about her ankles.

In my defence, all I can say is that I thought I was acting for the best. I thought I was doing the honourable thing. Love is hell isn't it?

It's either you that gets hurt or you that does the hurting, and they're both awful. If I had to state a preference, I think that ultimately I prefer to be hurt. I am used to it. I have had my heart broken many times over, and in time I know that it will heal itself. But breaking the heart of someone I've loved: I do not have much experience in it. But on the few occasions when it has occurred, the memory is still as fresh as if it's just happened.

CHAPTER 15

So I had cleared the decks. My heart was pure. My motives were honourable. I was ready to offer myself up to Elise.

But I still felt like an absolute swine, and the more Steve crowed, the worse I felt.

"You've dumped Jess?" He was incredulous. "Jess was sensational! I loved Jess!"

He swilled more wine. He was fascinated. That a guy should come to work in New York City and then wilfully, purposefully, opt out of the fabulous love banquet... It was beyond his comprehension.

"And now you're all set to fall in love with Elise."

"I'm at least halfway there."

"She's probably met her match. Professionally. Physically. Though obviously not on an intellectual level."

"That goes without saying."

"Would you mind then listening to a piece of advice from your old Uncle Steve?"

"I'm sure I'll have to hear it anyway." We were in one of the many unmemorable bars on the Upper West Side. It's funny about those bars in Manhattan. I can recollect nothing at all about them. They all seem to blend into this blur of light varnished wood and fey lagers. New York does most things brilliantly, but when it comes to watering-holes, it has never come close to matching a traditional British pub.

"From what I've seen of Elise, and from what I know about women, I wouldn't push her too hard," said Steve. "It's like when you're negotiating: the first person to name a price gets crucified. You never name the price."

I crossed my arms and leaned back on my chair. I was listening all right, but none of it was going in.

"You could show some interest," Steve said.

"I'm listening."

"Yeah, well, it's only your hide I'm trying to save." Steve gestured at me with his glass, ignoring the slopped wine. "I just happen to have this funny feeling that if you're telling Elise 'I love you' before she's in as deep as you are, well, my friend... it will be painful. Have as much sex as you can! Buy her flowers! Declaim a bit more of your Shakespeare. But please, please don't let the love word fall from your lips."

If only it were so simple. If only we could hear sound, sage advice from our friends and were then able to heed it.

But good advice is wasted on most people, unless, of course, they're paying through the nose for it. And as for myself, it almost becomes a goad, pricking me on to ever-greater acts of self-destruction.

Me, Kim, not wear my heart on my sleeve? It is not in my nature. When I am in love, I must declare it immediately. It's all I can think of, and eventually out it must come. The words seem to bubble from my lips; there is no method of stemming them. I may have known a woman only a matter of days, but once I know she's The One, I must – must – look her in the eye and whisper my love across the table. Sometimes it works. Sometimes it works quite well. It may be forcing the pace, but what woman in the first flush does not want to be told that she is loved?

My love is like my kisses. I kiss a woman as soon as I dare; and that is also how I declare my love. That is what we plungers do. We do not probe the bottom or check to see if the water's warm: we put our trust in love and be damned to the consequences.

I was besotted, and having Elise on the other side of America was only helping to stoke the flames.

Though love and lust aside, there were more pressing matters to discuss when next I spoke with her. Elise was staying at the Beverly Hills Hilton. It had taken an age to track her down.

"You need a new knee then?" said Elise.

"For thirty grand," I said. "Out of my price range."

"You'll be transformed!" she said. "I'm sure Tony will be able to cut you a deal."

"Tony?" I said in disbelief. Somehow the thought of Tony cutting me a good deal seemed unlikely. "Anyway. you don't happen to have any idea how the *Mirror* has already got wind of our Nick Spitz's attempted suicide?"

"They have? How do you know?"

"It's in their bloody showbiz column!" I said. "They're onto it! They know he tried to kill himself, and they know that he was saved by a 'hapless hack', as they decided to call me."

"Really?" she said.

"If this story gets out, and I don't have it first, then I won't just be up to my neck, I'll be drowning in it."

"I'll call Nick," said Elise. I could hear her writing into her notebook. "If it's all going to come out, then obviously you'll have it first. I'll sort it out."

"Well I can't say I'm too happy about this, you know Elise."

"It's fine," she said airily. "I said I'll sort it, and I'll sort it."

"Okay. If it were anyone but you Elise, I'd have run it days ago."

"But I am me, and you have held it over and I love you all the more for it."

I paused to take in what she'd said. 'Love me all the more for it?' Was that really what she'd just said? It was as good as a declaration of love... or was it? PR women are forever spouting "love you for ever" as they try to place one of their stories, but that didn't even guarantee a kiss. But Elise... she *had* kissed me. Could she be in love with me? It was possible. Stranger things have happened.

"When am I going to see you again?" I asked.

"Back on Friday," she said. "If I chase hard out of JFK, I might be with you by seven o'lock."

I liked this sort of language. There were none of the usual smoke and mirrors, shadowing each other's moves in a futile attempt not to get hurt. But you can twist and you can turn and it makes no odds, because although love is the most majestic thing that life has to offer, it comes with a price. You fall in love and one way or the other you're going to get burned, so stop whining and get used to it.

"I better make sure the sheets are clean," I said.

"You better," she laughed. "I am a woman of refined tastes."

I called in an army of cleaners and gave them 300 dollars to blitz the flat. They spent all morning. It was amazing how much lighter the place looked. Windows had been cleaned, blinds had been dusted, and even the speckle of black mould had been removed from around the rim of the shower.

I loathe shopping – it is one of the many delights that Satan will be lining up for me in hell – but I even spent one lunchtime mooching around Bergdorf Goodman for duvets, under-sheets and towels. "What colour do we reckon?" I asked the shopping assistant. "Navy?"

"Is this just for you?" she said, which I presume was a polite way of saying, "Are you going to be having sex on these sheets?"

"Err, no," I said, which was my polite way of saying that I did indeed plan to be making love on the sheets.

She trailed her slim fingers over the duvets. She was pretty; I was surprised at how much I was enjoying myself. "Go for white," she said. "Perhaps a little blue piping on the edge of the duvet cover?"

"I'll take two of everything."

"You're English, aren't you?" She scooped up the towels. "Put a vase of freesias by the bedside. You can't go wrong."

"Freesias it is," I said. "Any other tips?"

"Candles are nice. You can't have too many candles."

"So where, pray, is the candle department?"

She laughed. "I wish my boyfriend went to so much trouble."

"And you're offering a full money-back guarantee if she doesn't turn to mush?"

She smiled coquettishly. "If she doesn't turn to mush... then I will personally come round to see what the problem is."

My. God. My God! It was as if, by committing myself to Elise, my entire body had been sprayed with love-musk. If I had been a little looser with my morals, then I could have been seeing Elise, and Jess, and Ingvild, and quite possibly – unless I was very much mistaken – this pretty assistant. It seemed that now that I had voluntarily quit the dining room, women were clamouring at me to join them at the legendary Manhattan buffet.

But I was virtuous to a fault. I prided myself on my virtue. I had Elise in my sights and no-one else would do. Other men, I know, would have snapped up everything in sight. They'd have been asking Ingvild out for a drink, and following up on the pretty Bergdorf assistant's banter and... generally been making hay while the sun shone over the Manhattan skyline. And meanwhile if anything came of the relationship with Elise, then all the other women might well just have to fall by the wayside... but *until* that moment, and not until that moment, then where on earth was the harm in fooling around with a few other women? I love that term 'fooling around'; it covers such a multitude of sins from a stolen kiss to a full-blown orgy.

A haircut on the Friday morning; new pairs of pants and socks from Barney's; a bag full of plain ivory candles; two bottles of Bollinger and a bottle of Sancerre chilling in the fridge, along with smoked salmon, a side of gravad lax, a cold lobster and roast chicken; a loaf of wholemeal bread and a pack of salted organic butter; enough exotic fruit to have outshone Carmen Miranda's headpiece; two tubs of the most expensive ice-cream that money could buy; a posy of the Bergdorf Goodman-specified freesias; and I even went to the trouble of buying a small filing cabinet in which to stuff the thousand and one bits of paper that I'd accumulated during my year in New York. Well, Elise may or may not have been thrilled with what was on offer, but this was about as good as it was going to get from me.

Now all I needed, of course, was for the wretched phone to ring, so that – minutes before Elise's arrival – I was sent abroad on yet another wild goose chase. Doubtless my mad-masters were that very minute dreaming up some new hell to fly me to. "Kim's got a hot date planned for the weekend, so let's mess it up: but where, oh where, shall we send him?" The globe is spun. A pin is stuck in at random. "Alaska? I hear it's minus forty in January! That would be *perfect*!"

So there I sat, all aquiver as I tried to watch the television. I felt my chin. Stubble? How could I possibly have stubble when I'd only shaved an hour earlier? Vague memories, possibly apocryphal, of the lives of our submariners. It is said that when they're coming home after three months at sea, they're so excited at the prospect of being reunited with their loved ones that the testosterone starts coursing through their bodies. Their beard growth doubles.

I had a second shave, wiped the stubble from the sink, and continued to wait. I licked the heel of my hand and smelt it. It was rank! I'd got halitosis! Halitosis to stun a mule! Even the coolest guy in the world couldn't have won over a woman if he had rank bad breath. I gargled on Listerine till my gums stung.

The phone rings. I'm absolutely certain it's London. Who else could it possibly be? To my absolute amazement, it's her.

"Elise!" I said.

"Were you expecting somebody else?"

"No," I said. "No! How are you? Where are you? What are you doing?"

"Just got in. Shall I go home and freshen up?"

"No!" I said. "Come on over. Bring the bag. Bring all your souvenirs. But the main thing is, bring yourself."

"I'm on my way."

You know that feeling you get at the airport as you're awaiting the return of your lover? You sit there in the café, sip your coffee and attempt to read the newspaper: but it's hopeless because at every sentence you are pausing to look up at the arrivals gate. You return to your newspaper, only to be lost in a reverie about what your lover will be looking like, and what it is, precisely, that you'll be doing with them as soon as the front door has been slammed behind you. Or is there time, even, to make it back home? Not that delayed gratification doesn't have its charms... but might not it be more romantic to rent a room in the airport hotel? Perhaps they even do rooms by the hour...

And those happy thoughts occur, needless to say, when you're meeting up with a long-term girlfriend who, not a week earlier, you were sending off on holiday.

Your thought-processes tend to get more frazzled when you are dreaming of your reunion with a woman whom you hardly know. I didn't know it, but even then I was close to falling in love with her. And, I suppose, I guess, there was also that tiny matter of the sex thing.

I find that I am slightly torn. On the one hand, I do not wish to sound salacious or tawdry. But on the other, I must be candid. For if you are to understand anything at all of what happened with Elise – and just *how* it happened – then you may as well know now that the sex was pertinent. Not, by any means, that it was the whole of why I came to love her. But the sex was tied up with so many things – the love, the ecstasy and this absolute gut-churning agony – that I cannot be mealy-mouthed when I write about it.

The bell rang. I jolted out of my daydream and leapt for the door. "It's me," she said. I buzzed her up, and my heart is hammering as I open the door and hear her coming up the stairs. I stand there nonchalantly leaning against the door frame; cool, casual, not trying too hard. But what am I thinking of? Elise's got her bag. I must help her up with it.

I dash down the stairs and there she is coming up to the next landing. The bag drops to the floor. "Hi," she says. Is there just a moment of tentativeness as we look into each other's eyes – Does he? Does she? – and then I think to hell with it, and she's in my arms and I've kissed her firmly on the lips. I inhale her scent. Is that a sigh of contentment that I hear?

"Let me take you to my lair," I said.

"Take me to your lair." I take her bag and, holding Elise's hand, I usher her into my flat. The door is firmly shut behind us. For the first time we are alone together.

I could talk, but I have no words to say, and instead instinct just seems to take over as there, by the door, I enfold Elise into my arms and we are kissing, kissing most artfully, like sexual veterans who know each other's needs. She does not stop until she has satiated herself upon my lips.

We drew back, smiled at each other and kissed. "Let me look at you," I said. "I'd almost forgotten what you looked like."

She struck a smouldering pose, red lips pouting, hand on hip, one knee bent. "Like what you see?"

I took in her clothes. She wore creamy moleskins and a straining burgundy V-neck; not that I had any clue, but they looked rather expensive. Her coat was lying on the floor, testament to our debauchery.

"Very much," I said. "And you?"

It was now Elise's turn to give me the eye. As with my flat, I had done the best I could: Chino's and a sky-blue shirt.

Elise's head tick-tocked from side to side, Comme-çi, Comme-ça. "You'll do." She came over to me, slipping her hand round my waist. "Show me your castle."

It was not much of a castle, just the lounge and off it the two bedrooms, the bathroom and the kitchen. The parquet floor was an asset and so were the high ceilings and the windows. A sudden awareness came to me that it was probably all pretty small beer compared to the flats in which Elise was usually entertained.

Elise made admiring comments as we entered each room, though she saved her most lavish praise for my bedroom. The candles were already lit and the freesias in position on the bedside table. "It's lovely!" she trilled, before taking a closer look at the duvet. She lifted it up and inspected the bed-sheet. "And not just clean sheets, but new sheets!" Laughing, she broke off to look in the en-suite shower. "New towels and new candles too!"

"Don't be ridiculous!" I said. "You think I'd go to all the trouble of buying new sheets and towels..."

"Not forgetting the pillow-cases and the candles and the flowers..."

"And of course not forgetting the pillow-cases, the candles, the flowers, as well as the Bollinger, the Sancerre, the salmon, the chicken, the lobster, the fruit-basket, the two tubs of very expensive ice-cream..."

"What flavour?" Another kiss to my lips.

"I thought you'd be a Mint Choc Chick, but I bought the chocolate too, just in case."

"And anything else?"

"No, that's it... though actually, now that I come to think of it, in an attempt to clear up my mountain of paperwork, I did also purchase a very fine filing cabinet."

She looked up at me, hand upon my cheek, and kissed me. "Thank you."

"So, the big question is: would you like to eat? You've been here fifteen minutes and I haven't offered you so much as a glass of champagne!"

She kissed me — all those kisses that we shared in New York! Would that I had counted them; I treasure every one. "Or..." she said. There was this most delightful pause. "Shall we make love?"

A Fourth of July volley of fireworks seem to explode in my head. There have been a few moments in my life that I will treasure till my dying day. This was one of them.

I kissed her again. "Eating or making love? Of the two options, I think I'd go for the latter."

"Or perhaps…" Again, another exquisite pause. "We could do both? The Bollinger? And the ice-cream?"

"Just wouldn't be the same without a tub of Haagen Daz."

"No it would not."

We collected our booty from the fridge-freezer.

"Do we want plates?" I asked.

She considered the matter. "Perhaps a knife and spoon," she said. "I'm never good at eating ice-cream with my bare fingers."

As we sat there on the edge of the bed, my hands shaking a little as I fumbled with the champagne cork, I did fleetingly think of Jess, Ingvild and, well, others… and at that moment, I felt as if I would have traded in the lot of them for my Elise.

"I do have quite high hopes about this," said Elise. We chinked our glasses.

"But do be sure to have very low expectations," I said. "I'm a little out of practice."

She gurgled with laughter. "I don't believe that for a moment."

"Where would you like to start?"

She eyed me up, almost professionally, like a farmer sizing up a steer. "I thought, perhaps, that I might help you out of your shirt."

"A very good place to start."

She stretched back – I could see a ripple of bare skin between her shirt and her trousers – and carefully placed her glass on the bedside table. She swings back, kisses me, and one by one starts to unbutton me. "Why is it," she said, "that men's buttons go up the wrong way to women's?"

"Ladies like their buttons on the left so that it's easier for their hand-maidens to dress them."

"You just made that up!" She leaned over, helping me out of my cuffs as she swooped down to kiss my chest.

"I am a vast mine of the useless and the trivial." I shivered at the sight of her. Elise – Elise! – was kissing my shoulder-blade. She swept back the hair from her face.

"Maybe you are," she said. "But you're also a blagger."

"That is also true." I helped her off with her jumper, tossing it onto the armchair. "When I am stumped for a fact, which does not happen often, I have a tendency to make things up. Your shirt?"

"Please."

The banter helped to calm my nerves. I like to banter, yet had never used it in such extraordinary circumstances. We were teasing each other as we went about the wholly serious business of making love for the first time: when, as all lovers know, one tries to show that one is competent, proficient, considerate and even sometimes, as occasion demands, selfless.

"Your fingers are trembling," said Elise. She watched me fumble with her buttons.

"Freezing isn't it?" I was so ham-fisted I might as well have been wearing mittens. "It is a little unexpected. Fifteen minutes ago I was sitting on the sofa dreaming of you coming through the door: and now, here you are…"

"Wanting to make love with you."

"Yes. Obviously you must have been having a very lean time of things in Los Angeles." She slipped out of the shirt; golden skin, soft to the touch. I unclipped her black satin bra.

"Not a single kiss in La-la-land," she said. "As I was flying back, I thought that if I asked nicely…"

"Did you even say please?"

"I'm not sure I did." She leaned into me, skin to skin. "Please?"

"Please what?"

"Please let's make love."

"Then maybe I should help you off with your trousers?"

She stood in front of me. I unbuckled her belt and unbuttoned her trousers. They slipped easily down her legs.

"Lucky they're not skin-tight," I said. "That might have been a problem."

"You might have had to cut me out."

I weighed the trousers in my hands, my senses so alive. "What would have been best: scissors, razor or a carving knife."

"They were rather expensive," she said. "Perhaps olive oil?"

"What an erotic image," I said. "You, lying in a bath of olive oil."

"Let me see about your trousers."

"Though socks first."

"Always socks first."

"Could Clint Eastwood look cool in just socks and no trousers?"

"Not even Dirty Harry."

We lay on the bed side by side, her black underwear melding with my white boxers, and as our hands explored we either kissed or talked.

"I'm hungry," I said.

"We have no plates," said Elise with a kiss. "What ever will you eat off?"

I dolloped a scoop of Mint Choc Chip into her navel. She squealed.

"I hope it doesn't ruin your knickers," I said.

"They're La Perla too," she said. "Fresh on at JFK."

"At JFK?" I said. "You were planning ahead."

"Like somebody else with his new boxers. But since they are La Perla, and since I am rather fond of them, then it might be best to take them off."

She lifts up, and I still have this most unbelievable vision in my mind of Elise lying there naked on my bed, while on her belly is this dimple of ice-cream. The ice-cream was beginning to melt, with a trickle of Mint Choc edging down her belly.

Elise propped herself up on some pillows. First she looks at herself; then she looks at me.

"I've got no clothes on," she said.

"Doesn't the ice-cream count for anything?" I said. "And you're still wearing your gold cross."

"And you, darling Kim, are still in your boxers."

"My new boxers."

"Your *new* white boxers."

"Is that a problem?"

"Well not yet," she said, her hands straying to her flank. She stopped the trickle of ice-cream and licked her finger. "Though it might be in a few minutes-"

"When we're making love..."

"Yes, when we are making love." Her fingers eased inside the elastic of my boxers. "But keeping your boxers on doesn't seem very neighbourly."

"Never thought of it like that," I said. "But now that you mention it, keeping on my boxers seems downright unfriendly."

Our eyes never leave each other. I am drowning in them. And to me it is one of the truly incredible things about making love. It still never loses its edge. With every new love, it is as if I have been reborn a virgin. I mean that the excitement, the sheer thrill, is absolutely of a match with that time, half a lifetime ago, in a Windsor park with a beautiful piano mistress. And with Elise, I am abrim with, yes, *love*.

"That's better," Elise said. "Lovely though your boxers were, they look better on the floor. About that Mint Choc Chip?"

I kissed her. "I have been extremely concerned about my duvet."

"Your *new* duvet."

"I think we should take it as read that everything in this flat is new and has been bought with the express purpose of winning your heart."

"And hasn't it paid off?" she said. "Go eat your ice-cream."

In such moments, it is very difficult to stay in the moment. For on the one part, your every nerve ending is suffused with pleasure. You're aware of all these different bodily sensations, from the taste of ice-cream and musk, the scent of her perfume, and the sight of Elise and those bright eyes flickering; and on the other... your mind still cannot quite believe that you are so intimate with this beautiful woman... and then your mind drifts off to the St Regis.

"And how is it?" she asked.

"I will never have it any other way again." I moved up the bed. She kissed me lasciviously. "Tell me: where we shall go for our first holiday?"

"Our first holiday? Isn't that rather presumptuous?" she said. "And to think: we haven't even made love yet."

I cupped her face between my hands and kissed her. "No... but we are making love."

"Yes, *we* are making love." She laughed as she looked up at me. "Kim is making love to me: or should that be 'with me?' Though it definitely wouldn't be right to say that I was making love *to* you; or *at* you; or *under* you. No: at this precise moment, I am making love *with* you."

"In such circumstances, it is of course essential that prepositions are used correctly," I said. "Can there be any greater turn-off than the incorrect use of a preposition?"

She was smiling. A deliciously sexy smile. I've only just realised, all these years later, that a smile is the most beautiful thing that you can see on a woman.

Elise cooled my ardour with chocolate ice-cream, lapping it off me like a wanton. And – remember this – it was only the very first time that we'd made love; is it any wonder that I fell so hard and so deep?

She wiped a dribble of ice-cream from her chin. "I like your armchair. Is it time to continue our discussion on the appropriate use of the phrase 'making love'?"

She led me over.

"On the armchair, I am about to make love with Kim," she said.

"Are you now going to decline that for me?"

"Decline that?" she said. "Conjugate, surely?"

A vague echo of English lessons past. "I'm sure you're right."

"Don't you even need O'level English to join the *Sun*?" she chided. "Nouns, adjectives and pronouns are declined; verbs are conjugated."

"Well conjugate away."

"I am making love with Kim on the armchair," she said. "You are making love to me: on the armchair; and, upon this same chair, Kim is making love to Elise."

"Should Kim be taking any contraceptive measures?"

Elise let out a little moan and kissed me. "Kim, who is still making love to Elise, has most thoughtfully asked if he should be taking any contraceptive measures: but there is no need." She winked at me. "Thanks for asking."

"This is the first time that Kim has ever listened to a running commentary of his love-making."

"Really?" she shivered. "And normally you're so chatty."

"And are you going to still be talking when you have been brought to the brink of this much vaunted orgasm?"

Her fingers were biting deep into my arms. Her eyes fluttered, watching mine as she gave me the most delicious smile. "I am making love with Kim." Elise clutched at me. "Kim is making love with me, and…"

Despite all of Steve's warnings and despite all my best intentions, there was only one thing that I could say as Elise and I melded into one: "I love you."

I did, indeed I did, and though I may well have been a plunger, I can say that the sex… the sights along the way… it was worth it. Later on, certainly, there was absolute hell to pay. But I don't have any regrets. I do know, however, that there are some things that I should have done differently. But wistfully wondering about what might have been, what *should* have been… it's as wasteful as regret itself.

I hope that this sex scene has not been too graphic, too distasteful, but I want you to have some inkling of the astonishing drug that was Elise. And after that first night with her, I was completely hooked. I craved Elise and Elise alone, and nothing else, not work nor women, could ever hold a candle to her.

Though it was not entirely a one-way street. For I did have my own charms: charms that I had learned from one of the Hollywood greats, Marlon Brando.

We had gone back to the bed, and kissed and drunk Champagne, and after a light supper, Elise's arm snaked down my chest. "Elise has an overwhelming desire to make love for the second time with Kim."

"Or, to conjugate that *verb*, Kim is about to make love with Elise for the second time."

"Kim should not be standing on ceremony…" She stroked my earlobe between thumb and forefinger. "Kim is making love with Elise for the second time…"

A second time. After a few times, you don't keep count, though I always wish that I had. They say, as you may know, that when you are courting a woman, you should put a penny into a glass bottle for every time that you make love. Then, after you are married, every time you make love, you take a penny *out* of the bottle. And I have always been told that that married man will never run out of pennies. I wish that I had put it to the test. But my gut feeling, and indeed recent events, would indicate that the Rule of the Glass Bottle is correct.

And so we continued to make love… though to detail any more of it that night would be too much. It was more of the same, with new riffs, new arpeggios and fresh variations on a theme. But when we were finally – finally – spent, it was gone midnight, and like men the world over who have been sated by sex, I craved my sleep.

And this was when I remembered Brando's tip on how a man turns himself into a wonderful lover. It's not so much about what happens when you're in the throes of passion; it's about what happens *afterwards*.

So, while most men would have been turning over onto their sides and dropping straight off to sleep, Brando was giving his lovers the Big Elbow: he would firmly prop his head up on his elbow, he'd stay awake and he'd *listen*.

It wasn't easy. I may have been besotted with Elise, but after salmon, lobster and a bottle of Champagne – not to mention our bouts of love-making – my eyelids were weighted down with tiredness.

I excused myself. In the lavatory, I ran the water till it was ice cold and pressed my face into a wet towel. A few eye-drops and then, with at least a slight semblance of being bright-eyed and bushy-tailed, I joined Elise under the duvet, propped my head onto my elbow, and dreamily stared at her.

She smiled impishly as she kissed me. "I've been doing my research on you," she said.

"Find anything good?"

"No, nothing at all. Nothing of even the remotest interest," she said. "What a dull little life you've had these past thirty-three years…"

"Thirty-two, actually."

"Thirty-two then," she said. "Birthday soon?"

"Next month. The day before Valentine's Day… and since you ask, I was indeed born on Friday the 13th. Will you share it with me?"

"Yes." She kissed me. How we used to kiss in those days! And how different it all is now. It was as if, with each kiss, we were reminding ourselves that such snatched kisses were now positively welcomed. "Anyway, before you interrupted me, I was just talking about the humdrum little life that you've led. I mean: the Eton schoolboy who ends up at the *Sun*..."

"How dull is that?"

"And who once wrote in the newspapers about how he was seduced by his piano mistress?"

"Did I?" I stretched out to play with her crucifix. "That was an error."

"And who is sent to New York, and has five straight splashes in a row from the Louise Woodward trial..."

"You *have* been doing your homework on me!" I said. "You've done a cuttings check?"

She stretched for her glass. "It's known as due diligence. You think I'm going to start seeing a *Sun* reporter without knowing the first thing about him?"

"Fair enough." She tilted the glass of Sancerre towards me and I sipped.

"And who, within two hours of meeting me, saves one of the world's biggest superstars from killing himself at the St Regis."

"That's classified information," I said. "Who on earth told you that?"

She stretched over and held me tight. "I've never had so much fun in bed before." She held me tighter.

"Nor I," I said. "I hope that we always talk when we make love."

"Speaking of which..." She rolled on top of me.

"It seems I'm at something of a disadvantage then," I said. "You've done a full cuttings search on me, and yet I know next to nothing about you."

"A woman must have her secrets." She smiled, hands upon my chest. "Though I'm sure that a Red Top reporter must be capable of making deductions and inferences..."

"And assumptions."

I looked up at her, and I found that I was drawn to the challenge. I began with the obvious starting point: the crucifix round her neck. This was more, though, than just a gold crucifix; it also had on it a tiny figure of Christ.

What else did I have to go on? Her name, Elise: a little unusual. Her accent: sort of a mid-Atlantic hybrid. And another tiny detail:

the way she'd picked me up on verbs being conjugated rather than declined. Well, I didn't care what she said, that sort of grammar certainly seemed like university level to me.

"You're a Catholic. Your mother's American and..." I'm watching her closely, searching for any telltale signs that might reveal I'm on the right track. "Your father's English. Somehow they met in Britain. They fell in love. Naturally they sent you to a convent. How am I doing so far?"

"No clues," she said.

"But when did you come over to America?" I asked. "Perhaps university; but you must have had a thorough schooling in the UK. You speak with a slight American accent, but your manner of speaking is very much English..."

"That's only because I'm mimicking you."

"Don't distract me, I'm on a roll!" I kissed my finger and pressed it to her lips. "You went to university in America: Ivy League. Probably. And from your bedroom manners and the way that you are so immaculately groomed, you've stayed in America ever since.

"There's something about your mother though, isn't there? I sensed something. What's happened? What could have happened? She..." I trailed off. "She's Catholic. And she's split from your father. And – of course! – she can't get a divorce! So she's back here in America."

"In New York City." Elise applauded me, lightly clapping her hands. "Have you been nosing through my dustbins? That's illegal over here."

I cupped my fingers and modestly blew on my nails. "And your dad's in the UK? Living with someone? But you took your mum's side in it all?" I watch her every move. "You're very close to your mum."

"You're unbelievable!" she said.

"So some people say."

What joy it was talking, laughing, and caressing that extraordinary woman. How she lit up my life. At length, when we were both spent, we drowsed in each other's arms.

I woke up as she kissed me on the cheek. It was six a.m. and Elise was fully dressed.

"What?" I said. It took some moments to get my bearings. I was at home; and this was Elise by my side, kissing my cheek in the darkness. "What are you doing? Where are you going?"

"I've got to go back home," she said. "I have breakfast with mummy in the morning."

"I... what?" I'm wide-awake. So many questions are suddenly charging through my head. She's going to have breakfast with her mother? Does she *live* with her mother? "When... when will I see you again?"

She kissed me one last time on the lips. "Soon... I hope." Soft as a sigh of wind she slipped through the bedroom door.

CHAPTER 16

Those next three weeks went by in a chaotic whirlwind of love such as I had never known. Perhaps I do my previous girlfriends an injustice. When you're in the heat, all else seems tepid by comparison. I was so in Elise's thrall that I didn't give a thought to any of my old loves. No, you only start dreaming of past passions when your ship is in the doldrums and there's not a breath of wind in the air to move you.

But let's make no bones about it: when I was with Elise, we spent most of our time making love. I had never seen the like. Within a few days, we had not only christened every room in my flat, but every chair, every table, every stick of furniture. On a point of principle, we also sated our lust in the cupboards and upon the window sills and even in the laundry room downstairs. We went down into the darkness and switched on a drier. How it all comes back to me: the heat, the juddering vibrations and the clattering rumble that was loud enough even to mask our ecstasy. Not that I need to describe any of these sex scenes in graphic detail. But I mention it because the sheer volume, quality and, I guess, outrageousness, of the sex that we were having is pertinent to my tale. There was nowhere, seemingly, that was off-limits: broom cupboards of five star restaurants; steamy saunas in private clubs; rooftops that could be seen from a thousand office windows; and even my cramped little office was deflowered, as we skulked in one night after dinner. For me it was a revelation. For every dare that I offered up to Elise, she sent it zinging straight back at me, with added top-spin for good measure.

Elise and I were not by any means inseparable. She had her work and I had mine, but in so far as we could, we made time for each other. And there was one date, of course, that we had booked up quite early on in our relationship: my birthday, the day before Valentine's

Day. It's the story of my life, you know: I've always aspired to the romantic, but somehow I always end up just that little bit short.

She didn't tell me what she'd planned, but she'd told me to keep the evening free.

I'd spent the morning on a story, having a chicken burger with Ivana Trump in a stretch limo. Ivana was fantastic. Some celebrities leave me cold, but Ivana was funny and flirty and in under five minutes I totally understood how she'd managed to cast her spell around The Donald.

We had just fifteen minutes together.

"It's your birthday?" she'd said. We were snuggling up together, as if we'd just been on a date; these are the things that celebrities have to do if they want to promote New York's latest chicken burger.

"Yes, Ivana, it's my birthday," I repeated.

She had a huge smile, all teeth, as she beamed at Ali.

"Well come here!" She kissed me on the cheek. "How old are you?"

"Thirty-three."

"The perrr-fect age," she said. "For me."

And perhaps I was; soon afterwards, Ivana was stepping out with a young man who was actually younger than me.

After the pictures were in the bag, I went straight back to the office to write up the story.

Elise called just before lunch. There was a pause and then she started to sing.

"Happy birthday to you." She was singing in sultry imitation of Marilyn Monroe crooning for President Kennedy. "Happy Birthday to you. Happy Birthday, darling Kim, Happy Birthday to you."

"Very impressive," I said.

"What are you doing tonight?" she asked.

"I'd love to see you tonight, Marilyn, I really would, but actually I'll have to pass. I've got this hot date with this woman I'm very keen on... and you know... much though I'd love to sleep with a superstar, my date tonight might be a little peeved."

"Oh, what a shame," said Elise, though still in Marilyn's breathy voice. "She must be a special lady."

"Special? She's not special!" I said. "She's extraordinary! A potentially lethal combination of brains and beauty. She's taking me out tonight. It's going to be great!"

"And where is she taking you?"

"She has yet to tell me."

"I think you're meeting at her place," she said. "Seven o'clock and don't be late."

"I've heard of it," I said. "But I've never been there."

"Well, you'd better dress smart."

"Jacket and tie?"

"Just the jacket," she purred. "Though it won't stay on for long."

That night as I dressed for dinner, I had the exquisite feeling of knowing that I was on a promise.

Though as we all of us eventually learn, even the most fervent of promises are only made so that they can be broken.

As I'd used to do with Jess, I walked through Central Park. By chance, Elise lived not that far from Jess's apartment: perhaps fifteen blocks away. But from the exterior alone, I could tell that this was no grubby block of bedsits. With its grand white brick façade and green gabled roof, it looked as if it had been plucked straight out of a Paris boulevard.

A doorman let me in and the lobby reeked of old, understated wealth. I caught the lift up to the tenth floor. There were just two flats on the floor and Elise was waiting with the door open. She wore a red halter-neck dress.

I appraised her for a moment. "Lady in red," I sang.

"Oh, this old thing." She smirked; we kissed.

I crooned the Chris de Burgh song into her ear. "I've never seen you looking so lovely as you did tonight."

"I must wear this dress more often." She took my hand and led me into her apartment. It was one of those moments where you have to pause to readjust the sights.

I'd fallen in love with an extremely wealthy woman. It wasn't just the size, it was the sheer opulence of the place. The pictures, the furniture, the very thickness of the plush cream carpet. This was living on a grand scale. My little Upper West Side flat suddenly seemed cheap and tatty by comparison.

So that was my first impression: money, and lots of it. But let me give you some of the detail, because it wasn't just the money. Everything, but everything, was in the most exquisite taste. In the hall: an oval table such as I had never seen before. It seemed to be black marble, but was, I later discovered, made from a rare type of coal called coalite. On it were some ivory-coloured candles and a vase of parrot tulips. But of course it wasn't just a 'vase' of parrot tulips: it was a beautiful piece of cut crystal. And on the walls, some pictures and an antique gold gilt mirror; and again, I find it hard to do it all justice. It had that whiff of effortlessness that comes with extreme wealth.

Now, just to put this all into context. I've been around enough smart houses in my time to carry my own. But this was the first time that I'd ever knowingly dated an heiress.

Elise took my hand and led me through to her... I don't know... to call it a lounge or a sitting room doesn't come close to doing it justice. It was perhaps a drawing room, low-lit and awash with costly trinkets and the rest, any one of which would have been worth more than the entire contents of my flat. You know the general impression that I had? Elise was living in a proper 'adult' flat, whereas mine smacked more of the student dive. Hah! It's amazing how relative these things all are, isn't it? If she'd been living in some Jess-style bedsit, I wouldn't have given it a second thought; but as it was, all I could think was how paltry my own flat seemed by comparison.

As ever, I turned it into a joke.

"Like me, you've been out spending."

"I hope you appreciate the effort."

"Let me see then. You must have been to Christie's..."

"They needed a pantechnicon to bring it all back."

"And champagne too?" There was a bottle cooling in a solid silver ice bucket by the window.

"Will you open it?"

We smiled at each other as I busied myself with the foil on the bottle; it gave me a moment to take in the full grandeur of the room. It was, as I remember it, at least double, if not triple the size of Jess's entire bedsit. I have haphazard memories of the room: costly rugs on an oak parquet floor; furniture dotted about, some old, some new, but not too much; a wall of books; a gas fire ablaze; two sumptuous sofas in grey velvet; four high windows that looked out into the night; and a mantelpiece with a selection of family photos.

I eased off the cork, tilting the glass as I poured.

"Happy birthday," she said.

I was about to kiss her when there was a knock at the door. It was a white door, set off to the side of the fireplace. I'd seen it, of course, but had not thought anything of it. Above the door-handle was a large golden bolt.

I raised an eyebrow to Elise.

"That'll be mummy," she said.

"Right," I said. I tried to keep my voice neutral, expressing neither surprise nor annoyance that we were about to be joined by Elise's mother. Of course it might all just go swimmingly; it might turn out to be the most perfect birthday party ever. And yet... I certainly hadn't envisaged Elise's mother joining in the celebrations.

Elise slid back the bolt and opened the door, and in came Elise's mother. It was as if we'd been tooling along the motorway at 80mph and Elise had suddenly applied the handbrake: the one moment fooling around with Elise, admiring her flat, kissing her lush lips; and the next, I'm suddenly being introduced to her mother.

"Mummy, I'd like you to meet Kim," she said, guiding her mother into the room. "Kim, this is my mother Velda Stewart."

We shook hands. I tend to alter my greetings for the person that I'm meeting: and for Elise's mother, I kept things very formal. "How do you do?" I said.

"How do *you* do?" she said. She spoke with the same Mid-Atlantic voice as Elise, though veering towards America. "I understand it's your birthday, Kim. Have you enjoyed it?"

"I've had a lovely birthday thank you..." A red warning light went on. I'd been about to use her first name. But a little whisper told me to stick with her surname. "Mrs Stewart."

She nodded and gave me this tight smile. She was not about to say, "Do call me Velda."

I looked at her properly for the first time. She was older than I would have expected, perhaps in her Seventies, with a helmet of auburn hair that was slightly darker than Elise's; gimlet eyes, I certainly remember those as they lasered through me. A grey skirt and a cream shirt and a crucifix about her neck that was a match with Elise's. A formidable woman. And cold. Very cold, as if she'd once had her heart broken and was determined never to make the same mistake again.

Elise fetched another glass from the drinks cabinet and poured her mother a glass. There was an awkward silence. Velda did not seem to mind in the slightest. She never took her eyes off me.

"So are you… are you staying with Elise?" I asked.

"No, I live here," she said. "We are neighbours."

"Ahh," I said. "And you have a door connecting the two apartments?"

"Quite so," said Velda.

"Though we each have our own bolt on the door," said Elise. "We have to be on speaking terms before it can be opened."

We'd sat down. Elise was sitting next to her mother on the sofa, her hand casually tucked into Velda's arm, while I was in the interview position in an armchair.

"I hear that you work on the *Sun*," said Velda. She took the tiniest sip of Champagne before placing the glass on a coaster on the antique side table.

"For my sins," I replied.

"It is not a paper that I care to read."

"Not many people I know do care to read it," I said. "It's an acquired taste." I finished off the Champagne in one. I don't know what I'd been expecting for my birthday, but I certainly hadn't thought I'd be in for the Third Degree from Elise's mother.

"And you live on the Upper West Side?" she went on.

"Elise, I'd no idea that you'd be keeping your mother so well informed."

Velda, eyes still on mine, huddled in closer to Elise. "We have no secrets," said Velda. "She tells me everything."

I goggled at the thought. Everything? *Everything?*

I hedged. "How wonderful to be so close."

"Are you close to your mother?"

"She's dead, I'm sorry to say," I replied.

"How sad." Velda's voice remained completely flat as she spoke, with not a vestige of either empathy or emotion.

It sounded like a bit more was wanted, "She died when I was quite young. My father re-married..."

"And your step-mother?"

"Edie? I don't tend to share my secrets with her, no."

"How sad."

Elise, for all her closeness to her mother, was concentrating on her glass of champagne. Was she aware of all this sparring that was going on? Or was this just the usual standard fare that was dished out to any young man who'd been invited back to Elise's?

My phone rang. I have never been so relieved to receive a call from my mad-masters.

"Excuse me," I said. "It's a work call."

"Shall we leave the room?" said Velda.

"No, no, I'll take it in the hall."

It was Campbell, the night news editor. "Got your bag packed, old boy?" he asked.

"Of course," I said. "Where's it this time?"

"Halifax," he said. "Halifax, Nova Scotia. You're off to a graveyard; the flight's leaving in an hour-and-a-half."

"I'm on my way."

I had to make a conscious effort to wipe the smile from my face as I returned to Elise and her mother.

"I'm sorry. I've got to go to Nova Scotia."

The two ladies stood up and said the right things.

I shook hands with Velda.

"How nice to meet you, Mrs Stewart."

She gave me a nod. "You must come again."

And even at the time, I remember that her tone struck me as rather odd; as if she were the lady of the house and it were within her gift to invite me over.

Elise followed me through to the hall. "I'm sorry you're going," she said.

"I'm sorry too."

"And I'm sorry about mummy, I'd no idea she was going to pop round. She must have wanted to inspect you."

"Don't worry about that." We clung to each other. "She's charming."

"You're going to have to improve on your lying if you're ever going to fool me."

"And I used to be so good."

I'd all but said goodbye when Elise remembered something. "Your present!" she said. "I've got you a present! Happy birthday!"

She went to a beautiful tea caddy, with mother-of-pearl inlay and took out an envelope.

"A spa voucher for two?" I asked.

"Much more useful than that," she replied. "It's a new knee."

"A new knee?"

"You'll be running marathons in no time."

Yes, oh yes, it was indeed a new knee, and at first blush it was such a wonderful present, thoughtful and also costly. Extremely costly. And I suppose, also, that it boded well for our future. It would be reasonable to presume that giving a man a new knee for his birthday shows that you have high hopes for the future.

And yet... and yet, and yet. That new knee would cause me so much hurt, so much anguish, that at one stage in my life, I'd have ripped it out for sheer rage. Though it was not a physical hurt. After two months, that 30,000 dollar knee was as good as new. No, the hurt was all in my head: for every time I glimpsed my knee, there came with it a memory, and even now the thought of it still makes me wince.

CHAPTER 17

When looking back on a courtship, it is impossible to tell which elements were crucial, and which were mere detail. Though does it make much odds? Sometimes it feels like Elise and I were destined for each other from the moment we met, so that no matter which direction I set off on, all roads would ultimately lead to Elise.

Oh for a glimpse into just a few of those parallel universes to find out how Elise and I would be getting on now if I had happened to do one thing, or another thing, just a little bit differently. Let's put it this way: I don't think things could currently be any worse.

Of course I know it's all fruitless. It's meaningless. There is just this one universe, and we have to make the most of what we've got. We make mistakes and we damn well have to learn to live with them.

But if I could... if I could change just one single moment in my life, I know precisely the day, the hour and the very minute. I don't have many regrets in my life but that, undoubtedly, is a big one: it gnaws at my innards.

Not that anyone died. But I think, perhaps, that a little piece of me died that day, and what was left of my beating heart turned to shards of ice.

Anyway: Halifax in Nova Scotia, in freezing Canada in February 1998, and I am there to visit a graveyard: the Titanic graveyard, no less, last resting place for some 121 of the Titanic's dead.

It was the year that the world was going crazy for all things Titanic and in a couple of weeks' time, James Cameron's blockbuster would soon be cleaning up at the Oscars. Elise and I had already seen the film. While I quite liked it, Elise absolutely adored the movie. She was a complete sucker for romance. Her favourites were romantic comedies, where the lovers end up happily ever after, but dramatic romances, such as Titanic, were a pretty good second best.

First though, a brief explanation as to why on earth the *Sun* was sending a crack team to investigate a graveyard filled with Titanic dead. It's all perfectly simple. In the film, Leonardo DiCaprio plays a character called Jack Dawson... whose name, by coincidence, was shared by an actual stoker on board the Titanic... who just happened to be buried in the long line of Titanic graves in Halifax.

All fairly straightforward so far, but what had turned it into a *Sun* story was that the girls of Halifax had convinced themselves that Jack's grave belonged to *The* Jack Dawson. They'd turned it into a shrine, complete with garlands of flowers, candles, scarves and ticket stubs. Though I daresay that my mad-masters' interest in the story may have been piqued by the fact that the movie had been part funded by Fox... which just so happened to be another Murdoch company.

It was bitterly cold. So cold that after just a few minutes outside, I had my hands about my ears.

Ali and I wasted an hour at the Fairview Lawn Cemetery before eventually going off to a café and doing what any sensible reporter would have done from the first: we treated some girls to lunch and they returned the favour by posing for pictures at the side of Jack's grave. Not, perhaps, the most ethical journalism I've ever done. But ethics is so very similar to a relationship. Not black and white, but just a hundred different shades of grey.

I tramped about the graves as the girls artfully swooned for Ali. I reread the hand-written card that Elise had given to me. "Good for one new knee," she'd written. "With much love on your birthday, Elise."

I was amazed. Astonished. Nobody had ever spent this sort of money on me before; *I'd* never spent this sort of money on me before. We'd known each other for less than a month, and she was giving me a 30,000 dollar present. And not just any old trinket, but something that would be with me for the rest of my days. It showed how much she cared.

I waited and I waited in the cemetery; I believe it's impossible for a photographer ever to take too many pictures. And as I glanced at Jack Dawson's simple grey gravestone, I wondered what I'd have done if it had been Elise and me on the Titanic. The ship's slipped beneath the waves and Elise and I are paddling for our lives in the ice-cold Atlantic. Would I have given up my life for her? Would I have been the hero like Jack Dawson?

The cold in that graveyard may have numbed my brain. But I realised that I most undoubtedly would: if it ever came to it, my life or hers, I would have died for Elise. And though I knew all about love, I can't ever remember thinking that about a woman before.

It was a small but critical milestone in my relationship with Elise. I was in love with her. And I'd have done anything for her. *Anything?*

It's funny how we make all these grandiose promises, yet never think that one day our cards might be called. I wonder, I wonder. Would Elise have forced such an extraordinary pact on any other man? Would any other man have agreed to it?

✦

The time has finally come to pen the scene that I have been dreading ever since I first started on this manuscript a month ago. Some memories blur with age, but this one is still perfect to the last jagged detail.

It was a few days after I'd returned from Nova Scotia, and Elise and I were having dinner in a little French-style restaurant. I hadn't had too much to drink because I had my usual six a.m. start the next day. We'd already made love before we went out and would doubtless soon be doing it again when we returned to my flat. I was abrim with love. All I wanted to do was kiss her and tell her that I loved her, over and over again.

We were both having French onion soup, with toast and melted cheese on top; I remember that detail too. The toast was just a little bit too big, so you couldn't quite get it into your mouth in one. Elise tried to bite it in half and a sensual trail of warm cheese flicked from her lip onto her chin. She laughed as I scooped it up with my finger and placed it into her mouth.

"Have you booked yourself in for your new knee yet?" she asked.

"I love you."

She sipped more soup. "You're going to need two weeks off work."

"I adore you."

"Why didn't you get it done years ago?"

"Because I want you."

Very delicately she placed her spoon by the side of the bowl and leant over the table and kissed me. "I want you too."

That moment, with that woman, I was so happy I could have cried. No, that's just a ridiculous cliché. I couldn't have cried. Never in my life have I actually cried for joy. "A new knee!" I said. "That's thirty thousand dollars!"

"Not quite that much actually," she said. "I get a discount. He calls it 'Mates' rates'."

"Still!" I said. "Discount or no discount, it's unbelievably generous."

One last blissful moment of innocence. As we gaze into each other's eyes, I can't ever recollect such a love; have never seen such beauty.

"It's quite a big investment," I said, very lightly, jokingly even. "You probably want some collateral. Wouldn't it just be terrible if I got my new knee and hightailed it out of Manhattan?"

She laughed.

"So, Elise, I would hereby like to place it on record that as of this moment, I am dating you, and exclusively you. All those other girls, all those other numbers in my little black book: they're all gone, every one of them."

I smiled. I thought I'd said it well. Although I'd spoken lightly, I had been making a serious point. Though I had, of course, been dating Elise and Elise alone, I wanted to put our relationship on a more formal footing.

I presumed – assumed, even – that she would want to do the same.

And Elise... her reaction was odd. She smiled, but it wasn't quite a smile, and then she looked down at her soup and took another mouthful. Was she playing for more time?

"And have there been so many?"

I laughed uproariously. I sensed the tension in the air. "Since I met you?" I said. "Well of course I've had heaps of offers. But there's never been anyone but you."

Again, she looks me briefly me in the eye, before attending to her soup. She spoons up another piece of toast and daintily starts biting into it. A thought occurs to me. She couldn't care less about the soup. She wants to seem as if she's absorbed by it.

And why… why could that be?

A horrid, horrid question comes to mind. I hate to ask it, but I just have to know the answer. And if I don't ask it now, then it might be an age, a lifetime, before I can ever steel myself to ask it.

"And you?" I said.

"And me?" She looks at me, a picture of innocence. How could I even think to ask such a question? Why is it even necessary?

"And you…" I trailed off. "Is this exclusivity mutual? Has it been mutual?"

There, the question was finally out. I was shocked, almost, that I'd dared ask it. And up until about a minute earlier, I would have been 100 per cent certain about her answer: why would Elise be seeing someone else when she was obviously, palpably, having such a fantastic time with me?

But with this sudden skittishness, I was beginning to wonder. She couldn't be…

And yet why was she so awkward? Why wouldn't she look me in the eye?

Did it count for nothing that I loved her and that, though she had never put it into so many words, I believed that my love was reciprocated?

And what possible reason could she have for seeing another man? What could he give her that I could not?

I was watching her very carefully now. She was still staring at her soup. She placed the spoon on the plate. It was absolutely perpendicular to the edge of the table. She ran a finger across her lower lip, and a trace of scarlet lipstick stuck to her nail.

Finally she looked at me. And even before she's spoken, I could tell it was going to bad; the mood at the table had turned to a bleak, grey winter.

"I'm sorry," she said.

"Ahh." I was at a loss for words. She didn't need to say any more. I was already fast filling in the rest of the pieces.

"I'm sorry," she said again. "When we started, I didn't think… I didn't think it would turn out like this. There was another guy…"

It wasn't great. It wasn't great at all. I swallowed. And I remember how the blood appeared to be thumping in my ears – whomp-whomp-whomp – while at the same time, I was possessed by this peculiar calm. I felt almost disembodied, hovering above the table as I watched this little tragedy unfold.

As my brain so often does at times like this, I went onto autopilot. I wasn't really thinking. I just seemed to be spouting the words that I ought to say at such a time.

"That's okay," I said. "It doesn't matter. I understand. Sometimes it takes a little while to extricate yourself from…"

I tail off. I am mesmerised by the sight of Elise lightly biting her lower lip.

"I'm sorry," she said.

Very, very quickly now, I'm starting to see the whole picture in all its awfulness.

"You're still with him?" I said.

She looked down. She played with her onion soup, gazing at a piece of bread that was in her spoon.

She nodded.

"And… and you still don't know whether you'll be breaking up with him any time soon?"

Another nod. And another apology. I'd never heard a woman apologise so much in such a short space of time.

"That's okay." I took her hand. "I understand."

All just words, mere words. I don't know why I was so hell-bent on making life easier for Elise at that moment; perhaps I was terrified that then and there she'd call an end to it. In my defence, do please remember that I was besotted with the woman.

"I just need a little more time." She stared dolefully at her soup. "I'm very sorry."

"Have as long as you want," I said. Ebullient. Flush with bravado. I never for a moment expected that she would take me at my word.

"Thank you," she said. "It's… I don't know… I don't even understand it myself. It's…" And then she said it. The only words which could utterly disarm me. "I love you," she said. "I don't know why I have to see him, but I do."

"I understand." Her hand is between mine now, and as I'm stroking her fingers, I'm still in shock; because, finally, after all my copious protestations of love, Elise has said that she loves me too. And that of course is wonderful… but then she's also just happened to drop in the fact that I have a rival. God, as I look back now, I can see how she skewered me; perhaps she did not plan it that way, in fact I'm certain she didn't, but I was like a beetle pinned on its back.

I pressed her hand. She squeezed my fingers back. She doesn't look at me, still absorbed by her French onion soup. "It won't be long." She said it again, almost as if to reassure herself. "I'm sure it won't be long. I just need a day…"

My heart is thumping with, I don't know, outraged hurt; and yet it is also going out to Elise in her pain. I'm not good when women cry; it unnerves me. Disarms me. I do my best, but it usually falls short.

"One day a week," she said. "I just need to know."

"You know I love you," I said. "And if you need more time to… to work things out… then that's fine. I understand."

"Thank you," she said.

She looks at me, her eyes sparkling with tears; I had never seen a woman so… vulnerable? Is that the word? At that moment all I wanted to do was enfold her in my arms and shield her from the world.

She leaned over and kissed me passionately on the lips. Nothing more needed to be said. I paid the bill in cash and a minute later we were out on the street and walking back to my flat, where we made love and Elise repeated several times over how much she loved me.

And so the deal was done. I don't really know how I came to agree with it, but I did, and even now there's not a day goes by when I don't regret it.

CHAPTER 18

The next morning, as usual, Elise left the flat before I was awake, kissing me on the cheek as she slipped into the night.

I had plenty of time to rue my mistake.

For it was a mistake, a colossal error, no doubt about it, and on so many counts.

You can have no conception of the whirlwind of arguments and counter-arguments that chased through my brain the next day. I still had to write my stories, but always churning away in the background was this peculiar deal that I'd struck with Elise.

It's not often that I can remember the actual stories that I have written for the *Sun*. Generally in New York, it felt like I was filing copy into this bottomless pit. But I do remember the story that I was writing that morning. It involved two celebrities who'd just got engaged. And, as with Nick Spitz, for various legal reasons that will soon become apparent, I'm going to have to change their names. They were two actors, she much younger than he. I shall call them Adam and Scarlett.

It was the manner of Adam's proposal that had particularly whetted the *Sun*'s interest. The pair of them had just attended the New York premiere of Adam's latest movie, and just at the end of the film, as they were running through all the various funny out-takes, Adam's co-star suddenly started talking direct to the audience, "Scarlett," he says from on the screen. "Adam's got something to say to you."

The camera pans over to the entire cast, where Adam is standing centre-stage. And Adam sings a love-song and sings it well: Robert Burns' 'My Love is Like a Red, Red Rose'. And you can forget all the schmaltzy modern ballads, for there is not a lyric in the world to touch it: "And I will love thee still, my dear, till a' the seas gang dry."

The audience was in tears of ecstasy. But then Adam caps it by getting down on his knees. He looks direct into the camera, and asks, "Scarlett, will you be my wife?"

Absolute pandemonium. The audience was shrieking with delight. And it gets better! They've now got a camera-crew on Adam and Scarlett in the auditorium, and she's in tears and he's in tears, and then they're up on stage and waving and laughing...

As proposals of marriage go, that's a hard one to top.

I remember it well. First and foremost because Adam and Scarlett had made such a public show of their tender, mutual regard. The contrast was stinging.

But there is one other reason why I'll never forget that story. To put it bluntly, it would directly lead to the rather dramatic termination of my posting in New York. All to come, all to come.

While I wrote up this tear-jerking story about Adam and Scarlett, it was like I was having to contend with this wall of background noise: my worries and my fears, all of them griping to be heard.

On the one hand this... and on t'other hand, the other. Any way I looked at it, the whole thing left me sick to the stomach. It was bad enough knowing that, these past three weeks, Elise had been seeing another man. But then to *continue* to see him?

Just how did I torment myself that morning? Let me count the ways.

Well first of all: I'd declared my hand. I had said that I wanted Elise to the exclusion of all others and had officially put myself off limits to any woman but her. And how had she returned the compliment? She'd said that if I still wanted to see her, then I'd have to share her with another man...

And on the other hand: Elise had said that she 'loved me'. Did she love this other man too? Perhaps she didn't love this guy in the slightest. Perhaps – hideous thought – he was a tyro in the bedroom...

How had I ever agreed to such a deal? Had she bamboozled me into it? Had she sweet-talked me, or was it I myself who'd done the talking? Was it her tears that had won me over?

There was also that small matter of professional pride. I wasn't just some Wall Street hireling, I was a reporter, a *Sun* reporter, a gunslinger who worked with words and who took no prisoners. I walked tall. So was this really the sort of man who suddenly found himself such a hostage to a woman's whims?

And – just another thought to join the giddy cavalcade that was stampeding through my head – was it too late? For what was done could most certainly be undone. Elise might have caught me the previous night when I was delirious with love. But what was to stop me calling her up now – right now – and saying that actually, all things considered, it would have to be me and exclusively me... and if she didn't like that, well, I wished her well with her ventures.

There was also one other point of view which was probably summed up best by my Australian colleague Steve.

It was about ten a.m. when he ambled into my office, his lumberjack shirt hanging out of his stained jeans. Bloodshot eyes and a wild hedge of hair. He picked up the last bit of my bagel and started to eat it.

"What's happening?" he said, still eating.

"Adam and Scarlett got engaged last night."

Steve came round to inspect the copy on my screen.

"Do you have to eat in my ear?"

"What?" He continued to chew. "She hasn't dumped you already? You haven't even been dating a month!"

"No I have not been dumped by Elise." I continued to pound at the keyboard.

"You've misspelt Scarlett's name." He pointed at the screen. "It's a double T. So what has she done?"

"Elise?" I said. "She's done nothing."

"Don't try and kid a kidder."

I broke off from my pathetic attempt to be engrossed by my story. "Okay. I'll tell you."

Steve finished off the last of the bagel and raised his eyebrows expectantly.

I swivelled my chair to face him. "I asked her if we were dating exclusively. She said no."

"Tough break," he said.

"It wasn't ideal."

Steve strolled over to my map of America, removing the new pin in Nova Scotia and placing it in New Mexico. "So she's going to see whoever she likes."

"It's only one guy," I said tetchily. "One day a week."

"That's just fine then?"

"It won't be for long."

"Were you born yesterday?" he said. "Only a pussy rolls over like that."

"She just needs some time to sort things out."

Steve hummed to himself as he continued repositioning the pins in my map. "Look on the bright side," he said. "All the more time for you to carry on playing the field. Most guys would kill for that!"

I shook my head.

Steve looked horrified.

"You're *not* going to play the field? You're going to stay faithful and then one day a week you're going to let her carry on seeing lover-boy?"

"I'm not interested in anyone else."

"Irrelevant," he said. "You've either got to fight for her, or show her that two can play at that game. Women never respect a wimp."

Justin the *Times* correspondent, dapper in jacket and tie, entered the room.

"Who don't respect wimps?" he asked.

"Women!" said Steve. "Hear what he's done? He's given Elise full bloody permission to bang her other boyfriend!"

"Oh dear," said Justin.

"One day a week she's got! And meanwhile lover-boy here is going to stay faithful!"

Justin screwed up his face with distaste. The thought seemed to pain him. "Is that wise?"

Steve stood over me. "You've got to draw a line in the sand, mate." He poked me in the chest. "And once you've drawn that line, then you defend it to your last breath."

"Well it's a view."

"It's more than a bloody view! It's the only position to take. Anything else is a serious mistake. You think it's what she wants? Don't be ridiculous! What she wants is for you to take her in hand. You're an idiot!"

How I wish – how I wish, how I wish – that I had followed Steve's advice. I should have given Elise a piece of her own brinkmanship and thrown the thing right back in her face. You want to see this other guy once a week? That's fine, sweetie! See him as much as you like, see him every night! But, please, please, just don't count on seeing me again any time soon.

I have seldom told anybody about the pact that I made with this temptress, this houri, this woman who was always mistress to the man. I think, perhaps, I am a little ashamed. But the few friends who know of what happened just roll their eyes with – what? – disdain and the most uncomprehending disbelief.

You should know, though, that even the most extreme reactions of my friends have not been a gnat's bite compared to the torment that I have put myself through this past decade. How could I do it? Had my first year in New York left me temporarily unhinged?

I will do my best to explain for, of course, it is on this one point that my entire tale hangs.

As I hope you have already gathered, I loved her. It helped, I suppose, that our extraordinary sex-life just seemed to be getting better and better.

But there was more to it than that, a whole number of reasons in fact, not much in themselves, but together they swayed me just enough to give Elise her head.

For a start there was my first love, my piano-teacher, India. Though it is another story from another time, even sixteen years on, its shock waves continued to reverberate. What had occurred was that, through my jealousy, I had single-handedly managed to destroy our entire relationship. And ever since, this matter of jealousy had become a very raw point for me.

I had determined that I would never again allow it to be my master. So though I was not immune to jealousy, I had buried it so deep that I was no longer able to hear its insidious hiss. Yes, I buried it deep and left it to fester, and it has been festering now for over a decade. Perhaps through these words alone, you can get a sense of how noxious I now find its smell.

There was also something about New York in the late nineties. It seemed to be a city, a nation, of bed-hoppers, with the merry dance being led by our charismatic Commander-in-Chief. So why should I take exception to Elise's transgressions?

There were other reasons, and I will come to them. But the one that I remember for now is that in New York in 1998, I was living in the moment; I was incapable of doing anything else. My life was so hand-to-mouth that I didn't care what had happened yesterday and I cared even less about what was going to happen tomorrow. The only thing of import was the very moment that I was living in: here, now. And when I was with Elise, it was always fantastic, and when she was away, then what did it matter to me what she was doing? Out of sight, out of mind.

We find all manner of ways to delude ourselves, do we not?

✦

For a few days, the subject was not mentioned again. We saw each other a couple of times and drank and ate and made love just as we had always done. I remember being possessed by this gay, reckless abandon, determined to show Elise that I was indifferent to her other love. We had a magnificent time when we were together; I was happy to share. Hurt me? She hadn't even touched me a glancing blow.

It was towards the end of February, however, that I began to appreciate what I was up against. It was a Thursday, just after lunch, and I was about ready to head back home.

I called Elise up at work. "How we getting on?" I asked. There were so many things that I was striving to convey in those four words: cheeriness; optimism; vigour; spunk; spark; and, above all else, good-natured, irrepressible fun. This was a guy who lived life to the max. He didn't dwell on life's miseries. Where was the next party?

"Very well," she said. "And how are you?"

"As perky as a rat in liverwurst," I said. "Got time to see a *Sun* reporter tonight?"

"I can't," she said. Though a little quickly. What was it, what was it? I didn't know why but suddenly my antennae were quivering. Don't try and analyse it though, just go with your gut.

I could have ducked it. I could have said, "well have a nice time and see you tomorrow". But I had to know the worst... because immediately I knew: this was the night. This was the guy. But who was he? What hold was it that he had over her?

"So you're seeing him tonight?"

"Yes. I am."

"Tell me about him." I was doing my best to sound interested; not coming across as the jealous lover, but rather the intrigued friend who's curious for more detail.

"You don't want to know."

"Elise, I'm really cool about this," I said, telling the most barefaced lie ever to have fallen from my lips. "If you need time to sort things out, then I understand."

"He's a restaurateur."

"And Thursdays are his night off."

"Yes, that's right."

"Thursdays it is then." Thursdays. Bloody Thursdays. Most people are not too happy about Mondays, and for some it's Sunday evenings. But for me, even now, it's always Thursday nights that are the worst. It's just the memory, that's all, jangling at my nerve endings and reminding me of what once was.

I was still trying to sound jolly, though it must have all sounded so transparently fake. "What's his name? How old is he? Is he tall, is he short, is he funny? How long have you been seeing each other? Come on, Elise, tell me what I'm up against."

Elise sighed. "Honestly Kim, you don't want to know."

"Well I'd rather know something than nothing at all."

Another pause, but this time as if she were composing herself. "His name's Georges," she said. "He's French. A little older than us. I – we – started seeing each other on and off a few years ago, and... and I still care for him."

A Frenchman! Instantly I had conjured up an image of Georges. I pictured him as smaller than me, but much more muscled; swarthy with strong, capable fingers; good with his hands; an epicurean who loved both food and wine; exceptionally skilled in the bedroom. On that last point, there could be no doubt.

I was both enthralled and disgusted at the same time, and also a little ashamed at my total lack of self-control. I should have feigned complete indifference.

"And does he know about me?"

"He does," she said. "Yes, he does."

I could only hope that Georges was on a similar bed of nails to the one that Elise had prepared for me.

I'd heard enough now, more than enough to be able to flesh out my most obscene nightmares. I did not wish to know any more.

"Well…" I said. "Thank you for being so honest."

"I can't promise much, Kim, but I can promise that I'll always be honest with you."

The phone is returned to the hand-set. I trudge back home through Central Park in the rain. And I ponder how best to occupy myself that evening so that I will not have to spend too much time dwelling on the fact that Elise was having sex with Georges the Frenchman.

Go out and get drunk? Hit the bars with Steve, Justin and anyone else from the crew who wanted to tag along? I didn't really feel in the mood for company. Or perhaps some form of exercise, beasting myself at a gym until I only had energy enough to curl up and sleep? Or distracting myself with a solo trip to the movies?

In the end I opted to walk. Wrapped up warm, with money in my pocket, I intended to follow my whim. I might walk right down to Wall Street, bar-hopping along the way.

My knee was aching before I'd reached Central Park South Side, a vicious pain that began at my knee and gradually worked its way up my leg. It was painful. But not painful enough to block out my projections of Elise. Eight p.m. They'd be sharing a bottle of Champagne: Krug, probably, in Georges' honour. Eight thirty p.m. Does he kiss her as often as I do? Does he tell her that he loves her? Nine p.m. Are they having sex now? Do they talk when they have sex? Is she doing those things to Georges which once, I'd thought, were exclusive to me? Ten p.m. They must be having supper now, of some sort or another. Is he smoking a fat cigar? Is she naked on his lap? And where are they now? His place? Her place? Or perhaps they're at the chef's table at Georges' own restaurant?

By now, I've stopped in three bars, I've had six shots of whisky, and my knee is screaming as if Elise has buried an axe into it. Ahead of me, rising up sheer in front of my face, are the Twin Towers: strange to think that two such vast monoliths could be destroyed in a single morning. In 1998, they seemed destined to last forever... and perhaps they will, though only in that eternal sphere of the human consciousness.

I wasn't used to that amount of walking, but still I hobbled on, and still I continued to torture myself. When I looked at my watch, I would first register the time, and then I would wonder what Elise and Georges were doing to each other. Eleven p.m. Were they drinking Armagnac; Elise, naked, while Georges supped from her navel? Or were they having sex: again, for the second, third, time that night? Perhaps they'd never stopped. Perhaps they'd been having sex since they'd first kissed.

As I think I have mentioned, I have the most vivid imagination.

And believe me, there was no scenario, no matter how unsavoury or how warped, that did not at some stage drift through my mind.

I only had to have the very smidgeon of a thought, and there it would be playing up on this vast Imax movie screen, exact to the very last detail. The more perverse my imaginings, the more graphic it all became. The words 'Kama sutra' might skim bird-like over the horizon, and the next thing, Georges and Elise are acting out every conceivable pose in the book.

And then my knee's hurting like hell... and as surely as night follows day, I would start to wondering whether Georges ever hurt Elise. Did he tie her up, whip her? Was that why she'd taken me to La Nouvelle Justine?

And the truth is: I don't know. I never once found out what Elise did with her Georges, because I never asked her another question about him. Though actually, now that I think of it, that's not quite true. There was the one time, and all I can say in my defence is that I had been severely provoked.

CHAPTER 19

You would not credit it, but something occurred the next day which distracted me from my ceaseless navel-gazing.

Though it was one hell of a distraction.

As you might possibly deduce, the only thing that was ever going to distract me from Elise and her Georges was an even more spectacular dose of misery. And that's exactly what I got: the full lorry-load.

The next day, Friday, I didn't call up Elise in the morning. I'd thought about it, of course. Just call up and pretend that absolutely nothing had happened: "Oh hi Elise, how are you? Fancy going out for dinner tonight?"

But I did have *some* pride. Not much… that must obviously be apparent. But I had enough pride to prevent me from extending an olive branch to Elise. No, since it was she who had spent the previous night with Georges, then I thought it was very much up to her to make the first call.

By mid-afternoon, we still hadn't spoken to each other. That was fine by me. If Elise wanted to play it cool, then that was my kind of game; I'd mastered it before I was even out of short-trousers.

So when my mobile went at five p.m. I snatched at it, as eager as any young swain who has sewn his heart upon his sleeve.

Not Elise, however. But of considerable pertinence to her, nevertheless.

It was Campbell, the night news editor. "Shit's hitting the fan here, old boy," he said succinctly. "Trisha wants a word."

I'll try and explain the thought processes that a Red Top reporter can go through in that single second after he hears the phrase "the shit's hit the fan", or it's equally repellent twin, "It's all gone pear-shaped".

It had to be some sort of cock up. Was it a libel writ? A complaint to the Press Complaints Commission?

I checked my watch. It was past ten p.m. London time. The first editions must have just dropped. Which in all probably meant... I'd been scooped. Still ... chin up. Worse things happen at sea.

"What's happened?" I said.

"Splash and a spread in the *Mirror*," he said. "Nick Spitz trying to top himself in the St Regis."

He might as well have hit me over the head with a sledgehammer. I remember being so shocked, I actually had to sit down. I'd read about this 'weak at the knees' reaction in books and I had seen it in films, but until then I'd never experienced it myself.

"Nick Spitz?" I said. This one had been so far off the radar, I hadn't even had a sense of it coming.

"Full spit and cough," said Campbell. "Hang on a sec. Trisha's just in her office. Putting you through."

And now all thoughts of Elise and Georges and indeed my knee have been completely erased from my ever-fertile brain, as I'm scrambling, scrambling, to make sense of the avalanche that is rumbling towards me at the speed of sound.

"Kim?" She sounded clipped and in control.

"Hi Trisha." I wished Campbell had told me a little more about the *Mirror* story. How much did she know? How much of a hole was I in?

"So..." she said. Another long pause. "About four weeks ago, I asked you if anything unusual had happened during your interview at the St Regis with Nick Spitz. And, correct me if I'm wrong, but you told me that precisely diddly had occurred there."

"What have the *Mirror* got?"

I could hear her turning a page. "I would say that...the *Mirror* has got pretty much everything."

"What?" I was flabbergasted. "They've even named me?"

She pounced. "So it was you?"

It has been a long, long time since I have felt like quite such a rookie.

"Well..." Was there any way out? "What does it say?"

She was now at her most polite, her voice turning to this cold clear shard of ice. And a memory begins to chime. I've heard this tone of voice before... it was after the Christmas party. We'd made love in a hotel suite near the *Sun*'s offices; it was the first time I'd ever seen her come over girlish and coy. And then, as she'd asked me out for lunch and I'd politely turned her down, her voice had turned to this same diamond hardness.

"Rather than asking me questions, why don't you give me some answers," she said. "If you don't tell me precisely, exactly, what happened at the St Regis, you will have just served your last day as the *Sun*'s New York Correspondent."

"Right." I peered into the abyss. "Can you give me a moment?"

"Of course," she said. "Take *all* the time you need. We're only clearing the Splash and the centrespread as we wait breathlessly for your copy, but no hurry. No hurry at all."

"Well…"

I felt like an old con who's been picked up for the umpteenth time by the police, and who has finally realised that the game is up. "It was like this…"

Trisha asked the occasional question on some point of detail, but she heard me out in almost complete silence. She was almost certainly taping me, just in the possible event that I still refused to co-operate with the story.

After I was done with unburdening myself of the whole crazy saga of that night in the St Regis, there was a very long pause.

"So that's it?" said Trisha. "Nothing else you're hiding from me?"

"Nothing else," I said. Which was almost true for I had, of course, kept one minor detail to myself.

"This is what we are going to do then, Kim" she said. "First of all, I am putting you through now to the copytakers and you are going to file every single thing that you have just told me for the third edition. You will then file a second story, a first-person piece, on why it was that you sat on this world exclusive: which is because, of course, for the first time in your life you were trying to behave like the perfect gentleman. Do you have that?"

"Yes Trisha."

"When you have filed, come back to me. We will decide then what we are going to do next to try and salvage something from this disaster… and what, more to the point, we are going to do with you."

"Yes Trisha."

A minute later and I'm talking to the copy-takers. If you were a reporter in the field with no access to a computer, you dictated your copy straight over the phone to the copy-takers. They'd type it all up and then plug it into the News International system. Even today, if you're really tight up against a dead-line, it's still the fastest way to file a story.

The copy-taker was Andy, and though I had never seen him, I must have spoken to him at least a hundred times. He asked for the name of my paper and the story catch-line.

"Ready when you are," he says.

This hiss of Atlantic static. I feel like a high-diver at the edge of a cliff. What am I going to say? What am I trying to say? At such times, it's important not to dwell on the fact that ten million people will be reading your story the next day.

"World exclusive," I said. "Hollywood superstar Nick Spitz tried to kill himself in a New York hotel, and I was the man who saved him." I ended with the words, "Point, par," which is to say, "Full-stop, new paragraph. With copy-takers, all punctuation must be spelt out.

"Really?" High praise indeed from a copy-taker. They normally limit themselves to the one word, "Yes", which indicates that you're clear to continue dictating.

"Yes, really." I carried on with my tale, filing it in four takes, so that the subs could start knocking the story into shape. The only thing that I left out was the cocaine that Spitz had snorted before he'd tried to kill himself. As for Elise, she was of course very high up in the story. She was one of the stars of my tale.

The second story required more finesse. The first story had just been the nuts and bolts of what had happened with Nick Spitz the superstar. The second was an explanation of why I hadn't written the story in the first place, and why I had suddenly decided to write it up now.

"Ready," said Andy.

Another deep breath. Always, with the copy-takers, it's the first sentence that's the hardest. Once you've taken the plunge, it all comes much more easily.

"When I was sworn to secrecy about Nick Spitz's suicide attempt in the penthouse suite of New York's St Regis hotel, I had every intention of keeping my word," I said.

Not a bad intro for a first-person piece; should leave the readers wanting to know more.

I continued: "I thought that it would not be at all helpful to Nick's recovery if news of his overdose was splashed all over the front page of the *Sun*. That is why, for the past month, I have not told a soul about how I dragged Nick from a bath before binding up his slashed wrist with a towel and some telephone cord. So, after keeping Nick's dark secret for nearly a month, you can only imagine my frustration on learning that the story was all over the front page of a rival paper, and that it was Nick himself who'd given it."

Just so: exactly as I could have predicted, it was Nick Spitz who had leaked the story. He had been filming in Texas and had spent the afternoon with a feature writer and a photographer from the *Mirror*. The afternoon had turned into Nick's usual evening of excess and somehow he had ended up spilling the entire story to the *Sun*'s greatest rival. Throughout the *Mirror* story, there was no mention of the *Sun*, and I was referred to merely as 'a reporter'. That is the way of the British Red Tops: we never mention our rivals by name unless they've blundered.

"Nice story!" said Andy. "Should run for a while."

"Perhaps," I said.

He transferred me back to Trisha.

She did not thank me.

"What you are now going to do, Kim, as if your life depends on it, is fly to wherever Nick bloody Spitz is in the world. You are going to get a picture of yourself standing next to him. He is going to be having his arm round your neck, and he is going to be saying, "Thank you Kim, the *Sun* saved my life."

"Right," I said. "Where is he?"

"Two days ago, he was in Houston. So you've got about forty hours to get that picture. We'll be needing it for Monday's paper." She added sweetly. "Is there anything else I can help you with?"

"I'm on my way."

"Tell me one thing though. Why didn't you file the story?"

"I told you. I'd given them copy approval. The man had just tried to kill himself. I thought it might push him over the edge."

"You're lying," she said. "So... What was the reason?" I could hear her clicking her fingers. "It must be the PR! What's her name... Elise! There's a picture of her in the *Mirror*. She's very pretty."

"Elise?" I was aiming at a tone of slight wonderment. "Elise was there, but... there's never..."

"Are you dating her?"

"No I'm not dating her."

"It's like getting blood from a stone. Okay, Kim, one more question, just tell me the truth. Have you ever had sex with her?"

And you know who, not a few months later, was to undergo the exact same grilling? None other than President Clinton, as, red-faced and splenetic, he so famously denied ever having "sexual relations with *that* woman".

For my part, I try to keep things succinct when I lie. "I've never had sex with Elise," I said simply.

"I know you," she said. "You've always been a sucker for beautiful women."

"Especially after Christmas parties."

It was the first time in three years that I had ever alluded to our night together. But I heard, I think, an amused snort. She thawed.

"You must have spiked my drink," she said. "Anyway, Kim, if you're lying..."

"I'm not lying."

I don't think she believed me, even then.

✦

I'd been on the phone for over an hour and as soon as Trisha had done with me, I called Elise... and, though it may sound odd, I was very much looking forward to the call.

For a kicker, I had been utterly vindicated. I'd said that Nick Spitz's story would get out, and not even a month later and it was already whistling round the world. It seemed that I had kept my side of the bargain, whilst Elise and Nick had most singularly failed to keep theirs; they owed me.

And... one last thing. Now I know this may sound petty, but after what she'd put me through with Georges, I was not averse to the thought of making her squirm. This may strike a peculiar tone, seeing as I've been saying how much I loved Elise. But even when you've met the love of your life, there is still always scope for some tit-for-tat.

"Hi Elise," I said. Business-like.

"Hi Kim." Also business-like. She was testing the temperature of the water. Was I warm, cold; did I want her... or was I going to call time on the whole thing?

"How are you?" Still formal. Even when there's important news to impart, it's still best to retain the social niceties.

"Very well," she said. "And how are you?"

"I'm chipper," I said. "I'm afraid I have bad news. Nick Spitz has spilled the story of our night at the St Regis to the *Mirror*. It's all over tomorrow's front page."

I took savage delight in dropping this bombshell. There was a satisfyingly stunned silence from the other end of the line.

"What have the *Mirror* got?"

I turned the knife.

"They've got everything, Elise! He's told them everything! It's the splash and a spread. The only thing that they appear to have left out is my name. But everything else, it's all there. You, apparently, are also in the story, alongside a very fetching front page picture."

This time she was much quicker on the uptake.

"I'm so sorry," she said. "I should... I should have guessed this would happen."

"That's all right," I said. "These things happen."

"What can I do to help?"

"I think it's all done," I said, before adding, almost as an after-thought. "Though actually there is one thing."

CHAPTER 20

Elise was too tied up with the arrangements to see me that night, so we met up the next day at JFK with Ali. I'd had to get up at five thirty a.m.

I was not at all sure how I wanted to greet Elise. I hadn't seen her in two days, but in that time there had been a lot of water under the bridge, not least of all her Thursday night with Georges.

As she bounded up to me at the airport, I was fully intent on giving her a hug and a peck on the cheek, but Elise was having none of it. She clung to me as if she hadn't seen me in a month, all thought of Georges forgotten. When I came to kiss her on the cheek, she turned her face to catch me full on the lips.

I had never known her so passionate. We held hands as we walked through the terminal; at the check-in to Houston, she kept her arm tight about my waist. Luxury of luxuries, we even had time for a coffee; she cocked her leg so that her knee was over my thigh.

I don't know how I'd expected her to be after her night with Georges, but I certainly hadn't expected this storm of tenderness. This public display of affection was something that I had never seen before. It felt like I had just returned safe and sound from two months in a war-zone.

Apart from her kisses and her caresses, Elise also solicitously inquired after my knee.

"You're limping so badly," she said. "What have you been doing?"

"Just walking."

"We've got to book you in for that new knee."

"As you've already told me, I'll need two weeks off."

"Well book up the holiday then."

"Could do."

"Must do." She kissed me, her hand teasingly pressed against my belt.

Looking back, it puts me in mind of a badly behaved girl who has displeased her father, and who is now desperate to make any possible amends. Daddy's slippers, daddy's pipe and daddy's tot of whisky are all brought over as the little girl even feigns interest in daddy's day at work.

Ali didn't turn a hair as she was introduced to my new girlfriend; in fact, you might almost have thought it was a normal state of affairs for me to be travelling with a PR who also happened to be my lover.

We checked into the Sheraton in Houston. I have no idea what it was like. I have stayed in hundreds of hotels in America and, like the shops and the cars, they all blend into this blur of pap. Though it was much warmer than New York City, I remember that. I basked in the spring sunshine.

As soon as the bedroom door had closed behind us, Elise was all over me. We had a couple of hours till we were due to see Nick Spitz on set, and what better way to spend it than by making love?

Except.

Two things.

I have always hated taking a girlfriend on a job. I am not good company when I'm on a story. The story is king. And even though the story may have been perfectly gift wrapped – as it was, seemingly, in this case – I still fret about all the many things that can go wrong.

There was, of course, one other reason why I couldn't focus on our love-making: was I just supposed to forget that, not 36 hours earlier, Elise had been doing all this and more with the Frenchman?

Elise pushed me up against the wall and a moment later her hands were working away at my belt and my shirt-buttons. Normally I would have loved it and would have thrilled at the way that Elise was taking control. Yet in my perversity, the only thought that was running through my head was, "Did she do this with Georges on Thursday?"

Elise's every action provided me with a fresh means to torture myself.

She was more assertive than usual; a trick that she'd picked up from Georges?

"I love you. So much," she said.

And Georges? Was he also loved so much?

I had never known her so passionate. Was this going to be the way of things in the future? For putting up with Georges, was I to be weekly rewarded with this most astonishing sex?

In truth, neither my heart nor my head were really into it. Oh, it would have been just perfect if I could genuinely have been living in that moment and been able to cut off all thoughts of past or future. But I am not some beast in the bush. Sex is never just about sex. Each act comes with its own unspoken history, and so even as Elise was offering herself up to me, all I could think of was, "What of Georges two days ago?"

Am I not contrary? I spurn everything that I have and yet yearn for all that I have not.

I don't know how it might have ended. My brain was so fried that I was on the verge of calling it quits. If Elise really loved me, why did she have to see Georges? Might it not have been easier on my tender heart to have split up immediately? For if we were in any sort of long-term relationship, then I was going to have to endure this hell for some time to come. How long was Georges going to be in the picture? Weeks? Months?

And yet it wasn't the sex that redeemed Elise, it was her loyalty.

A limo had been laid on to take us to the set in downtown Houston. We breezed through security. The star's trailer was parked up on the side of the street, and Nick himself was having lunch. We were supposed to be getting thirty minutes.

Nick himself opened the door to his silver bullet trailer. As I often am when I'm on a big story, I was nervous. "Just don't mess this up," I was thinking to myself. It didn't help that Elise was there.

"Hey!" said Nick. The first thing to hit you was the smile. Here was a guy who'd been reunited with his best friends on earth. Or at least it was the world's number one actor putting on his most fulsome impression of perfect happiness.

Nick's movie role was, as I remember, some hotshot lawyer, and he was wearing a blue suit and button-down shirt. Not a hair, nor an eyelash out of place. There was no trace of the cut upon his wrist.

"Come here you!" He gave Elise a bear hug. "Just look at you! Isn't she fantastic?"

It was my turn next. I got another bear hug. "Good to see you man!" He thumped my back with his fist. "How are you Tim?"

Tim. Of course he was going to call me Tim. Why for one single second should I have believed that this superstar had anything other than feet of clay? Of course he had feet of clay, for why should he be any different from me, Elise and the rest of us mortals?

Then an outstretched hand for Ali. "Good to meetcha!"

Inside the silver bullet, there was a sofa and a couple of reclining armchairs, as well as a vast flat screen TV and a kitchenette at the back. It was about as luxurious as you could possibly make the inside of a caravan.

"So guys, what can I get you to drink?" He stood by the open fridge door. "We got juices, coffee? Hey Tim, do you want a beer?"

But, fortunately, old habits die hard. Since I was already well acquainted with the flakiness of stars and their timetables, I did not want to waste a moment on being put at my ease.

"Love a drink," I said. "Though shall we get the pictures out of the way first?"

"Cool by me!" he said. "Where's good for you?"

I turned to Ali. "Where shall we go?"

We followed her out of the Silver Bullet.

"Wow!" said Nick. "Feel that sunshine! A little hotter than NYC!"

"You can say that again!" If Nick wanted to be the happiest man alive, then I was delighted to play along. Elise just smiled.

"So, that night," he said. " Can't remember a thing about it."

My heart sank. So this was how he was going to play it.

"It must be very distressing for you," I said. "And also for your family."

Ali found a place off down a side street that had a fine backdrop of the city. She squatted down low, while Nick stood between Elise and me with his arms comfortably about our shoulders.

"Hey, can't you stoop a little," he said.

"Of course." I stooped at the knees.

Ali fired off a reel and then got off a few shots of just me and Nick. Ideally we'd have tried some frames somewhere else, but we were already tight on time, and I still hadn't had one word of the promised interview.

Back to the silver bullet. The tape recorder is switched on. I've only got a few minutes.

"So Nick," I said. "How are you? Are things any better with your family?"

"Things are just great." The smile did not change by even one scintilla.

"Quite a turnaround, then, from a month ago."

His eyes never left mine. He didn't say a word.

I tried another tack. "Do you reckon you lost one of your nine lives at the St Regis?"

"I don't know," he said. "Why don't you tell me what you think."

Such is the madness of celebrity. Nothing is ever as it seems.

"Me?" I said. "I remember breaking the door down to the bathroom. I remember finding you in the bath, and the blood and the pills on the floor. It was awful."

"Is that how you remember it?" said Nick.

I thanked my stars that we already had the pictures in the bag. I wasn't sure which way the interview was heading, but it certainly had all the hallmarks of another disaster.

"No?" I asked. "Well that's pretty much the story that you gave to the *Mirror*."

"Can't believe anything you read in the papers these days, Tim!"

"What do you think happened then?"

"I can't really remember." The Aw Shucks grin never left his mouth.

"Elise," I said. "Perhaps you could refresh Nick's memory?"

And this was it. This was the moment. If she didn't back me up on this, then it was over, no doubt about it. I had, at least in theory, soaked up Elise's tryst with Georges. But if she was also going to choose Nick Spitz over me then, in all honesty, we were finished.

I turned to Elise, but Nick was still looking at me.

What was she going to say? Now that I was forcing her off the fence, which way would she jump?

"Kim saved your life," she said. "And it's Kim, not Tim. Kim. And though I may have helped, it was Kim who broke down the door, Kim who pulled you out of the bath, and Kim who bandaged your bleeding wrist. And if he hadn't... well you'd probably be dead."

"Okay," said Nick.

Elise wasn't nearly done. I've often wondered what was going through her mind. Was she trying to make amends for... do I really need to spell this out? Georges? Was she outraged at the ingrate Nick's sudden distortion of the facts? Or was it... Did they have a past? Was this payback for being another of Nick's cast-offs?

"I think it was shitty to give the story to the *Mirror* and I think it's even more shitty to be playing these games. This guy saved your life, Nick! A little gratitude might be in order."

"Just say it like it is, why don't you?"

She shrugged, playing with her crucifix. "I think you've been in films too long, Nick. Every day in the movies, you're saving the world. I've seen you do it over and over again. But in reality... have you saved anybody's life? Anybody at all? And this guy, this guy Kim, he did just that for you, and I think he behaved pretty damn honourably about the whole thing. It was a front-page story and he didn't run with it. And now, because you went and talked, you've landed him in the shit, and what we're trying to do, Nick, is make some sort of amends. It's that simple. We're trying, for once, to do the decent thing."

Well, as I look back on my life with Elise, there are a number of things on the debit side. But on the credit side, that one speech is right up there. It is not often that a superstar gets to hear the unvarnished truth, least of all from his own PR.

Nick nodded, looking first at me and then back to Elise; Ali was sitting unobtrusively off to the side. She was not saying a word, though how she must have been revelling in the turn of events.

And I have perhaps an inkling of what was going through Nick's mind at that moment: where was the screenwriter? Where was the line? When a star is in character, he can effortlessly deliver the lines that have been written for him. But in reality, can they dream up the lines themselves? Or are they as empty as sounding brass and tinkling cymbals?

"You're right Elise," he said. "You're right, you're right, you're right. Kim..." He smiled at me. "Kim, I owe you."

"I... you're welcome." I said.

"I don't know why I did it. But, you know, it did help put things into perspective. You realise what matters: the kids. Barbara."

"How are things with Barbara?"

"They're good," he said, before adding, almost carelessly, "I've split with Cat."

I tried not to seem surprised. This was an astonishing turnabout.

"I'm sorry to hear that," I said.

"We'd run our course."

"And... and Barbara?"

"Wouldn't that be nice?"

I had another five minutes before one of the runners knocked on the door, and after more hugs all round, Nick was back off into that ethereal realm of the superstar, and Elise and I were delightedly staring at each other before we both burst out laughing.

And that, I suppose, was when I decided that, even with Georges, Elise and I might be able to make a go of it. She was funny, she was loving and above all else, she was loyal; and so long as her liaisons with Georges were never actively thrust in my face, then I thought, I hoped, that I might be able to handle it. If only – if only – it had been that simple.

CHAPTER 21

It would be a few months before I saw Nick again, and when I did he would do me a small but critical favour. Not that it worked out well. But few things in my life do tend to work out well.

As for Nick's story and his possible rapprochement with Barbara, it ran for a few days, and for the space of a week I was a minor celebrity, interviewed by the magazines and the trashy TV shows. I tasted my fifteen minutes of fame, but on balance, I think I'd rather skulk in the shadows. I prefer reporting on the news to actually making it.

And the Kim-Elise bandwagon trundled on. After what she'd done with Nick, I was smitten.

The Thursdays did not necessarily become any easier for me, but I learned to live with them. Georges was never referred to, either directly or indirectly. The usual routine would be that we might talk in the morning or the afternoon and, while carefully neglecting to say anything at all about what was going to be occurring that evening, we would chit-chat about our days. Save for this elephant in the room, we were almost like any other couple in love.

I tended to spend my Thursdays with my friends. And as men do when they want to forget, I would get drunk.

On Fridays, Elise and I would again go through the same ritual of the phone-call, only this time carefully neglecting to ask, "So what did you do last night?" Elise was also unable to ask me what I'd done the previous night, because that would then have raised the uneasy spectre of what it was that she had been doing...

Not so much the elephant in the room as this giant blue whale, stranded there on the floor, still wet, still raucously breathing its last, and yet somehow we forever managed to avoid talking about it. You might think it odd that, for weeks on end, I never brought the subject up with Elise, but really it was the only way that I could deal with it. In hindsight… well that's a different thing altogether. When it comes to listing the things that I would have done differently in my life, I hardly know where to begin.

I realise I may well be contradicting myself. In my defence, I can only quote the Walt Whitman line with which the besotted President wooed his Monica: "Do I contradict myself? Very well then, I contradict myself. I am large. I contain multitudes."

At the time, I found it easier never even to mention Georges' name; as if, by not doing so, he might be conveniently expunged from my thoughts. How facile it now seems: for Georges was going to be rumbling through my head whether I talked about him or whether I didn't.

As he still continues to do.

I wonder if Georges ever had any conception of what he put me through. Hand on heart, I can say that in the past decade, there has not been one single day when Georges' spectre has not drifted through my dreams.

The Clinton-Lewinsky road-show continued to snowball; I continued my endless zigzag across America; and after some chivvying from Elise, I finally booked up two weeks' holiday. This was a very unusual situation for me. Elise was dating me, though not exclusively. And yet on the other hand she was buying me a new 30,000 dollar knee. I knew she was rich, but…

"It doesn't feel right," I said.

"You need a new knee." She stroked my back with a feather. We were lying in my bed, a quiet Friday in before the operation the next day. "I want you to have a new knee."

"But it's so expensive!" I said. "It's ludicrously expensive!"

"It's a present. Can't you accept a present?"

"I love presents. It's just a little pricier than any other present I've ever been given. It makes me feel uncomfortable."

"Well don't be."

"I feel beholden to you."

"Beholden!" She cuffed my back. "Why don't you behold my body?"

"I'd rather be holding it."

"Touché!" she said.

"I have the most incredible urge to make love with you again."

"With me?"

"Or perhaps on you?"

"No, this time I would like you to make love under me."

Just as with Georges, the matter of the knee or the operation was not mentioned again. It has been one of my more idiotic beliefs that it's generally easier not to talk about things that are unpleasant: as if somehow, by not talking about them, they will disappear. They never do, though, they just rot.

By now it was April. It had been three months since I'd last seen Dr Tony Steele. I had forgotten all about him. I had forgotten that he was the perfect all-American beefcake, the sort of guy who bench-presses 300 pounds before breakfast. He was a mirror to my inadequacies.

I still was unable to put my finger on what it was about Dr Steele that set my teeth on edge. He seemed, I think, to be the embodiment of not just America, but New York City, with this sense of perfect entitlement, as if he were worth every ounce of all the good stuff that came his way.

I wonder if I, the posh Limey, grated with Steele in the same way that he grated with me. Perhaps. I find that gut feelings tend to be mutual.

I was in the same mid-town skyscraper that I'd first met Dr Steele, though on a different floor. It was a very exclusive private hospital, with operating theatres, nurses, surgeons, anaesthetists… and, I suppose, kitchens and porters and everything else that a patient might require. I was staying for a week.

I'd already changed, stripping out of my clothes and now wearing nothing but sandals and a white hospital gown. I had my own private room, plain white with a bed, television and a view into the Fifth Avenue canyon. Elise had dropped me off in a taxi an hour earlier, and had promised to return in the afternoon.

Elise! I smiled at the thought of her. What a tonic she was. Who else but Elise would have spurred me on to get myself a new knee, and then paid for it into the bargain?

There was a knock at the door. Before I could answer, Tony Steele walked in followed by another man. They were both in white coats.

"Morning Kim, how you feeling?"

"A little nervous."

"You won't regret it, I promise. This is your anaesthetist, Dr Baker."

We shook hands and said our hellos. Steele drew a big black arrow on my leg pointing to my shattered kneecap, and then ran through the schedule. In an hour I was going to be wheeled into theatre where Dr Baker would be administering a general anaesthetic. The operation itself was intricate and would take four hours. I'd need a week in bed and in about ten days, I'd be on crutches.

In my time, I have mixed with Hollywood superstars, cabinet ministers and Rock Gods, but none of them have had the same effect as that model of Alpha Male excellence, Tony Steele. It had been a long time since I'd felt so out of my depth.

"All set then?" Steele clapped me over the shoulder. "We'll just go and scrub up. They'll bring you through shortly."

I have a memory of being helped onto the trolley by a nurse. I'm wheeled into the theatre. The two surgeons in green scrubs; stainless steel shimmering under the bright arc lights; and a nurse pottering by some wicked-looking instruments.

Steele winked. "Sweet dreams."

Injections are made. I think I'm going to be out like a light, but I'm not. Though my eyes are closed, I can still hear.

Steele is talking. "This is the one I was telling you about," he says. "Elise bought him a new knee for his birthday."

"They must be a real love match," replies the anaesthetist.

"More fool him."

More. Fool. Him. What a thought to set me off into the dark chasm of my unconsciousness.

CHAPTER 22

It seems like only a moment when I'm waking up in my private room. I'm in bed, my knee is throbbing, and Elise is reading a book in the armchair beside me.

For a while, I didn't move. I watched her through half-closed eyelids, struck afresh by her beauty. As she read, her red lips moved very slightly.

"Do you like what you see?"

"Very much." I was slurring my words, as if my tongue could not keep up with my thoughts. "I never knew you mouthed the words when you read."

"Only the dialogue." She clipped a silver bookmark onto the page and kissed me as she moved over to sit on the edge of the bed.

"The tip of your nose moves too."

"I didn't know that. In a sexy way?"

"It would be impossible for you to do anything in a way that wasn't sexy."

"You charmer."

"I'm only giving value for money. You've spent a fortune on me; I'd hate you to think you'd made a duff investment."

She kissed me again, the tip of her tongue dancing along the edge of my lips. "If you hadn't just had a very large scale operation – and if you weren't slurring your words so much – I'd think you were trying to bed me."

"Well, now that you mention it... Is there a lock on the door?"

We never did have sex in the hospital, but this week of enforced inactivity was blissful, with nothing but the television and my books for company. Even the hacks deigned to visit, with Ali and Justin and my oppo correspondents from the *Mail* and the *Mirror* all coming round with fruit and chocolates. Steve visited most lunchtimes, polishing off any food that was going.

Tony Steele also came round a couple of times to admire his handiwork, though he didn't spend long with me. I sensed that he was not a guys' guy. He was primarily a ladies' man.

Elise, of course, was the perfect visitor. Almost every night she would come round for two or three hours after work, abrim with gossip and anecdotes. We played backgammon and I annoyed her by winning.

The Thursday, of course, was a different day to all the rest. I'd hoped it wouldn't be. I'd hoped that Elise might for once forego her night with Georges. It seemed not.

She came round at lunchtime, sensational in a black coat, doubtless designer, though its brand was lost on me. I immediately knew that this lunchtime visit meant she'd be elsewhere in the evening.

"You're spending lunch with me!" I said delightedly, puckering up to kiss those same lips that within a few hours would be kissing Georges. And yet although Georges was never mentioned, the whole tenor of our conversation seemed to change, for now that it was Thursday, every word that I uttered had to be set against the context that she would soon be having sex with the Frenchman.

Every moment that I'm thinking about her beauty, there is a correspondingly bitter-sweet moment as I realise that for today she is off limits.

Elise played along with the charade. She would happily chatter about what she'd done last night, or what she'd be doing to me as soon as she got me back into the bedroom, but there was this unavoidable black hole in the conversation: what, exactly, she was going to be doing that night?

Or at least, that's what I used to think. I used to think that she was happy to play possum. But, looking back, the events of the next Thursday rather proved otherwise.

It went like this. Elise had taken a week off work to nursemaid me. She had all but moved into my house. She would still go back home early in the morning so that she could be with her mother for breakfast, but by about eleven a.m. she would breeze back through the door with coffee, cakes and kisses. By now, she not only had her own keys, but her own drawer. We were almost like a proper couple. What a superlative week that was: in the heart of New York City, and yet cocooned with Elise away from all the madness.

You know what's coming next. It's Thursday and by now Elise has got me so well trained up that I'm certainly not expecting her to be spending the night in with me; though in the event, I certainly wasn't expecting what *did* happen that night either.

It had been twelve days since the operation and I was hobbling around on crutches. Elise and I had just had lunch when Steve rang from the front door. "Get yourself downstairs!" he said. "I've got you a wheelchair!"

Elise smiled. Boys will be boys.

"Come along too!" I said to her.

She wrinkled her nose. "He wants to tell you about his latest girlfriend," she said. "I better not cramp his style."

Steve was at the door. He kissed Elise on the cheek before slinging his arm round my chest, propping me up as I hopped downstairs. Elise followed with the crutches.

I marvelled at the wheelchair. It was battered, rusty, older than I was, but it did nevertheless have four wheels and a seat.

"Did you steal it?" I asked.

"Found it in the basement."

Elise handed over the crutches and I kissed her. "Thanks lover," I said. "See you later."

"Have fun."

As Steve wheeled me along, I looked over my shoulder. She was still standing on the steps of my brownstone. She blew me a kiss.

Steve wheeled me off into Central Park. It was the first time that I'd been properly outside in over a week. We went through the John Lennon memorial, Strawberry Fields, and down to the café by the boating lake. We drank beer in the dappled sunlight.

"It's quite an asset having you in a wheelchair," Steve said. "Have you seen the amount of interest we're getting?"

"Girls smiling at you are they?"

"Girls always smile at me. Come out with me tonight. I can be the long-suffering hero who's taking his crocked buddy out for a drink."

"Don't you have enough girlfriends?"

"In New York? You can never have enough girlfriends." He belched as he swilled back the last of his beer, simultaneously gesturing to a waitress for a refill. "Come on, come out."

"I don't know…"

"Why not? I'll share the girls fifty-fifty."

"I don't want to go fifty-fifty. I've got Elise."

"Today's Thursday."

The statement of fact hung pregnant in the air.

Steve was remorseless. "You've got nothing to lose… and everything to gain."

"I love her," I said. "I don't want anybody else."

"Thank you." Steve smiled at the waitress. "It's not about whether you want anyone else or not. If you just carry on doing what you've been doing, then she'll just carry on doing what she's been doing. Unless you do something, Georges isn't going to be leaving the picture any time soon."

He was right. I know he was right. It would have been better for me to have done anything at all rather than just roll over and give Elise her free pass on a Thursday. Better if I had brought the whole dubious business of Georges out into the open; better if I had told her that, come Thursday evenings, I also would be out playing the field; and better still if I had made the ultimatum that I should have given from the first: it's Georges or me.

By the time Steve wheeled me back, it was late afternoon.

He helps me up the stairs. I drop the key, fumble it, drop it. We go into the flat. The lights are still on. A trace of perfume that is not familiar to me lingers in the air. Steve gets a couple of beers from the fridge. And as we're sitting in front of the TV, we simultaneously hear the sound of Elise singing softly in the bathroom. She's singing what was once one of my favourite songs, 'New York, New York'.

Yes, it's that same scene that I began my manuscript with.

She's getting ready for her date with Georges.

In my flat.

In my own bathroom.

It dawns on me that for the first time, I'm going to see Elise as she really is on a Thursday night. Up until then, I had no idea how she looked for Georges.

"She's doing this on purpose," said Steve. "She's pushing you. Seeing how far you'll go. Seeing how much you'll put up with."

"I don't think so."

WILLIAM COLES

"Look mate, it's bizarre enough that she's seeing Frenchie every Thursday, but then for her to be actually getting ready for this hot date in your flat? She's rubbing your nose in the shit! You're mad if you put up with it."

Mad?

Or madly in love?

The toilet flushes, Elise comes out and I have to say she looks as beautiful as any other unattainable woman. She's wearing jeans and a light brown leather jacket that I don't think I've seen before.

"Oh, hi Kim," she says.

I can't tell if she is genuinely surprised to find me in my own flat or whether she is shamming.

Things are now decidedly awkward. Should I be getting up out of the sofa and kissing her, just as I normally do every other day of the week when we're about to part?

Or should I be saying, "Don't see Georges tonight, stay with me instead"?

Steve is concentrating on the television. I can sense how he is urging me to take action.

And Elise... she lingers.

Looking back, this was the moment that I'm sure she wanted me to take control. I may not know much about women, but there are times when a man must assert himself.

I gazed at her, but said not a word. It wasn't just my aching knee or the shock of finding her still in my home; a part of me couldn't believe that this was really happening. That Elise, here, now, was about to go off and have sex with another man.

"Well, I'll be off then."

I raised up my bottle in casual salute. The door closes behind her. Steve urging me, urging me, to go to the top of the stairs and to call for her to come back.

I did nothing.

Later, after a kindness from Steve, I wept. But that is what Elise did and what she still continues to do: she is the woman who makes men cry.

152

CHAPTER 23

The next day, I had a stroke of luck. At least, at the time I thought it was lucky. I was sent to Barbados.

"You don't have to do much more than watch him," said Kent, the news editor. "Enjoy the sunshine."

"I'm on my way," I said.

What had happened was that the owner of a Premier League football club had been caught making derogatory remarks about his fans. He had spent two days fire-fighting in the UK before belatedly realising that he'd only been fanning the flames. He then went to ground. His plan had been to lie low in Barbados' luxurious Sandy Lane hotel, in the hope that by the time he returned home a fortnight later, the story would have blown itself out.

Unfortunately for him, the *Sun* had got wind of his holiday plans, and so, before he'd even touched down in Barbados, Ali and I were already on our way.

I'd not seen Elise before I left, but we had spoken on the phone. It had been affable enough and there had been no mention, of course, about the previous night. But I was hurting and I was angry, and no amount of pretty words from Elise could make up for the fact that the previous night she'd been with the Frenchman.

Barbados was as hot as I'd ever known it. It was right at the end of the season, and walking out of the plane was like walking into a wall of heat.

A taxi took us to the Sandy Lane, which in those days had a touch of class. It's all been knocked down now, to be replaced by another ubiquitous five star hotel, and all that remains is that exquisite crescent of golden sand. But in 1998, the Sandy Lane was still very much the grand hotel of old, with the odd touch of quirkiness. I still have a few memories. A wide, open lobby, white marble, an air of spaciousness, and beyond it a glimpse of an azure sea. Ali and I were booked into a couple of single garden rooms which, though they were the cheapest in the hotel, would still have paid for a comfortable room at the Ritz.

I made the various check-in calls to the news desk, and then I went down to the beach, my crutches sinking into the sand. It must be the most expensive piece of beachfront in the whole of the Caribbean, if not America.

Ali was already out on the beach, lying on a sun-lounger. Next to her was a towel and a large zipped-up sports bag which contained her camera and biggest lens.

"Seen him?" I threw the crutches onto the sand and gently eased myself onto the lounger.

"No," said Ali. She passed over a faxed photo of the man. He was fat and balding: a description which could have applied to most men on the beach.

"But he's here?"

"Suite thirteen, on the top floor."

"Good work!" I said. "So now all we have to do is sit here and wait."

Which is exactly what we did. For day, after day, after day. Three days of sitting on the beach from practically dawn to dusk, but our man never once came out to have a swim.

Occasionally we might see our quarry having dinner and I once spotted him in the bar. But the only way that the story was going to work for a paper like the *Sun* was if we had a picture of our football tycoon sunning himself on the beach. Pictures of him drinking or playing golf were all well and good, but the only thing that would justify the huge expense of sending both Ali and me to the Sandy Lane was a front page picture of him, fat, pink and happy, lolling on his sun-lounger.

It should have been the most idyllic time, recuperating from my knee operation, but it was hellish. Apart from my general frustration with the story, I was stuck on one of the world's most beautiful beaches, and yet completely unable to have a dip. Because of my new knee and the raw wound, I could never once go into the sea. Instead, I would lie there on the sun-lounger, exercising my knee as all the while I quietly fumed. There was nothing else I could do.

I tried to read, but every time I finished a page, I realised that not a word of it had gone in. So instead, I would gaze out at the sea and would wonder just how it was all going to turn out with Elise. And occasionally, of course, I would inspect my fellow holidaymakers. Most of them were couples, but right from the first, I was struck by a rather odd pairing. There were two women who seemed to be together, but who never spent any time in each other's company. One of them was a redhead, who I did not see much because her fair complexion meant that she couldn't spend any time on the beach. And the other...

Ah yes. The other. She was strikingly beautiful, an Indian, with long black hair, a white swimsuit, and the most mesmerising almond eyes that I have ever looked into.

In and about the hotel, we would pass each other and would smile but never would speak. On the beach, as I waited for the man who never came, I would gaze at her from afar. She would never lie in the direct sun, but would sit reading under a sun-lounger. Every hour or so, she would swim to the Sandy Lane raft, about a 100 yards out from the beach, and would sit there by herself staring out at the ocean. She intrigued me greatly. What was she doing at the Sandy Lane? What country was she from? And she was... single?

On the third night of our stay, Ali had already gone to bed and I was morosely nursing a rum punch at the bar. I was vaguely watching the football tycoon have dinner with his wife. They were already on the third bottle. I was bored beyond belief.

"Tell me, what are you doing here?"

I turned to see who was talking to me. It was the woman, the beautiful Indian, in a flowing floral dress. She slipped into the chair next to me, and I caught a whiff of coconut oil.

"I don't know." I turned the thought over in my head. "What am I doing here?"

"I haven't been able to work you out." She was English. She smiled. A lovely smile.

"Well, a touch of mystery isn't a bad thing. Anyway, what are you doing here?"

"I'm on a honeymoon."

I looked at her ringless fingers. "But you're not married."

"My friend's honeymoon. Jilted a month ago. As she'd paid for the holiday, she took me instead."

"So that's why she looks so miserable."

She laughed, sweeping her hair over her shoulder. "Your turn now," she said. "You're not on holiday. You're not with your lover. So what are you doing here?"

"You don't want to know." I sipped some punch. "What will you drink?"

"I'll have a punch too," she said. "And I do want to know."

There was a lull as I ordered her drink.

"Maybe I'm a cop," I said.

"I don't think so."

"Maybe I'm just here recuperating after my knee operation."

The barman placed the drink in front of her and she thanked him before having a sip. Her eyes slid down my legs

"You've definitely had a knee operation," she said. "But that isn't why you're here."

"How did you work that out?"

"I see you – on the beach, in the hotel, occasionally talking to your colleague –"

"My colleague?"

"So I was right!" she said. "Do you have a girlfriend?"

"Do you have a boyfriend?"

"Do you answer every question with a question?"

"Only when sparring with someone like you."

And that was the start of it. Her name was Neeraja. She lived in London and she was a copywriter with one of the big advertising agencies. She had a boyfriend and was expecting him to propose within the year. She didn't know if she'd accept.

And she was extremely interested to hear about my relationship with Elise.

"You must really love her," she said the next day. We were having a late coffee after breakfast.

"I do really love her."

She was wearing a white cotton gown and, underneath it, her white swimsuit.

"And does she really love you?"

"She says she does."

"And yet on Thursdays…"

"Yes," I said. "On Thursdays, she loves somebody else."

"Why don't you do the same thing?"

"I don't know. I guess because I love her. And I guess because I haven't really fancied anyone else." I paused, drank my cold coffee, looked at her. "Until now."

Even now, I don't know what made me say it. It just seemed to come out of nowhere.

"Until now?" she repeated.

"Until now."

"Well isn't that a shame?" she said. "I think that in time I might have come to fancy you too – and yet we both of us have our lovers waiting for us back home."

I laughed. "What an impossible position for us," I said. "If we were both single, I'd simply lean over and kiss you right now."

"But as it is, you've signed this pledge of fidelity to your unfaithful girlfriend."

"And I wouldn't want to compromise your relationship with your soon-to-be fiancé."

"Perhaps I should be the judge of the limits of my relationship with my boyfriend."

"Indeed you should."

"But you're right. If I were single and if you were single, then a kiss would be…" she drummed her fingers on the table as she searched for the right word. "Appropriate."

"So all we have to do is wait until that happy day when we are both single, and then we could make a go of it."

"We'll have to synchronise our split-ups."

"Absolutely. Someone like you would be snapped up the very moment you were back on the market."

"Ditto."

"But nothing could ever come of it though," I said. "You live in London. I live in New York. It would just be a completely meaningless fling."

"A completely and utterly meaningless fling." She smiled. Without another word needing to be said, we had reached the most total understanding.

"What a shame."

"Quite."

Neeraja got up to go and as she walked past me, she bent over and kissed me on the lips.

"I think you deserve better," she said.

I stroked her cheek.

"I'm in Room 14," she said. "I'll be waiting."

I watched her sashay out of the restaurant. She was very beautiful. I wanted her.

I continued to sit there, staring out the sea, weighing up what to do next. I was amazed at the sheer acceleration of what was happening with Neeraja. But it wasn't just her kiss or her lovely offer. I was suddenly questioning the whole essence of my relationship with Elise. It boiled down to one very simple question: why on earth did I put up with it? Was I that desperate; that much in love?

But if Elise had her freedom on Thursdays, then perhaps I could have a taste of it too.

And I thought about Neeraja.

I wanted to kiss her again. I wanted to kiss her again very much. I wanted to feel her lips on mine. I wanted to hold her; to see her naked; to look into her eyes as she ravished me.

I didn't waste another moment.

I slouched out of the restaurant, past the reception, and went up to the first floor. I wondered what might happen when I got into her room. Maybe we'd just kiss.

Maybe we'd do something more. I didn't really care; all I knew was that I wanted her.

I knocked on her door. I was both nervous and very excited.

Neeraja opened the door. She was still wearing her white gown and her swimsuit.

"You came." She smiled and took my hand as I walked into the room.

I closed the door behind me. We looked at each other for a moment, almost shyly, and then we lunged at each other, clinging so tight. And I smelled her hair and it was a new scent, a fresh scent that I had not smelt before and that alone was intoxicating. And fresh curves and new skin, and a different kind of warmth to that of Elise.

I wanted her.

Neeraja looked up at me. "You know the Kama Sutra?" she asked.

"I might have heard of it."

"We are going to play a game that newly-weds play on their wedding nights. It helps to break the ice."

"And we do need an ice-breaker."

She kissed me. "All you have to do is gently bite my lower-lip."

"Is that all?"

"And at the same time, I will be trying to bite your lower-lip – though perhaps not quite so gently."

"Bite away."

Our arms still slung about each other's waists, we eye each other up before our lips move closer and closer, and as I watch her lips breathe into my mouth I feel almost disembodied. I've never played this game before. It is erotic. If you are trying to bite your lover's lower lip, you have no option but to duck your chin and open your mouth wide, and very quickly it becomes very intimate. Tongues start to dab and soon all thoughts of biting are forgotten.

Without taking her eyes off mine, Neeraja slipped her hand down the front of my shorts.

"That's very forward of you," I said.

"May I pleasure you?"

"How do you intend to do that?"

"Ohh…" She tailed off as she did something magical with her fingers. "In the normal way."

"Or in the not so normal way."

She helped me step out of my shorts. I was fumbling at her swim-suit, but Neeraja did not want that. "This isn't tennis."

"Isn't it?"

Her eyes glided from mine and for the first time, she looked down. "Well, well, well."

"Three holes in the ground." I was trembling with excitement. I didn't know what was going to happen next. I was with someone new; just about anything could happen.

She led me over to the side of the bed. For the first time, I noticed the room. It was white, opulent, airy, with a light sea-breeze sighing through the open windows. It was extraordinary, surreal – a million miles from what I'd expected to be doing that morning. I could not take my eyes off this beauty as she nestled between my knees.

"I'm going to make you cry," she said.

I looked down at her. And, even now I can see her there, for in my mind's eye, I still have a snap-shot of that very moment. "And how are you going to do that?"

"I'm going to make you cry." Neeraja's hand stroked my waist. "With ecstasy."

I laughed. I couldn't take my eyes off her. She was holding my gaze very steadily, eyes completely locked on mine. For the first time I noticed her lipstick. It was fresh on, absolutely scarlet. "That'll be different."

She broke off. "Ever cried from ecstasy before?"

"I'm not so sure I have."

"I find it a real turn-on."

"That makes two of us." I stretched down and tried to slip my hand beneath her swim-suit. I wanted to stroke her breasts. "No," she said. "Maybe later."

She was a beautiful woman, but it was her eyes that were the knock-out. A lock of dark hair fell across her face and I stroked it away, so that I could still continue to look at her. They were Siren eyes that you could have drowned in.

And then, as surely as night follows day, my phone rang. In those days, my mobile was with me always. I never thought to think of turning it off.

Though at that moment, at that critical moment, I certainly had no intention of taking the call.

"Take the call," said Neeraja. Knowingly. Lasciviously.

So I took the call, thinking, perhaps, that Neeraja would break off, but she did nothing of the kind – in fact she only seemed to move up a gear.

"Yes?" I breathed.

"What the hell are you doing?" It was Kent, the news editor.

"Writing copy."

I looked down at Neeraja. She stuck her tongue out at me.

"Good," he said. "So you know Ali's got the pictures. File everything you've got. Then check out. Then front him up to see what he's got to say for himself."

The phone clicks off. Neeraja raises an eyebrow in query. And I would so love to be continuing with what we have just started, but already I'm thinking about the story, thinking about my opening sentence… and, well, really, those sort of thoughts are not conducive to ecstasy.

"You heartbreaker," said Neeraja.

She gave me a hug as I left the room and gave me a peck on the lips. "I'll see you later?"

"Of course you will!" I waved as I scurried down the corridor. Dead-lines have always made me do the most insane things.

I was still pounding out my story when Ali came into my room an hour later. The pictures were perfect, showing the football tycoon in all his corpulent glory. I filed, Ali sent her pictures, and then with my bag packed I went off to find out what the man had to say for himself. He was apoplectic with rage. They often get like that when they realise they're going to be on the front page of the next day's paper. I half expected him to hit me. But he didn't. He just screamed a lot.

And after that, everything came to a sudden and rather dejected stop, and there was nothing left to do except for the final thing that had to be done.

I found Neeraja on the beach. She had a book in her hands but she was not reading it.

I sat down heavily on the sun-lounger next to her. She was just in her swim-suit, very serene, almost regal, so very different from the woman that I'd just been with in her bedroom.

"I'm leaving," I said.

Very slowly, she took off her sunglasses and looked at me. "How sad."

"It is sad – but also probably easier for both of us."

"Easier not to have the temptation. I'll miss you."

"And I'll dream of what might have been."

A little snort, a little nod. "You never told me what you were doing here."

"Just a reporter," I said. "And now my story is done and I'm on my way home."

"I guessed it was something like that. You've been stalking somebody. And your colleague is the photographer."

"Correct on all counts." I smiled.

I stood up, leant over her and kissed her on the lips. She held my hand.

"I never did get to make you cry," she said.

"Though I was pretty close to ecstasy."

She smiled at that. "It's been nice not quite knowing you."

"Goodbye."

Without a backward glance, I stumped off back to the hotel.

I wonder if Elise had somehow intuited what had happened, because for the first time she was waiting for me at the airport.

I held her tight and inhaled her scent. Until that moment, I don't think I'd realised how much I'd missed her. We went back to my flat and had made love twice within the hour.

"Has something happened?" she asked as we drowsed in bed.

"It's good to be back," I said.

I never mentioned my beautiful new friend. And that, or so I thought, was the end of Neeraja.

CHAPTER 24

Elise's mother was a problem.

Since I did not have a mother, I had no-one to compare with Velda.

But she did seem to go out of her way to be objectionable. I was never quite sure if it was personal.

As I had surmised, Velda had split up with Elise's father some seventeen years earlier. She had been rifling through his bag after a business trip and had found just what she'd hoped to find, a fresh packet of condoms. Within the hour, she had left the house and never set foot inside it again. I don't want to judge the father, Jack, and I don't especially want to judge Velda. Not so, Elise. For her, an only child, her father's infidelity was the ultimate betrayal. Their relationship collapsed, and Elise moved to America with Velda soon afterwards.

To my knowledge, Elise had not even spoken to Jack in four years. That's a long time not to speak to your father.

That's a lot of baggage.

After her divorce, I think that Velda had foresworn against men and was happy to live with her cats and her Elise. They had adjoining flats, though to all intents and purposes they might as well have been living with each other.

On the surface, Elise adored her mother. Velda was her rock. And yet I had this sense that Elise longed to be free of this stifling weight, not so much a rock as an anchor dragging her down.

If at all possible, I tried to avoid going round to Elise's flat, and I think that she also preferred it like that. When we were in Elise's flat, Velda would forever be popping round for a chat. If Elise had locked us in, Velda would just start knocking. Then, ten minutes later, she'd come back again to check if the door was still bolted.

Velda was well practised in the art of the passive-aggressive. In the short conversations that we had, she would never make a full frontal attack; instead, it felt like I was being assaulted by a sniper, as this whip-crack of bullets whistled over my head. I rarely rose to the bait, and instead would sit there soaking it up.

But you can only soak things up for so long before you become saturated.

By now it's summer. My knee is almost completely mended and preparations are underway for the New York nuptials of those two Hollywood superstars Adam and Scarlett. Adam, as you may remember, was the star whose show-stopping marriage proposal had made headlines around the world.

They were getting married at The Plaza in front of 500 guests, and without doubt it was going to be New York's wedding of the year. Elise, whose firm represented one of the stars, had already received a note through to keep the date free. Elise could not resist gloating, but consoled me by saying I'd be able to read the highlights in *Hello!* magazine.

I, meanwhile, had been sent to Peru for the most unusual story that I have ever covered. Ali and I were to find our way to the town of Cusco and once we'd acclimatised ourselves to the altitude, I was to venture out onto the Inca Trail. To eat a guinea-pig.

Such were the whims and indeed the limitless pockets of my mad-masters. It seemed that a small amount of UK lottery money had been sent out to the Peruvian guinea-pig farmers to help them breed a giant guinea-pig known as a Mauro Minha. The *Sun's* readers were incensed that their hard-earned lottery money was being spent on turning these family pets into finger-food. I was despatched to interview the guinea-pig farmers.

We'd walked seven miles up the Inca Trail before I found an old woman who would sell me a Mauro Minha (named, I believe, after a Peruvian heavyweight boxing champion). It was about the size of a large rabbit. The woman wrung its neck, par-boiled it, and then plucked all its hair out. The skin was rubbed with spices and its offal was turned into tiny sausages. She spit-roasted the guinea-pig for an hour and we had it for lunch with boiled potatoes. It was one of the most delicious meals I have ever tasted.

Another night in Cusco, and then a flight back to Lima, and then another flight on to Houston. We'd been away four days. I was already tingling at the prospect of seeing Elise again.

I was just in the act of checking in my bag at Houston Airport when I remembered the cardinal rule for all of the *Sun's* foreign correspondents. What with dreams of Elise, it had all but slipped my mind. We were never allowed to board a flight without first calling London.

"You couldn't hang on a second," I said to the check-in girl, getting out my mobile.

Campbell the night news editor picked up.

"Okay to go back to New York?" I asked.

"I'll just check, old boy."

I could overhear various mad-masters talking in the background. "It's Kim in Houston. All right to fly to New York?"

"Think so." The sound of fingers tapping at a keyboard. "Haven't they just found that schoolboy runaway in Florida?"

"Kim's got Ali with him too." says another

"Shall we send to Florida?"

"The freelances in Miami are pretty good."

"Nah, let's send."

Campbell was on the line again. "You're off to Miami, old boy."

I love the sheer arbitrariness of news stories; the one moment I'm flying home to Manhattan, and the next, just because some tearaway has happened to call home to his mother, I'm off to Ernest Hemingway country in the Florida Keys.

"I'm sorry." I smiled at the check-in girl, as if swapping flight destinations was a regular occurrence. "Would it be possible to get us on the next flight to Miami?"

Florida. *Sun* readers are addicted to Florida, though personally, I hate it: the heat, the theme parks and the sun-burned Brits all hell-bent on having the holiday of a lifetime.

Ali and I spent five days chasing round the Sunshine State. A fourteen year old schoolboy from Essex had eloped to Florida with his 33-year-old lover. All had gone well for one week, until the boy had foolishly called his parents to tell them that he was okay. Within minutes, the call had been traced and the Florida police were sent storming into the couple's love-nest in Key West.

What a sad little tale. The woman was a married housewife, and though she'd only been in custody for twenty-four hours, she looked much older than her years. I inspected her carefully as she shuffled into the courtroom, manacled at both hands and feet and wearing an orange jumpsuit. She was 33, the same age as myself; another sorry example of the sheer lunacies that we are capable of committing when we are in love.

By the time I was eventually allowed to fly back to New York, I had been gone for ten days. I'd been speaking to Elise every day and I had bought her a large conch shell from the Keys. Two holes had been drilled into the side and when you blew into it, the conch boomed like an alpine horn. I planned to tell Elise that the conch would be her call sign; the moment I heard it, no matter where I was, I would come running Tarzan-like to her side.

I'd been away so long that I'd forgotten what day it was. And the day that I got back to Manhattan was inevitably a Thursday.

I had already left a message for Elise when I'd been at Miami airport, and I called her again while I was waiting for my luggage at La Guardia. Her mobile was off, so I tried her home phone. I'd all but given up, when her mother picked up.

"Hello?" A hard, suspicious voice. It was Velda.

"Hello." I was momentarily taken aback. "I... I just wondered if Elise was about?"

"Who's speaking?"

I'm sure she knew full well that it was me, but I played along with her. "It's Kim. How are you?"

"She's in the bath," she said. "I thought it was Thursday today." I detected what I thought sounded like a little laugh.

"What of that?" I asked. "Am I not allowed to speak to Elise on a Thursday?"

"I would have thought that it is more a question of whether Elise wished to speak to you."

"Well let me rephrase my question." Ali had retrieved our bags and was patiently waiting for me to finish my call. I gave her the thumbs up. "Could I possibly trouble you to ask Elise if she might deign to speak to me?"

"Don't you take that tone with me, young man."

I didn't know it at the time, but I can see now that it was the classic passive-aggressive move. You nip and you nip, and then when suddenly your adversary bites, you switch to outraged shock.

"May I ask you something Velda?" For the first time, I'd used her first name. "I know you don't like me. But I just wanted to know, is it personal? And if so, what have I done to annoy you so much?"

This was precisely – *precisely* – the moment that she had been waiting for. "How very ungallant of you," she said. "Not really the behaviour of a gentleman? Did you learn that at Eton? Or perhaps your father?"

After five months, I'd finally had my fill.

I was bitterly polite.

"Perhaps, Velda, you'd like to tell me how a lady behaves, especially on a Thursday."

"So boorish," she said.

"So charming," I replied.

"I very much look forward to the day when, as she undoubtedly will, Elise tires of you."

As I recall those stinging insults, which were still just plausibly within the bounds of politeness, it seems as if we were both possessed by this delirious desire to hurt each other in any way that we could.

"At least," I said, "I love Elise and I want the best for her"

"And what's that supposed to mean, you ill-mannered pup?"

"It means, Velda, whatever you take it to mean."

"Well good day to you. I'm sure that Elise will be having a lovely time tonight, just as she has for – how long is it now? – the past ten days."

Without giving me time to deliver some tart rejoinder, Velda cut me off and slammed the phone down.

I was simmering! How I seethed! I couldn't believe it!

For it seemed that Velda knew all about Elise's weekly trysts with Georges. They probably joked about it with each other. And what was that last little dig all about? Did it mean... did it mean that Elise had been seeing Georges while I'd been away?

I did not have to wait long to find out.

Within three minutes, Elise had called back; her voice, normally so soft, had a brittle quality about it which I had not heard since that fateful phone call all those months ago when she'd spiked my story on Nick Spitz.

There was no greeting. She dived straight in.

"What have you been saying to mummy?"

"What?" I hadn't thought that I would be so soon on the defensive. "What have I been saying to your mother?"

"She's in tears!" said Elise. "She's over seventy years old!"

It felt like I was floundering in a swamp. The more I flailed the quicker I sank into the murk.

"I'm very sorry to hear that your mother's taken it so badly."

"She's shaking like a whipped dog! I've never seen her like this! You should be ashamed of yourself!"

Always, in my arguments with women, I find that all too soon I'm on the back foot. My troops may be marshalled and my plan of attack clear and yet in a matter of moments, it seems that my flank has been turned and my army is in disarray. It makes no difference how thoroughly I have prepared my battleground, for the battlefield is never going to be of my own choosing.

But nevertheless, I did have a number of things that I wanted to get off my chest. And out they came.

"You think I should be ashamed?" I said. "What about you? Aren't you ashamed of how, week in, week out, you juggle me with Georges?"

"I'm not proud of myself, no; thank you for mentioning it."

"Well seeing as we haven't talked about Georges in quite a while, I thought that now might be as good a time as any to bring him up."

"And what do you want to say?" Visually, I could almost picture Elise folding her arms across her chest.

"I can't be doing with it any more," I said. "It's either me or Georges, and that's an end to it."

I was shaking from the adrenalin. I'd done it! I wasn't sure it was the best thing to do, but I had done it! I had issued the ultimatum that I should have made months ago.

"So be it," said Elise, before adding one final barb. "At the very least you won't be able to abuse my mother again. Goodbye."

She replaced the handset. But she didn't return it properly to the handset, so I overheard Velda's parting shot. And I'm afraid that, for better or for worse, she overplayed her hand.

"Well!" I heard Velda snap. "I hope that is your swan-song with that sick little man."

CHAPTER 25

You never break up after the first row. For that, rather surprisingly, was what it was. In over five months together, Elise and I had never once had a row, and now that we'd found ourselves embroiled in such spite, we were both a little shocked at how we had so set out to hurt the one we loved.

For one, two days, I was aglow with indignant pride. I'd soaked up her nights with Georges, not to mention her mother's insults, and what a relief – *what a relief!* – to think that I was finally shot of the whole thing. No more tortured Thursdays! For all I was concerned, Elise could go to hell in a handcart, and Georges could wheel her on her way.

There was, of course, that dull throb of the heart that comes when another love affair comes to a close. But on balance, I thought I was in credit. I'd miss her; miss her very much. Now that I'd had a chance to catch my breath, I was frankly shocked that I had put up with the Georges madness for so long.

And that would have been – perhaps *should* have been – the end of it all. But Elise, for whatever her reasons, was not going to let me go so easily. We might have split up, but I was still besotted. And all it needed was the slightest tug on the leash, and I couldn't help but come trotting back to her side.

That tweak came four days later. I'd spent my weekend stewing, part delighted and part appalled at what I had done.

Elise sent me a little e-mail. I pounced upon it.

"I'm sorry," she wrote.

Within moments I had written her back: "I'm sorry too."

My inbox pings. "Can I buy you a drink?"

Now if ever there was a moment to have paused for thought, this was it. Because I know what I am like. I am a total sucker for beautiful women and that is especially so when I have just split up with them. So if I had had any sense at all, then I might have just been that little bit more circumspect about seeing Elise again. Not that I never wanted to see her again. But only after a respectable cooling-off period, so that I might just be able to restrain any more of those damnable urges to kiss her.

Not me though. I am a plunger and I very much fear that I always will be.

I e-mailed Elise back. "A drink would be nice." So Dexter's it was again, the same bar where we'd met for our first date, and just like the first time, she'd arrived early and was drinking Krug. The moment I saw the bottle in the ice bucket, I should have turned on my heel and left, for it meant that Elise was not nearly done with me.

It was summer and she was barelegged, bare-armed and in a stunning white dress. I kissed her on the cheek. Without a word, she poured me a glass of champagne.

"Where we came for our first date." I sipped.

"It is," she said.

We stared at each other and she took my hand.

"I'm sorry," she said. "I didn't want to give up on us without a fight."

"It's your call, Elise," I replied. "I love you. But it's Georges or me. I mean it."

But the thing is about these ultimatums and these threats: you have to see them through. Otherwise you're in a far worse position than you were to start off with.

"I know," she said. She sips. She looks so beautiful. She plays with the hem of her skirt. I glance down to see just a little more of her beautiful legs. "You're right. I'm sorry."

"I'm sorry too." In my brain, it feels like these two raging forces are battling against each other. On the one hand, I know that it is essential that I stick to my guns; and on the other, well I have this crazy young man who is bawling in my ear to kiss her.

"I will deal with Georges," she said. "I'm sorry it's taken so long."

Now this was it. This was the moment when I needed to show her that I did have the smallest amount of steel in my soul. This was the moment when I should have said to her, "I am so happy to hear that Elise, and please, please call me when you have finished

171

with Georges." Then: a last swill of Krug; a peck on the cheek; and without a backward glance, I walk out of the door.

But no, I didn't. I used to console myself with the belief that I loved her, and that I lusted after her, but you want to know the truth? When it came to a battle of wills with Elise, I was utterly spineless.

So what I in fact said to Elise was this: "I am so happy to hear that." It felt like I'd been climbing up the north face of the Eiger and just as I was nearing the peak, I somehow lost my footing. I'm scrabbling and I'm screaming, but I'm on sheet ice and I'm heading off back into the abyss.

At the critical moment, I didn't have the stomach to see my threat through.

We kissed. It was lovely. Almost as good as the first time I'd kissed her in Dexter's. There was all the passion that you expect when lovers manage to rekindle the flame. But as I write about it now, it so sickens me that I hardly have the words to describe it. So although I suppose it was romantic and loving, as we both delighted in how we'd pulled back from the brink, I am only able to view it now through the most opaque lens. At the time, it was undoubtedly another of those beautiful Kodak moments. But it does also have to be set in context.

And as I see it now, the image of that couple kissing in Dexter's wine bar is so distorted as to revolt me. Because what I'd only sensed then, but now know for certain, is that that had been my chance and I'd blown it.

More kisses and more champagne, and now we're getting a taxi straight back to my apartment so that we can consummate our new relationship, and I suppose it was all just wonderful, but I can neither remember what happened and nor do I have the urge to write about it. We had sex. That's all you need to know.

Our relationship was back on track.

Except it took me two weeks to appreciate that our relationship was not just back on track but back on exactly the *same* track. Georges was still very much in the picture. For all of Elise's promises to 'deal' with Georges, nothing ever seemed to happen. Nothing was said of it, but come her Thursday evenings, Elise would inevitably be "tied up".

For myself, now that I'd broached the subject once, it was almost as if I didn't have the stomach for the fight. At the age of 33, I had become like the President's long-suffering wife: life was easier if I turned a blind eye to my partner's secret trysts. We adopted the Bill Clinton mantra for gays in the military: "Don't ask; don't tell".

Talking of which, the Clinton-Lewinsky saga was reaching its dramatic finale. The story had turned into an absolute monster: day after day of ever more astonishing revelations about the President and his intern. Stories which had at first seemed like nothing more than Republican spin and seamy tabloid excess turned out to be true to the last detail. The story had been running on the front page for weeks, and in the autumn it was all due to come to a frothing head when Bill Clinton's tormentor-in-chief, Kenneth Starr, published his report.

The story was so big that we had three people covering it, with the Political Editor and Jenny the Los Angeles Correspondent all shipping into Washington for the week. The city was sweltering; I've never known anywhere so muggy. The clammy heat left you wet with sweat.

The Starr Report was due to be released at eleven a.m. and News Corp had hired a conference room for all of its various foreign correspondents. Steve had been despatched off to one of the government buildings to pick up ten copies and there was a car standing by to whisk him back to the Ritz Carlton.

I remember the tension in the room as we waited for the report to come in. There were about a dozen of us sitting there waiting to get our hands on the report, and with the *Sun*'s deadline looming ever closer. All we knew was that they were clearing the first ten pages for this story, and we would have to work like demons to get the copy over in time.

We sipped coffee, glancing occasionally at the televisions. There was the most unbearable tension, for all the world like soldiers in the trenches in the last few minutes before they went over the top. I watched as there was this sudden dam-burst out of the building, reporters pouring out onto the street. The minutes tick by as we have nothing more to do but wait. The Political Editor, Mike, was doodling away on his laptop, playing with the various intros that he might use. But the truth was that we didn't have anything to write until we got our hands on the report.

It was noon before Steve finally walked into our news hub: not carrying our copies of the Starr Report, but pushing them on a trolley. I think the report was nearly a foot thick, comprising at least six volumes.

We dived in, each of us grabbing a different volume and then skimming it in search of the lurid and the sensational. The report was couched in Starr's stifling legalese and most of it was unreadable. We would flick through page after page, eyes scanning up and down the text looking for tabloid buzzwords.

"Got it!" I'd bawl to Mike, our team leader for the day. "Sex over a pizza!"

"Write it up!" Mike said joyously, revelling at being at the very epicentre of the biggest news story of the year.

"And he was pleasuring her with his cigar!" called Jenny.

"That's the headline!" said Mike, cackling with delight now that he knew how he was going to tackle the story. And as it turned out, it was indeed the front-page headline: "Cigar Sex, Pizza Sex, Phone Sex". In tabloid news terms, a story did not get much better than this.

By two p.m. we'd filed; thousands and thousands of blistering words pouring out of our laptops, and then came the lull... the calm after the storm. We'd stand up, stretch; you could feel the tension oozing from your pores. The Australians, of course, had quite different deadlines from us, so were still pounding away into the afternoon. For once, it was me who was able to chafe Steve.

We hounded the president for a week until he was all but impeached. At one stage it looked like Kenneth Starr had got his man, with Clinton like a stricken beast on the ground as that hound-dog Starr eviscerated his guts. But with a kick and a bound, Clinton was free, and I'm glad he got away, as I've always had a soft spot for the old rogue.

But the news never stops. Always there are the blank pages that have to be filled. We had excavated every morsel of marrow from the Lewinsky scandal, and after our week of merriment at Clinton's expense, the dog barked and the caravan moved on.

I called up Elise to say that I was on my way home. I'd be back in New York just in time for the nuptials of those two superstars, Adam and Scarlett.

"I'm sorry you won't be joining me at the wedding," said Elise.

"You'll see me out the front with the paparazzi."

"I'll take careful notes for you," she replied.

I blew her a kiss.

It was Ali, however, who was to plant the completely insane seed that I should try and crash the wedding.

We were drinking black coffee at nine a.m. as the Delta flight winged its way back to New York.

Ali was staring out of the window. I was reading. At first I didn't understand what she was saying.

"*Hello!* magazine are spending over two million on this wedding. Security's going to be real tight," she said. She sipped her coffee. "Wouldn't it be great to rain on their parade?"

"I loathe the way celebrities do these deals." I broke off from my newspaper. "There they are, for ever bleating about how they want their own privacy, yet when they've got a wedding, or a baby, or a new house, they always sell the pictures to the highest bidder."

"It's not as if they even need the money anyway…"

"Be a great one to gate-crash."

"Sure would."

And that should have been that; just another of those fanciful journalistic pipe-dreams which is mulled over and then discarded.

Except, for some reason, which even now I don't fully understand, I decided to take it a step further.

"So, from a purely theoretical point of view, Ali," I said. "How would you go about gate-crashing this wedding?"

"Three things." She ticked off on her fingers. "One, you've got to look the part. So being a Brit, you'll have more chance than most. Two, you've got to have a suite in the hotel. It helps to blend in. The security people see you milling around. They get used to you."

"And three?"

"Three's simple. You've got to be lucky. Chutzpah helps." She rolled the Yiddish word in the back of her throat. "But luck beats everything."

I mulled over Ali's words. The thought of Elise's astonished face as I breezed up to her table and gave her a kiss. And even if I didn't manage to gatecrash the wedding, I'd still have a suite at The Plaza. I'd be waiting for Elise upstairs as she schmoozed in the ballroom.

"So," I said. "Still purely from a theoretical point of view, I wonder if The Plaza's got any rooms left."

"Been booked up long ago," said Ali. "But you better give them a call."

I did, calling up The Plaza on Delta's extortionate in-flight phone system. And like those bizarre news stories that I used to chase after in America, it all now seems so ridiculously arbitrary. The Plaza was full. It had been full for months. But by chance, they'd just had a cancellation. One of their deluxe suites. "Would you like to book it, Sir?"

I dithered. Never for a moment had I dreamed that I'd actually be able to get a room in the place. The cost was also a factor. The room was substantially over 1,000 dollars.

But on the other hand – because there is always the other hand – why not live a little? Why not spend a night in The Plaza?

"I'll take it," I said.

Ali looked at me warily. "You're doing it?"

"Haven't worn black tie in months."

She delved through her bag. "You might as well take this." She handed me a disposable cardboard camera, the sort of thing that you see on the tables at parties. It took 32 pictures and had a little flash. You pressed the button and hoped for the best.

"What's wrong with a real camera?"

"You'll never get in with one. They'll have airport-style metal detectors."

"But this is supposed to be all theory, right?"

"All theory, and nothing but," she said. "You do know that the shit's going to hit the fan if a *Sun* staffer is found gate-crashing the wedding?"

"Better not get caught."

CHAPTER 26

I wondered whether to tell Elise that I was going to try and join the wedding party, but decided against. She could be quite a stickler when it came to celebrity etiquette. Besides, where would be the jaw-dropping amazement if she already knew that I was on my way?

I walked through the park, my hold-all slung over my back, and by now I had my game-player face on. Although I was in it for the fun and for the chance to see Elise, the reality was that I wanted to crash the wedding just for sheer devilment. I was a *Sun* reporter. I walked tall. I laughed in the face of *Hello!* magazine's hireling security men.

And as for the possibility of getting caught...

Perhaps I just hadn't had long enough to dwell on the task ahead of me, but I didn't give it a thought. Though if I *had* taken the time to think about it, I would not have gone within a mile of The Plaza.

There are a number of perks to being a staff reporter on the *Sun*, but the downside is that your behaviour has to be, if not beyond reproach, then at least plausibly deniable. All of us Red Top reporters will occasionally practise the dark arts, but when we do, we know that if we are caught, then we are on our own.

There is, however, a corollary to that: if you're caught, and the story is big enough, then you won't be on your own. You will still be up to your neck in it, but as you wallow in the mire, you will at least have some good friends for company: the news editor, perhaps, and possibly even the editor himself.

The Paparazzi had already assembled outside The Plaza, with their metre-long lenses and that other essential tool of the Paps' trade, the six-foot stepladder. With a baseball cap firmly pulled over my head, I scuttled into the hotel.

Inside, I was just like any other wide-eyed Brit who'd been invited to such a star-studded wedding. I stared about me before ambling over to the reception. Everything was in order.

My suite had a fine view up the length of Central Park, not that I had the eyes to see it. I sat hunched in front of the TV, nursing a gin and tonic from the mini-bar and contemplating the possibility that this might well be the last job I ever did for the *Sun*. I had not mentioned it to a soul on the paper. If it went pear-shaped, they might privately laud me, but they'd sack me all the same.

It's funny: I'd hardly given Elise a thought. I was so obsessed with gate-crashing the wedding that I'd all but forgotten why I'd set out to join the party in the first place.

It was a sweltering September afternoon, but I'd cranked the air-conditioning up so high that it was giving me goose-bumps.

I shower, hot followed by ice-cold. I shave, brush my teeth, clean my nails and moisturise before putting on my best dress-shirt. I wear the little adornments that have been given to me over the years by my father: some monogrammed cufflinks in eighteen carat gold and some mother-of-pearl studs that used to belong to my grandfather.

I spend ten minutes spit-polishing my black Oxford's, working the polish in with my forefinger in tiny circles. My hair glistens with styling wax, sleek as a sea otter.

A dab of Givenchy cologne. I tie my silk bowtie and I give my double-breasted dinner jacket and my trousers a final brush-down. They were another gift from my father, this time for my 21st birthday. The suit, complete with braces and old-style turn-ups, was made-to-measure by those very traditional London tailors, Johns and Pegg.

I place a white handkerchief – lightly crumpled, not folded – into my breast pocket and put a sweet-scented gardenia into my button-hole.

Last, but not least, I put on my watch, a silver Cartier with a black strap. This was not a gift from my father; it used to be worn by one of my past loves. Another story for another day.

The disposable camera was on the bedside table. I thrust it into my coat-pocket.

A last inspection in the full-length mirror. Not much, but the best I could do.

It was gone five p.m. The bulk of the guests would be arriving. My hands were sweating as I rubbed them together.

I thought I might have a drink or two in the Champagne Bar; see what turned up. That was it. That was my plan in its entirety.

I quit my room and as the door clicked shut behind me, I saw a couple already in the corridor. I paid them no heed. We were all heading to the lifts. They were obviously going to the same party.

So far, I'd only seen the man's back, but there was something slightly familiar about him. He pressed the button for the lift and the woman turned to look at me. Straight away, I knew who she was.

A moment later, the man looked at me and then did the most magnificent double-take. Maybe it was the tension, but I found it so funny that I burst out laughing.

"Kim!"

I'll say this for Nick: it may just have been an act for him, but if so, he played it for all he was worth.

"Kim!" he repeated, giving me one of his trademark bear-hugs.

"Honey!" he said. "This is Kim! He's the guy who saved my life!"

A truly remarkable piece of serendipity, but that's how it all happened, I promise you. It was my old-sparring partner Nick Spitz, and by some extraordinary quirk, we had both synchronised our arrival at the wedding.

Barbara was charming. "You're Kim?" She was delighted. "Now I finally have the chance to thank you in person!"

And so now it was Barbara, beautiful, a little older than me, who was clasping me to her bosom.

When Barbara was done with me, Nick gave me *another* hug. "It is so good to see you, man!"

We gazed at each other, and Nick cuffed me on the shoulder. Because it really was the most remarkable story: Nick Spitz had got it back together with his ex-wife Barbara. They'd started dating again in the summer and I suppose that, in a very, very modest way, I had played a small part in their rapprochement. They both certainly seemed to think so.

Together, we got into the lift and as we glided down to the grand ballroom, I'd hardly managed to say a word because Nick was still expressing his gratitude.

"So we had a few bumps along the way," he said. "Who doesn't? But we're back together, and we love each other."

Barbara beamed as she stroked his arm. "We love each other."

"And the kids are pretty happy too!"

"I don't know what you did," said Barbara. "But thank you."

I shrugged, feeling the first tinges of a blush. "You make a great couple."

Nick could see my discomfort. "He doesn't want to talk about that: he's an uptight Brit!" he laughed. "So you here in an official capacity or are you one of the guests?"

"I'm here with Elise."

"Elise?" He clapped me on the shoulder. "Now I did not see that one coming!"

"We've been dating pretty much since I first met you at the St Regis," I said.

He screeched with laughter. "Just don't blame me when it all goes wrong!" he said. "That must have been one hell of a night for you."

The lift doors opened and although in my peripheral vision I can see a wall of security men, my eyes are glued to Nick and Barbara. He still had his arm round my shoulder, was still laughing, and we were just walking straight into the ballroom. There might have been some kerfuffle over tickets, but I wasn't really aware of it; for after all, why did the security men need to check me out? Not only did I look the part, but I happened to be the best friend of Nick Spitz.

The briefest of pauses as we breeze through the scanners. The miracle has happened: in under five minutes, I'm in with the stars. I'm in with Elise.

I accepted a glass of Champagne and lingered for a while next to Nick, but although it was pleasant to be feted, I did not want to be pictured next to him. So as Nick and Barbara greeted some other Hollywood players, I discreetly faded into the background, and for the first time was able to take in this Aladdin's cave, packed not with gold, or treasures, but with the greatest stars on the planet. Everywhere I looked, there would be an Oscar winner, a Pulitzer prize winner, a Nobel Prize winner; actors rubbing shoulders with rock-stars, directors gossiping with oligarchs. Willowy supermodels, worshipped by millions, yet knowing that no-one was interested in a single word that they uttered. Actors' spouses, forever doomed to living in their partners' shadows. Big stars being cut down to size as they were ushered into the presence of even bigger stars. And as for me, gliding unnoticed through the throng, I felt untouched and untouchable; I was the cat who walked by himself.

The grand ballroom had been decked out to an advanced degree of splendour. I had never seen so many flowers festooning the walls, the pillars, and the tables; bottles and bottles of Krug; and jewellery and gowns that would have been more than a match for the Vanity Fair Oscar party.

I saw Elise off to the side talking to a woman. She was wearing a floor-length gown in shimmering grey silk. I don't know the designer, but it couldn't have cost anything less than 10,000 dollars. Her hair cascaded onto her bare shoulders. Even the superstars were left in the shade.

I came at her obliquely, from the side, slipping my arm round her waist.

"They're serving your favourite Champagne," I said.

She was so surprised that she gave a little jump and nearly dropped her glass, before throwing her arms round my neck and kissing me.

"Surprised?" I asked.

"Kim!" She could not have been more amazed if I had come back from the grave, and stood there gaping before finally introducing me to her colleague. Her name was Paula. I remember nothing else about her.

Arm in arm, Elise and I meandered through the stars. "I've got a room here," I said. "Will you join me later?"

"What sort of room?"

"A deluxe suite, darling. It overlooks Central Park. You might like it."

She laughed. "You are amazing!"

In the centre of the room, there was more noise and more swirling activity as the guests swirled on the periphery of that thrilling vortex where the bride and groom held court. Scarlett was in a slinky white gown with a train that coiled about her feet, while her new husband was wearing a tailcoat of navy blue.

As we lingered, it was interesting to witness the social dynamics that were in play. I had seen it before at Royal cocktail parties. The happy couple were talking to three people, but around the edge were about twenty different groups, all of them talking animatedly to each other, yet also keeping an eye on the bride and her groom as they waited for their moment in the limelight.

I was on such a high from crashing the wedding that I was Hoovering up the Champagne. After, I don't know, five, ten, glasses, it suddenly seemed like the most natural thing in the world to get out my camera and start taking pictures.

I excused myself from Elise and went off to the rest-rooms. And if I'd had any sense I'd have hurled the camera into the bin. Jeopardise my entire career, and all for what? A few rotten snaps of a celebrity wedding? For some world exclusive which, by the end of the week, would be just so much fish and chip paper? For the chance to rub *Hello!* magazine's face in the ordure?

I don't expect you to understand. Only journalists appreciate this demonic hunger for exclusives. Later, after the event, we can laugh with the best of them about the total inanity and the irrelevance of the news stories that we cover; but when the red mist descends, these stories are our very life-blood.

And now that I'd actually managed to crash the wedding, I'd be damned if I didn't see it through to the end.

I pulled out my camera and hid it in my handkerchief. It fit snugly into the palm of my hand.

Back in the ballroom, I avoided Elise. I didn't want to have her involved in any way.

The bride and groom, Adam and Scarlett, had moved a little over to the side. I sat down at a nearby table and with the camera on my knee, pointed it vaguely in the right direction. As carefree as any other reveller, I sipped my glass of Champagne and fired off a shot. Very casually, I slipped the camera under the table and clicked the film on with my thumb. Another shot and another shot; I'd no idea if I'd even got a picture of the couple, let alone if it was in focus.

I tried to get closer to the newly-weds, standing nonchalantly at the edge of the circle of power, with handkerchief and camera hanging loosely by my side.

I was still snapping away as the Master of Ceremonies called us over for the speeches. This was probably my last chance. The speeches were to be followed by a sit-down dinner. It would have been far too risky to have stayed.

I eased my way through to the front, standing behind a shimmering matriarch. As before, my arm hung loose by my side, the camera now not two inches from the woman's bottom. All eyes were on the bride and groom.

It was now much trickier to take the pictures, as I was having to roll the film on with just my right hand. The bride, of course, was the main picture that I was after, though if I could get them together, then so much the better.

The bride's father finished his speech and the couple kissed. I had time to fire off a single shot. By rights, the groom was due to make the next speech, but Scarlett, ever the diva, stepped in and said she wanted to say a few words.

She looked terrific. Not only did she have a glass of Champagne, but she was puffing on a cigar the size of a cucumber. This, without a doubt, was the picture.

The bride had said something funny at her husband's expense. He grinned and clapped and we all followed his lead. Scarlett milked the applause and took another puff on her cigar.

I was staring at the podium with a happy smile on my face. I clicked the camera and awkwardly started to thumb the film on. I don't remember a word of what she said. I would point and click, and point and click, until suddenly I realised that I was out of film.

Scarlett was looking at me and without a thought, I did what I do when any woman catches my eye. I winked at her.

It was a very stupid thing to do. I'm sure that Scarlett had been winked at by many strangers over the years, but what I had done was attract attention to myself. As I glanced over to the side, I saw that Adam was staring at me. I didn't know if he'd seen anything. But that was now an irrelevance. The first imperative for a paparazzo once he's got the pictures in the bag is to get the camera – or at least the film – off the premises.

But I wasn't at all sure whether I'd make it.

I started to edge back through the crowd, the camera up my sleeve.

I was desperately searching for somewhere to hide the camera – perhaps a plant pot, or one of the bouquets – when I caught a glimpse of Elise standing on the periphery of the crowd, over to the side. I worked my way over to her, gliding shoulder-first through the throng of the brilliant and the beautiful.

I caught her round the waist and kissed her cheek.

"You couldn't take this?" I whispered, thrusting the camera into her hand.

"What?" she said. A ripple of horror passed over her face as she realised what she was holding.

"I'm in room 542," I said. "A deluxe suite. I hope to see you."

"What?" she said. "You…"

But I wasn't there to hear anymore, I was sauntering off towards the exit, not a care in the world. And I still wonder why I landed her in it like that, why I turned her into almost an accomplice. It was undoubtedly just a thing that I'd done on the spur of the moment. I certainly hadn't planned to give Elise that red-hot camera, and if I had thought about it, I would have realised that it would have jeopardised her job every bit as much as my own. But I just didn't care. It might possibly have been the drink. But my abiding memory as I stalked out of the room was that I'd done everything I could. It was out of my hands. Win or lose, it was all now done to Elise.

They frisked me after I'd been through the scanners. I even passed the time of day with the security guard as he competently patted down my pockets and checked my keys.

And then, well, it was simply a matter of returning to my room, cracking open a bottle of beer. I lay on the bed, gazing out over that unmatchable Manhattan skyline, for once quite content. The dice may have still been in spin, but for now it was all completely out of my hands, and when that's the case, when there's absolutely nothing more that I can do, I am more than happy to sit back and see where the fates will wash me.

I wasn't at all sure whether Elise would come. I had certainly landed her in very deep water; and perhaps, I don't know, it's possible that Georges may have been a part of it. For once, it was I who was putting Elise through the loop, and making her squirm and fret and sweat and wonder what it was that would be the right thing to do. And actually, I didn't much care what she did; it was satisfaction enough to know that I had put her on the spot.

I had another beer and showered and luxuriated in the rich white cotton of the Plaza's dressing gown. But would there be anyone to come share the bed with me?

I wondered briefly what I would have done if it had been me who had been handed that fully loaded camera.

Tried to sneak it out of the building. Not a shadow of a doubt in my mind. Just for the hell of it.

But Elise?

It was certainly a test, I could see that. But what exactly was I testing? How much she loved me? Or how far she'd go for me?

I don't know. A whole lot of things. But I was certainly well content with my position as I watched dusk turn into brilliant Manhattan night. We would see what happened; we would see.

There was a knock at the door and I thought I heard my name being whispered.

I bounded to the door and opened it wide, a great beaming smile on my face. Elise strode past me, quite seething with anger.

She went over to the window, staring out over Central Park as she drummed her fingers on the sill. "Well," she said, very softly. "As good a way as any to wreck my evening."

I sipped my beer, now very cool. For as you can perhaps sense, this was nothing at all to do with the camera, the wedding, or the wrecked evening. That is how it is when you soak it up and you soak it up. Eventually it all comes out. It has to come out. But usually, the cause of that final explosion is entirely tangential.

"I'm sorry to hear that," I said.

"It's bad enough you crashing the wedding, but then to involve me in your puerile little games! It's pathetic!"

"I'm sorry you feel like that." Oh yes, I can be quite the master of the ducked apology.

"You're sorry I feel like that?" she said, turning on me. "Are you going to say you're sorry?"

I looked at her over the top of my beer-bottle.

"Probably not, no."

She started hauling up her dress, until it was way past her knee and up over her thigh. I didn't quite know what she was doing. Then, quickly she bobbed down and retrieved the camera. It was tossed onto the bed.

"Your 30 pieces of silver," she said.

"So you got it out?" I said. "Thank you."

"It's as well that I found out now how little I mean to you."

"On the contrary. I did it because you mean so much."

The hem of her dress fell to the floor and she pondered what it was that I had been saying to her. And being the bright woman that she undoubtedly was, Elise would have divined my meaning in a matter of moments.

"Goodbye," she said.

"Goodbye."

I did not attempt to stop her leaving.

And that, or so I thought, was the end of it all.

I can almost hear the gleeful howls as the Fates looked down on me that night.

The end of it all? I hadn't even started the main course.

CHAPTER 27

I checked out of the Plaza, a non-entity easing his way through the paparazzi and into the night. I was not interested in having a luxury hotel room to myself, and instead slipped off to a quiet bar on the Upper West Side. My euphoria was on the ebb and I tried to pick myself up with an Armagnac. I still didn't know then exactly what it was that I'd done with Elise, but there was no going back now.

I was on my fourth double by the time Ali arrived, swirling the Armagnac in a brandy glass the size of a melon.

She whistled as she took the disposable camera, downing the rest of my drink in one before going off to develop the film.

She called me an hour later.

"You've got some good pix," she said. "One beauty of Scarlett with a cigar. Do you want me to send now?"

Perhaps I should have paused a little longer before I decided whether to cross that particular Rubicon.

But I did what we cavaliers do. I just blurted out the first thought to come into my head. I told her to send away, and had been asleep for all of two hours when the phone drilled into the darkness. It was three a.m.

"Hello?" Bleary, still covered in a thick blanket of sleep.

"Kim." It was Trisha, most striking of all my mad-masters. "Tell me about the pictures."

"Yes." I paused. I could still smell the Armagnac. "Well... I gate-crashed the wedding and snatched some pictures with a disposable camera."

"*You* took the pictures?" she said. "On whose authority?"

"I... I did it off my own bat. It was a kind of last minute thing. I didn't want to get anyone else involved."

"You're a staff reporter! Never mind you, what was going to happen to me, to us, when you got caught?"

"But I didn't get caught!"

"You are such a liability!" I heard what sounded like her fist pounding the desk. "So is that it? Is there anything else I need to know?"

"I don't think so…" I tailed off, not even quite sure myself whether there was anything else I ought to mention.

"I want all this in writing, everything! How you came to be there, how you took the pictures, and how you got them away. And I need that memo, now!"

I spent an hour writing it all up. In black and white, and with the dull thump of a hangover, it didn't look so good. I even for a moment managed to forget about Elise.

I was sipping black coffee when the editor called in person to deliver the axe-blow. The editor rarely calls in person. But when he does call, it's usually bad news.

He liked the pictures; he liked the story. He liked them all so much that he was going to run with them in the next day's paper. He also, he said, liked me very much too.

Which was why when I returned to Britain, he was going to give me one of the best jobs going: I was to join the political team, working in the Westminster Lobby. With immediate effect.

"You've done an excellent job in New York," he said. "Terrific job on Clinton. Louise Woodward. You should be proud of yourself. But there's going to be a lot of heat when we run these pictures. It's best for you to get out of New York. Fly back tonight."

"Tonight?" I was dumb-founded.

"I'm sorry."

Fly back tonight? What about my friends, Justin, Steve, Ali, the rest of them? What about my freewheeling life, master of my own domain? And what, above all, about Elise? How would that leave us? Maybe, for better, for worse, it really was over. Certainly it was going to be easier on my heartstrings if I was out of Manhattan altogether.

I wrote my world exclusive about the wedding, describing in meticulous detail the couple's clothes, the star guests and the limitless Krug. It was all there, though even at the time, I knew it was all so much dross.

My belongings filled three bags. That was it. The accumulated detritus of nearly two years in New York. I stripped the bed and thought about taking the candles, but in the end I left them. The lease and the utility bills would be sorted out when I got back to the UK.

A last lunch for those friends that could come. They were shell-shocked, I think, at how a member of our merry little band had been culled so mercilessly. I got royally drunk. A group-hug, a wave, and I'm gone. I left Manhattan with my three bags in the trunk. En route to the airport, I put in a last call to Elise.

"I'm just calling to say goodbye," I said. "I'm leaving Manhattan today."

"Ohh," she said, the wind momentarily taken from her sails. "You're leaving? You're leaving tonight?"

"My time as the *Sun*'s New York Correspondent has officially come to an end."

"So they're running the pictures tomorrow?"

"They are," I said. "Thank you for smuggling them out. I didn't think you would."

Elise was still clutching at the enormity of what I was telling her. I don't know what she'd expected: perhaps another fight on the phone, perhaps another rapprochement in a week's time after she'd cooled down. But not this. She certainly hadn't expected this.

"If ever you come over to Britain, it would be lovely to hook up."

"But... but I can't live in Britain!" she said.

"I wasn't asking you to."

"No," she said, her tone almost becoming wistful. "No, you weren't. It might have worked."

"Well, goodbye," I said. "And thank you. I'm sorry it has to end like this."

"And I," she'd said. "Goodbye."

I checked in and found a bar overlooking one of the runways. Minute by minute, I watched the planes take off, soaring to a hundred different cities around the globe, a little reminder that my jet-setting days were now well and truly over.

And of course I was thinking about the car-crash end to my relationship with Elise. I couldn't divine her meaning. But no matter how awful a relationship, lovers always breathe a sigh of regret when it finally comes to an end. It is, for better or worse, the devil you know, and who knows what other monsters are lurking out there in the deep.

I wondered if it would have worked if Elise had come back to London with me. Perhaps. A fresh start with Georges turned into nothing more than a memory. But then... who knows what Elise had meant. Who knows what goes through a lover's mind as it dawns on them that this time really is the last time and that, for better, for worse, for richer, for poorer, this time it's over for good.

I ambled off to go through security and passport control: just meandering along, savouring the moment. Alone again.

I have seen it so many times in the films, and there in JFK, I was to have a movie-moment all of my own.

I heard the scream first: "Kim!"

I stopped, turned. She was bowling through the airport, tearing towards me, leaping into my arms. She held me so tight.

"I want to be with you," she said. "I want to be with you in London."

It was now my turn to be tongue-tied. With nothing at all to say, I kissed her.

"Will you marry me?" she asked.

My brain seemed to perform a complete back-flip. One moment I'd been preparing myself for a life of singledom in London and the next this vision, this woman, this love of my life was asking if she could be my wife.

"Yes," I said. "Yes. Yes! I'd love to marry you."

"Thank you," she said, now impish as she kissed me. "Was I really going to do any better?"

"I don't know," I said, and I too was smiling as I kissed her. "But I certainly wasn't."

"I wasn't going to do any better," she said, her lips no more than a few millimetres from mine. "And I could have done a lot worse."

We kissed and hugged and the minutes ticked by and perhaps I should have just caught the next day's flight. I looked at my watch. Bare minutes to spare.

"And… and…" How, delicately, to bring up the one other matter that was never far from the forefront of my mind? "This is real commitment you know. It'll be me and only me, till death us do part."

"After we're married?" she said. "I'm happy with that."

If I hadn't been in such a hurry, I might have paused for one second to ponder the implications of her words.

I was ecstatic. London meant so many things. It meant waking up in each other's arms. It meant having breakfast together. And also, without a doubt, it meant that Georges was over, finished, dead, buried and consigned to the history books.

That, at least, would be the Rom-Com ending.

In real life, however, even the sweetest pill becomes embittered.

CHAPTER 28

We were to be married in New York in February, and Elise and I spent five magical months shuttling over the Atlantic. We would try and meet up every fortnight, one of us flying to the other; how I loved those reunions.

I'd land at JFK, back at my old stamping grounds, and there would be Elise waiting for me in the arrivals hall. We would be practically tearing off each other's clothes before we'd even walked through the door. I bought her a diamond engagement ring. More often than not, the door through to her mother's flat remained locked.

It was the most civilised engagement imaginable, with a lot of sex and not a single row; if only our marriage had been the same.

The small matter of Georges did not come up. I still wondered, occasionally, whether she was seeing him while I was in the UK, but we were both still adhering to our "Don't ask, don't tell" policy. Besides, come March and the end of our honeymoon, we'd be living together in London in the new house that we'd found in Holland Park.

On the romantic front, things may have been going just perfectly. But at work, shoe-horned back into a pinstripe suit, you can have no conception of how stifling life was in Westminster. Tony Blair was still in his pomp, and his foul-mouthed spin-doctor Alastair Campbell treated the Lobby – and, indeed, the ministers – like a pack of hounds.

It didn't help that I'd come from New York. After a year of Bill Clinton and Monica Lewinsky, it was difficult to get interested in the stultifying grind of UK politics. My only stories that made it into the paper were crammed into the Page Two graveyard; I hadn't had a splash in months.

Speaking of which... the last time I *did* have a splash was of course my front page world exclusive of New York's wedding of the year. I will have to wait a long time before I manage to cap that story, and though it worked out very well for the *Sun*, it didn't work out quite so well for me. At a conservative estimate, I reckon those pictures were worth around 250,000 pounds. And what was there in it for me? A dull job in Westminster. And, exquisite irony, I didn't even get a byline.

And so we move onto my own dull imitation of New York's wedding of the year. Being a devout Catholic, Elise's mother had for a long time been pushing for St Patrick's cathedral, which was very close to my old work-place.

That was fine by me. I wasn't in it for the wedding, I was in it to spend the rest of my life with Elise.

The night before the wedding, Steve and Justin threw an impromptu party for anyone who cared to come. It was a great night out. My father and my half-brothers were there, as well as Elise's father Jack. He was not nearly the monster that Elise had painted him. As for Elise herself, she had declined to come. She said it was unlucky for a bride to see her groom on the night before their wedding and that she'd be spending the evening with her mother.

St Patrick's is a vast church, classic Victorian Gothic. Elise's side of the nave was packed, whereas I had to be content with my family and a motley assortment of reporters. Though there was a representative from the *Sun*'s London newsroom: one of my mad-masters, Trisha, looking very glamorous in a white designer suit and a huge black hat.

We had a brief conversation as I escorted her to her pew.

"Elise?" she said. "Isn't she in PR?"

"That's right!" I said brightly. "She's got a stable of stars, Nick Spitz..." I blushed as I stuttered to a halt.

"Nick Spitz?" Trisha seized on the name. "Nick Spitz from the St Regis..." She stared at me. "I knew it!" She poked me in the stomach with her finger. "I knew it, I knew it! Elise was the PR! That's where you met! That's why you didn't run with the story!"

"And hasn't it all worked out brilliantly?" I grinned sheepishly.

"I do hope so... for your sake."

Trisha scowled and then caught herself, brightening as she realised where she was. Her kiss just missed my lips; how much more attractive men become when they are on the cusp of committing themselves to another.

Steve was my best man, while Justin and my two step-brothers had been tasked with handing out of the programmes. Velda had insisted that we all wore black tails. And of that ghastly day, I also remember the flowers. I hadn't seen anything like them since my night in The Plaza.

Up strikes the wedding music. I'm in love. Elise and her newly rehabilitated father, back basking in the warmth of Elise's love after a full four years in the cold, are coming up the aisle towards me. She's wearing a very simple white dress with a garland of flowers in her hair. Radiantly beautiful.

During my first wedding, I had been beset by doubts.

But with Elise, there were no such doubts. Everything was right. When I saw her at my side, shaking a little from the nerves, I knew for certain that I was doing the right thing. She leaned against me as she repeated the vows, clutching onto my arm. I had a sense that she was on the verge of collapse.

As newly-weds do, we signed the deal with a kiss. Looking back, I think it was probably the high-water mark of our marriage. I loved her. She loved me. And now, and on record, she loved only me.

The organ strikes up. It's Bach, my one and only request for the entire wedding. Elise is beaming as she slips her arm into mine. A brief glance behind me and I observe an odd little cameo: my father and my new mother-in-law are supposed to be following us out of the church. But there's a slight tussle going on. By tradition, Velda should be taking my father's arm: but as it is, she's got her arm so tightly crossed about her chest, that it's as if my father has taken *her* arm. They'd only just met that morning; perhaps her dislike of me wasn't so personal after all.

Now that we were married, Elise and I had swapped sides. She was walking on the left past my share of the guests; and I, in my turn, was walking alongside Elise's friends and family. I was so happy that the smile, no, the grin, was fixed upon my face; Elise's friends delightedly reciprocated. I knew quite a number of the faces. They looked happy for me. They looked happy for us.

Towards the end of the aisle, the number of guests was beginning to thin. St Patrick's is a large church. Though I was still doing my duty. I was still smiling at everyone and anyone who had turned out for our big day.

My eye was drawn to a man sitting alone in the back row. Unlike everyone else, he stood with his head bowed.

I could sense that Elise was looking at him. He was the last guest in the church.

The man suddenly looks up. He's not looking at me. He's looking at Elise. His eyes are red, puffy, and the tears are running freely down his cheeks.

Elise twitches. It's nothing to the electric shock that's arcing through my body. I know this guy; I know exactly who he is.

We're in the car, some black stretch limo, all so tasteful and expensive and all now so utterly irrelevant.

Elise sensed immediately something was up.

"My husband!" she said with forced jollity. "How does that sound?"

I couldn't be doing with any more of the charade.

"Georges was in the church," I said. Not a question, but a statement of fact. "Or am I now allowed to call him Tony? Dr Tony Steele?

She did at least have the good grace to bow her head. "I didn't think he'd come," she said.

This chill of calmness descends over me, a black shroud to mask the molten lava that bubbles within. "Let me get this right." In lawyerly fashion, I precisely link my fingers together. "When we first started dating you said you'd never lie to me. And yet now, on our very wedding day, I discover that there is no Georges and there is no Frenchman, and that in fact your lover is a six-foot-five surgeon who's married with kids?"

"I'm sorry," she said, her hands twisting miserably.

She may have been on the rack, but I wouldn't let up. Couldn't let up. I had to know.

"I remember you saying..." I still couldn't get over the enormity of it. Tony! Tony Steele! In the Church! This was the guy, this Captain America, who she'd been seeing every Thursday? "I remember you saying that you'd always tell me the truth."

"I lied to protect you." Elise chewed on her lip. "We all do that."

"And my knee?" I asked. "Was that on the house? Did he give it me for nothing?"

"No, no," she said. "I just wanted you to get well."

"With a special discount for lovers." I stared out of the window. It was raining. February in New York City. Of course it was raining.

"I'm very sorry," she said.

There was, or so I thought, nothing more to be said, and for a minute or so we drove on up past Central Park in complete silence.

Though it occurred to me that actually there were quite a number of things that needed to be said.

"Tony was married," I said. "Where did you used to go with him?"

"Please," she said. "Please don't do this."

"I want to know," I said. "This isn't going away."

"Hotels. He had a flat."

I'm not going to cry. I can't cry. My guts are turning to ice. I've got one more question. And I have to ask it.

"When did you last see him?"

Maybe it was a lucky shot.

Elise, so stunning, so distressed, squirmed in her wretchedness. She did not reply.

But then she didn't need to. I already knew the answer. Where else would she have spent her last night of freedom but with her lover?

CHAPTER 29

I'm not saying Tony Steele was the cause of our problems. I daresay that even without the ugly memory, we would have had plenty enough problems of our own.

We did our best, we really did, to make a go of it. We have three wonderful daughters, so for at least a period of our marriage, we were still having sex with each other.

But there was a part of me that had died during our wedding day, and though I did my best to move on, I was never really prepared to surrender myself in quite the way that I had done before. It wasn't as trite as no longer being able to trust Elise. For on that awful wedding day, I resolved to draw back. Never again would she have my heart and I think she knew this.

If ever I found myself faltering, I only had to look at my knee to remind myself of Tony. It could curdle my love in seconds.

We had our house in Holland Park and we had our children; those girls, I'm sure, I will one day come to tell you about. And I was still at the *Sun*, though now I also had become one of the mad-masters, grinding away at the executive pit-face. No more scoops, no more world exclusives, no more lavish expense claims. The higher you climb up the tabloid tree, the less fun there is to be had.

As for Elise, she was still in PR, though not nearly so much. She saw a lot of her mother who, within a year of our marriage, had followed us back to Britain and now lived just round the corner. She had a key to our house; let us just say that I came to find that my work-life had its charms.

Our marriage was amicable enough. Georges – or Tony, as I shall now call him – was never discussed again. But as you can imagine, we did not spend our anniversaries reminiscing about our wonderful wedding day.

And our sex life, our once glorious sex life, just withered and died. It dropped away to nothing. I'm not blaming Tony. I'm not blaming Elise. I'm not apportioning any blame at all, I'm just stating the truth of things. Like many couples with children, the sex dwindles till it is nothing but a memory.

Not that I didn't have my secret lusts and my private fantasy-girls. It's hard not to these days, considering the sexual revolution that has occurred in the last decade. I would not have believed it possible, but my two years in New York now seem like a model of sexual restraint and sobriety. Thanks to the internet, you can fix up to have sex with any random stranger who lives within half-a-mile. It's not for me, but you are always aware that it's all going on; and you're aware, also, that you're seeing none of it.

I was very much ripe for the plucking.

It's lunch-time, a summery Wednesday, about a year ago now. I have a rare day off and I'm pottering around near Lord's cricket ground in St John's Wood. I've read the papers. I'm just wondering whether to have a coffee or whether to explore one of the bookshops.

A woman is walking on the other side of the road. She is, perhaps, Indian, with long dark hair, and she looks very happy. She almost glides along the pavement. I like her clothes too, expensive black boots, a snug black leather jacket, and very, very tight blue jeans.

She looks over her shoulder to check for traffic, and then crosses the road. Briefly, she looks at me, and all I'm thinking to myself is that she looks friendly, personable, when suddenly she breaks into a smile and says my name: "Kim!"

From nowhere, a name pops into my head. It's Neeraja. The girl from Barbados who I'd last seen, what, twelve years ago.

She gives me a huge hug. I haven't had a hug like that in years; certainly not from my wife. It's been so long that I've almost forgotten what it's like to be hugged like that. We laugh, we hold each other, as we head to a café.

Coffee turns into lunch. No rings on her fingers. She is divorced with a couple of kids; she shrugs as if it's neither here nor there. "I love my life," she says. "And you? That woman who had the lover on Thursdays?"

"I married her."

"Much scarring?"

"Just a little."

As we're finishing a second bottle of Pouilly Fuisse, she goes to the lavatory. I have a moment to myself. I like this woman. I like this woman a lot. And from deep down within my gut, I sense these long-forgotten stirrings.

When Neeraja comes back to the table, I see that she has applied fresh lipstick. I can't take my eyes off her scarlet lips. I have no idea what she's saying, all I can do is gaze into her face, looking first at her eyes, before, always, staring at her lips.

I'm thinking the unthinkable. What, I wonder, would it be like to kiss this woman?

When you're married, you make these vows of fidelity and, for as long as you stick with them, they seem to be writ in stone. You know that friends or relatives may be unfaithful, but for you it's not even an option; it's as ridiculous, say, as trying to swim across the Thames at night. It's something that you could probably do, but it would also be foolhardy; bordering on the insane. At the end of it all, there might well be some little thrill, but it would be risky beyond belief. So why chance it? Why jeopardise everything to satisfy a whim for adventure? Why do we do these things, take these risks? I'll tell you why. Because whatever we've got, we always want more. It doesn't matter how much we have in our lives, after a matter of weeks that merely becomes the benchmark; and then, a little while later, we take a look at life's grand banquet and we have a taste of something else.

But marital vows are another thing. Seemingly so easy to break. But that first time that you do it, you are aware that you are breaking a very big taboo.

I leant over and kissed Neeraja. It feels quite different. It has been a long, long time since I've had a kiss like that, for somehow, since we have been married, my kisses with Elise have never had the same savour.

"I live quite close," Neeraja said. Those red lips were moving again. I longed for another kiss.

"Do you now?"

"My kids are at school."

"Oh are they?"

"Like to come back for a coffee?"

I smiled. What an extraordinary turn of events. In over ten years of marriage, I had never been unfaithful; I had never even seriously contemplated being unfaithful. And now, in the span of one single lunchtime, I was willingly, actively, diving into the thrilling world of the adulterer.

Did I feel as if I was betraying Elise? A little. But when you are in your forties, you do not need to be reminded that we must seize each and every moment. And if we kiss, then why not take it a step further? Why not take the plunge, immerse myself? Now that I had crossed the line, it all seemed so seductively easy. In my mind, at least, my marital vows were all but forgotten. That day, in that restaurant, I had reached a tipping point where every boon and every delight had to be seized in that instant.

There was, of course, one other factor, though I know that this may sound like a sop. Let us not forget Tony. Even ten years down the line, Tony was still in my thoughts, and he still irked me. Though not, perhaps, for the reasons that you might imagine. The memory of Tony irked me not because he had been Elise's lover, but because I had been such a pathetic, juddering jelly of a man as to have put up with him. What on earth had I been doing? What sort of guy just meekly accepts that, once a week, his girlfriend has a right to see her lover? Couldn't I – even once – have fought for my love?

And I remembered, also, that one time when I *had* fought for her, when I'd issued Elise with an "It's him or me" ultimatum. I'd stuck to my guns for all of four days.

As for the wedding and Elise's lies, that was merely the icing on the cake. What did it matter if she'd been having sex with Georges the Frenchman or Tony the all-American beefcake? I couldn't blame her, because it was me, the wimp, who'd acquiesced to the whole damnable situation in the first place. It's funny how we can forgive our friends and our relatives almost anything. It's much harder to forgive yourself.

Neeraja led the way to her flat. We did not hold hands. That would have been far too indiscreet.

"What would you like to do when we get inside?" she asked.

"I thought you were going to make me some coffee," I said.

"And while we wait for the kettle to boil?"

"Yes," I said, my mind alive to the possibilities of what was being promised to me. "Water takes ages to boil."

She lived in a mews house off Marylebone High Street. It was almost entirely on the first floor, with a winding spiral staircase that led up from the front door. I followed her up the stairs, mesmerised by the sight of her legs in those skin-tight jeans. Lust bubbled up in me like water from a spring; I had not felt like this about a woman in over a decade.

Neeraja pushed me up against the wall, lips firm against mine. I did not pause for a moment, and did what we plungers do. I dived in. I remember her scent. Every woman's aroma is unique. I had forgotten that.

We were like seasoned lovers, plucking at each other's buttons and peeling off our clothes. We laughed as I tugged at her tight jeans.

"Next time, I might wear a dress," she said. I hurled her trousers across the room.

"Next time?"

"I certainly hope so."

Our affair had begun.

CHAPTER 30

I would meet up with Neeraja two or three times a week, often in the mornings when I was working the late-shift. Usually it would be at her flat, though on occasion we'd go to a hotel. I was surprised at how many five star hotels were prepared to rent out their rooms by the hour.

We never asked each other about our love lives. I did not know if Neeraja had other lovers, and for her part, she never asked me about Elise.

Our love affair was largely conducted in the bedroom. London, for all its vastness, has so many prying eyes that it would have been risky to have dined out together.

Sometimes she'd called me at work, but in general, we communicated by text messages. Ever the assiduous adulterer, at the end of each day, I would delete all the messages on the phone. I was certainly assiduous, but as it turned out, not quite assiduous enough.

For a long time, we never spent the night together, but then I engineered a lads' weekend away. Three glorious days together in Prague. I was a middle-aged man in love: which is to say that I was as much in love as I'd ever been. It never ceases to astonish me that, even the 20th time round, you can still be as deliriously in love as you were during that first careless rapture.

I was meticulous in covering my tracks. But I don't think it made much odds, because Elise, being a woman, must have soon sensed something in the wind. Perhaps I was more relaxed, more easily amused at life and its fripperies – who knows?

I'd just been to the lavatory. Ostensibly I'd been going through my ablutions, but in actual fact I'd been texting Neeraja. We were going to meet up the next morning, a Monday, before I went to work.

I slip the phone into my pocket. The toilet is flushed. I wash my hands and unlock the door. And as I step out of the lavatory, Elise just happens to be coming out of the bedroom. Just a comfortable couple who happen to run into each other as they go about their daily chores. But somehow, I don't think the timing was a coincidence.

"Oh hi Kim," she says. She's looking good these days, I have to admit, with perhaps a couple more lines about her eyes, but still in very good trim. She does Pilates, kick-boxing and other such exercises down at her gym. And her hair, her auburn mane, still gleams of gold in the sun. Not that I'm really able to appreciate Elise's beauty any more. Her looks for me are like an Old Master that hangs upon the dining room wall; once wondrous to behold, she has now become just another part of the furniture.

"Hi," I said.

"I've just lost my phone," she said. "I couldn't borrow yours?"

Well what am I going to say? I can hardly *not* lend her my mobile. If I don't give her the phone, then I might as well then and there confess that I have acquired myself a lover.

"Sure." I fish the phone out of my pocket and hand it over.

She scrutinises the phone for a couple of seconds. It's an old-fashioned Nokia.

"Oh look," she says. "Somebody's just texted you."

She clicks onto the message. "It's from Henry," she says. "Who's Henry?"

"Just a colleague."

"Henry is apparently looking forward to seeing you tomorrow morning. He blows you a kiss." She cocked an eyebrow, before busying herself with the contents of my inbox.

All is revealed.

"So who is it?" she asked. Her face was white.

There was no point in trying to deny it. "Just a woman I met."

"Just a woman you met? How long?"

"About a year."

"Do you love her?"

"I don't know."

She smacked the phone back and forth into the palm of her hand. "Right." Her mouth was a tight line. She walked downstairs.

The dam-burst came later that night; I was more than ready for it.

The girls were in bed and I'd just gone down to the kitchen to get myself a drink. Elise was watching television.

"Tell me, Kim." She did not take her eyes off the TV. "Do you think it's okay to have an affair like this?"

Now, this was the moment. Was I going to fall to my knees, beg for forgiveness? Plead and grovel and tell her that it would never, ever happen again?

Not on your life.

"I don't think it's perfect." Casually, I opened a bottle of beer. I had been rehearsing these arguments for quite some time. "But I'm not going to beat myself up over it."

"And what about our marriage? You think it's fine to bed who you want?" Also very calm, she drank her herbal tea.

"Like I say, I'm not going to beat myself up over it."

The teacup exploded against the wall. She stood up and faced me, shaking with rage. "Just what the hell is that supposed to mean?"

"Well let me ask you a question, Elise," I said. And, looking back, I wonder if I hadn't been wanting to get caught all along, just for the pleasure of this moment. I had been waiting for it for some time. "What about you and Tony? Do you think that was okay?"

"Tony?" she shrieked. "What's Tony got to do with this? We weren't even married!"

"Tony's got everything to do with this." My eyes flicked behind the television. The tea was slowly dripping down the wall. "Or should I call him Georges?"

"You agreed to Tony!" she said. "You agreed to it! You knew all about it! I said I'd sort it out, and I sorted it out! I haven't seen him since we married, not once! This is quite different!"

Ah, well, that is precisely the point isn't it?

I won't bore you with the rest of the tirade. By now we had both set out our positions and there was much more mud to be hurled, not least by me, as I finally dipped in to this deep vat of rage that had been quietly simmering since my time in New York.

As for Elise... I guess that there were many things for her to fume against. My infidelity was just the excuse, but with it there was also rage at, I don't know, the lack of sex, the lack of love, indeed our whole lack-lustre marriage. It is possible there may have been some guilt in there too.

We slept, obviously, in separate rooms, and the next day Elise did something which I could not have predicted.

She did nothing at all.

For a full week, we did not speak to each other. When the girls had breakfast, I would stay upstairs. When I got back from work, Elise would ignore me. I would get my drink and ignore her. It was as if Elise and I were made of glass. We looked through each other and never once into each other's eyes.

For seven nights, it continued like this and, given how angry I was, it might well have continued for another seventy.

Except on the seventh night, just as I was dropping off to sleep, Elise crept silently into my bed.

She was wearing nothing but a new perfume. Not a word was said in the darkness, but suddenly her mouth was on mine, her hands roaming about my body, and we were making love: though making love like we'd used to make love in New York, with enthusiasm and ardour and all those other things which had fallen by the wayside since we had married. It was remarkable. And when we had utterly spent ourselves on each other, Elise kissed me and left the room.

The next day: silence. It was back to how we were before. We may have been having Manhattan sex with each other the night before, but by day, she would not speak to me. She would not even look at me. In the kitchen, I stretched out a hand to touch her arm. She brushed me away.

That night, I am wondering what on earth is going to happen next when Elise again slips into my bed. Though we were still in total darkness, it was even more thrilling than the night before. Just like thirteen years ago, the whole smorgasbord was on offer. Twice in the night we made love, quite wild with passion.

Another day of not speaking, not touching. Elise spent the afternoon out shopping. And we now come to the third night. I have showered, shaved; I'm ready for her.

Ever so quietly, the door opened and she came into the spare room; moments later we were kissing. She had on a scent from another life and another world; could it be Chanel?

And this time, it was different. This time, she let out a little laugh, and then stretched for the light. She was lying naked on her back. Around her neck was a gold necklace that I had not seen in a long time, a cluster of entwined vine leaves.

"You," she said, "are going to make love to me."

I was not slow on the uptake.

"I am going to make love. With you."

"I am going to make love with you, because I love you."

I looked at her askance. Honestly, I can say that at that moment, I had never seen Elise so beautiful.

"I love you," I said, "Which is why I am going to make love to you."

"Make love under me?"

"Or perhaps make love on you?"

She let out a delicious shudder as she cupped my face. "You, Kim, are making love to me."

"I, Elise, am making love with you."

"We, Kim, should make love more often like this."

"That, Elise, is one of the most sensible things that I have ever heard from your lips."

"But though it is lovely to be making love, with you, Kim, here, now, I have always felt..." She bit her lip. "That beds were rather bourgeois."

"We could be making love on the sofa."

"And to think, we've never once made love on the sofa."

"And the kitchen table?" I asked. "Do you think, Elise, that it will hold up under the strain?"

"I think it's time we found out."

✦

Two days later, and our little marital ship was gliding smoothly over a calm silver sea. We were as cordial as can be. The sex was as good as it ever was. It's been a revelation to me: middle-aged sex can be just as good as it ever once was. You do it once, and you do it right.

And there were jokes too: little witticisms, sometimes at each other's expense, though always well meant. What did the girls make of the extraordinary transformation that has occurred in their parents? I have no idea.

I'm in bed waiting for my wife, my new-found love. She is showering off the dirt from a day's shopping. And as I wait for her, I wonder what might be on offer tonight; perhaps my office? In all our time together, we have never christened my office. A mistake, and one which should be attended to.

Odd, isn't it, how these things work themselves out? We hadn't been speaking to each other for years, and then after just a few phenomenal bouts of love-making, everything had clicked back into place. No need for any word of forgiveness either. We'd made love and we'd moved on.

Elise was singing to herself in the bathroom. 'New York, New York': "And if I can make it there, I'm gonna make it anywhere…"

And from on the other side of the bed, I hear another sound. It's a tiny sound, just a slight beep. It's come from Elise's Blackberry. The beep is so small; almost surreptitious.

There's no reason why, but I have a sudden urge to look at her phone. Quickly, I snatch it up. The sender does not appear to have a name. Just a letter. A single letter. The letter "T".

Elise is now out of the shower. In a few moments, she'll be back in the bedroom to put on her night-cream. I hear the bolt being drawn on the bathroom door.

I press a couple of buttons on the Blackberry.

Even as Elise comes back into the room, I'm returning the phone to her bedside table.

I roll onto my side of the bed.

She's wearing a white silk nightie. I've never seen it before. It looks expensive. Stupefied, I stare at her.

Elise sits on a stool by her dressing table and applies glossy lipstick.

Word for word, I am recalling the text message that I've just seen on her phone. I'd only had a couple of seconds to read it.

That's all I'd needed.

"You blew my mind," it read. "You always blow my mind. Any time, anywhere, you know I'll always be there for you. Love, and much of it." He'd signed off with his name and a kiss.

He was back. Tony was back. I wondered if he had ever been away.

And I was right back in my Manhattan days, stuck again with my perpetual Elise dilemma. Do I mention the lover? Or does the human sponge do what he has always done: soak it up. Soak it up, without complaint.

Elise winks as she catches sight of me in the mirror. "Doing all right over there, Kim?"

I take a deep breath and press the heels of my hands into my eye sockets. I see stars. My eyes thud with pain.

"I'm cool."

Hidden behind my newspaper, I wipe away the tears with my fingertips.

www.ingramcontent.com/pod-product-compliance
Lightning Source LLC
Jackson TN
JSHW020019141224
75386JS00025B/595